Playmaker

Playmaker

A HIDDEN ATTRACTIONS NOVEL

DEANNA FAISON

W by **wattpad** books

To those standing in their own way.

It gets better.

Playlist

Nonsense
Sabrina Carpenter

Wine Into Whiskey
Tucker Wetmore

Different
Joshua Bassett

For Tonight
Giveon

Back to Friends
Lauren Spencer Smith

Whiskey Glasses
Morgan Wallen

Slow It Down
Benson Boone

One

MADDIE

I just need to study.

That's all I need to do.

But how on *earth* am I supposed to do that with all that racket going on downstairs?

Slamming the textbook in front of me closed, I move to the window and part the blinds to observe the party going on below. With my parents away for their annual anniversary trip, my brother decided to throw a spring break *extravaganza* now that we're back from our respective colleges, but with the noise they're producing, I wouldn't be surprised if our neighbors tell our parents when they return, or worse, call the cops.

I don't understand how Ethan has even stayed in contact with the friends he used to associate with in high school. Since I graduated, the only person I've stayed close to has been Maya, but she's my best friend. The people I did lab projects with and spoke to during lunch were always kept in the background, and I was fine with that. If I had fewer people to hang out with, it allowed me more time to study. After all, I didn't get into Briarwood—the best pre-med school in the country—by smoking blunts and getting trashed every weekend like *some* people.

A shrill laugh echoes from the patio below, and I roll my eyes when I spot a girl draped across my brother's lap. Her hands are running through his hair, and she seems to cling to every word he says like it's the last time she'll ever hear him relay some irrelevant story about his glory days on the high-school football team.

Unlike me, my brother decided to attend community college until he figures out what he wants to do with his life, and while there's nothing wrong with that, it's days like this that I wish he'd grow the hell up already and focus on building his future rather than groping a random girl's ass.

He could have gone far with football. He was *great* at it. If he had just taken the scholarship he was offered, he might have been as good as—

No.

Absolutely not.

Despite my best efforts, my eyes stray to the guy sitting beside my brother, and I attempt to fight the surge of butterflies dancing in my stomach. Cameron Holden, also known as my brother's best friend, is the *epitome* of a fuckboy. He's red flag central, and personally, I think he should wear a warning label every time he leaves his house.

Cameron got into West Bridge for football, and he's already their star player, even if it's only his junior year. Everyone predicts he'll make it to the NFL, and maybe that's what makes him so conceited. Whatever the reason, Cameron thinks he's the greatest thing to walk the planet, but I'm always first in line to remind him that he's *not*.

The Cameron I used to know, back when he and my brother were kids, was much cooler than the version he transformed into once he hit high school. The nerd with glasses who was obsessed with collecting Pokémon cards was my first crush. I drew hearts with his name in them in all my diaries, and when I went to sleep, I'd dream of a life where he'd fall for me, too, and all the conversations we had when my brother wasn't around didn't make just *me* giddy and feel as if I was on cloud nine, but him as well.

There was a time when I thought we were more than friends until . . .

No.

I will not think about that day.

After he basically exiled me from his life, I felt embarrassed to admit I ever felt that way about Cameron, and when I get these random twinges of butterflies, I do everything in my power to shut them down. My heart doesn't seem to realize he isn't the same boy he used to be, or maybe it's reacting due to the science of attraction.

Any normal person would see Cameron on the street and fall head over heels for him. He's six three and ripped, with facial features that could have been chiseled by Michelangelo himself and a smile that could rival the hottest of deserts here in Arizona. Who *wouldn't* want to jump his bones? It's natural to want to pry his hand off the breast of the girl he's currently groping and place it on mine instead.

At least, that's what I try to convince myself.

The bass of the music gets louder, drawing me from my thoughts.

Doesn't Ethan realize I have the MCATs to study for? Since I'm only a freshman, I can't take the test until next spring, but

I don't care. Every moment counts, and I had planned to keep myself holed up in my room the entirety of spring break to take advantage of no distractions.

Clearly, that isn't going to happen.

With an annoyed huff I leave my room in just a pair of pajama shorts and a tank top, ignoring the fact that I look like a bum as I head downstairs and throw open the sliding door to the patio.

Ethan glances in my direction with a beer in hand, seemingly amused by the expression on my face. "Yes, Maddie?"

"I'm trying to study!" I attempt to yell over the music. As soon as the sentence leaves my lips, I realize how insane I sound. We all just got finished with finals for the semester, so the next two weeks should be time to wind down and celebrate.

The girls I've never met before snicker in the background, but I ignore them and keep my eyes on my brother.

"Why don't you have a drink?" Ethan suggests. He reaches over to grab one from the cooler and passes it to me, and I hate how the object feels cold and unfamiliar in my hand. "It's spring *break*, Maddie. Emphasis on *break*. Stop being such a bore all the time."

The girl sprawled across his lap bites her lip to keep herself from laughing, and it only fuels my anger. I don't like parties. I never have. At least not now, at this point in my life. My only goal is to become a doctor, and achieving that requires an immense amount of focus. I'll have time for partying and getting shit-faced *after* I graduate medical school.

"Mads has always been a bore." Cameron's emerald-green eyes glisten with humor, and damn him, his use of the nickname he gave me in middle school makes my heart falter for a beat. He arches a perfectly formed brow as he awaits my answer, almost

4

like a *challenge*, but I won't give him the satisfaction of seeing me riled up. He doesn't get that privilege. Not anymore.

With a roll of my eyes I dismiss him completely and turn my attention back to Ethan. "I'm just asking if you can turn the music down. That's it."

Before my brother can reply, Cameron clears his throat, and I can't help but wonder if my lack of attention is bothering him. I briefly glance his way, immediately cursing my urge to do so when he winks and opens his long, muscular legs wider in the chair. His lap looks inviting as hell, and the girl who left to get a drink moments ago seems to think the same. She plops her ass down in the spot I *refuse* to look at and hooks her arms around his neck.

Gross.

"What, you want to join too?" Cameron asks me with a devilish grin. "There's enough room for both of you."

Just like that any attraction that tried to crawl its way into my body evaporates instantly. It doesn't matter if Cameron looks like a movie star. Moments like these are a constant reminder that he isn't who he used to be, and although he has his reasons, they aren't enough for me to look past his repulsive displays of arrogance.

"Cameron, that's my *sister*," Ethan warns him.

The belly laugh Cameron gives in response shouldn't make my stomach twist into knots and bile rise in my throat, but it does. "Relax," he reassures Ethan. "I'd never go for Mads. She's like my sister too."

More snickers erupt from the two girls I'm seconds away from strangling, but thankfully Ethan shifts uncomfortably in his chair and sends me a look as if to say, *I'm sorry about him.*

There's not a single excuse in the book he can give for Cameron's behavior anymore. I used to listen to them and hold on to the hope that he would change, but Cameron has proven time and time again that he doesn't plan on overcoming the hurt he experienced after his mother's death. Instead, he let it fester and grow like weeds that I swear changed the chemical makeup of his brain. Ethan stuck by his side because Cameron's his best friend, and I did, too, until Cameron all but told me to get lost.

"I'll turn it down." Ethan relents. "It's fine."

For a moment there's a flicker of emotion in Cameron's eyes. I get the strange sensation that he might apologize, but then the music quiets, cutting off whatever moment we might have shared.

I can lie all I'd like, but deep down I'm hurt that he changed. I was certain he'd mature and grow out of this playboy phase, and then. . . . Well, I never let myself get that far into the future. My hopes would only be crushed for the millionth time, and even if he *did* mature and become more like the boy I used to know, my brother would be furious if he made a move on me.

I'd never go for Mads. She's like my sister too.

With his words playing like a broken record, I storm back into the house in a wave of fury. I'm too pissed off to focus on studying now. Instead, all I can think of are the fleeting moments Cameron and I have shared over the years. From him consoling me when I fell off my bike in the third grade to our moment at Myrtle Beach together on my family's annual spring break vacation six years ago. It was the summer before he started high school, right before his mom passed. I convinced him to sneak out onto the beach while everyone was sleeping, and that night I *swore* he had been about to kiss me. I wonder if he would have if that wave hadn't interrupted us, and if he hadn't become a different person a week later, I might have asked.

But those *memories* are exactly what they are—memories. At some point I have to let go and move on.

With a reluctant sigh I peel the blinds back to take one final look at the man who never seems to leave my thoughts.

It's only going to be this way for the next two weeks. Then we'll head back to our schools and I won't have to be reminded of the past like a knife to the chest.

The girl who was in his lap has moved, and as much as I want to look away from his gray sweatpants, I can't. The bulge there is *huge*. It's outlined like a piece of candy begging to be unwrapped, and I'm the idiot salivating over it.

I *knew* I shouldn't have looked. I avoided it for a reason, and—

Oh fuck.

I guess I'm not the only one plagued by memories.

The moment I drag my eyes to his, they're already locked on mine, and that same flicker of emotion in them downstairs comes back full force.

Any walls I built around my heart shatter with hardly any effort at all. With a single look Cameron can break through my defenses, and judging by the cocky grin that falls over his face, he knows it too.

And that's all the information I need to realize that this will be an *excruciating* two weeks.

Two

CAMERON

What is Little Miss Goody Good focusing so intently on?

We've been having a staring contest through her bedroom window for what feels like an eternity, but I can't seem to tear my gaze away from the way her cheeks turned a rosy pink and her lips parted, and how she looked curious as hell when I caught her staring at my half-hard cock.

Maddie is the one to blame for this. What the hell was she thinking coming downstairs without a bra on? I'm not *blind*, but I didn't get enough warning to avert my gaze in time before she threw open the sliding door with her tits practically falling out.

I've become *very* skilled at ignoring Maddie's tits, curves, and well, basically every feature of hers that seemed to become enhanced once she got into high school. She's Ethan's little sister, and even though she's only two years younger than us, it still feels wrong to be lusting after her. If Ethan knew I even once imagined Maddie bouncing on my cock, I'm positive I wouldn't *have* a cock anymore.

Yet I still do it. There are too many times to count when I've jerked off to the thought of her.

And now I'm bordering on full-on hard with images of curly blond hair and blue eyes heavy lidded with ecstasy as I fill her.

Christ.

I need to get a grip.

Thankfully Sadie falls into my lap, a welcome distraction. I've been drinking too much tonight, but Sadie has only had one beer. I don't ask questions when she attaches her lips to my neck and runs her hand down my chest, but my eyes stray to the window upstairs again where Maddie is watching the scene unfold.

I thought she had to study?

The woman never leaves her room whenever I'm home from college. It's rare we're both home at the same time, but springtime is the exception, given the fact that I've never missed a Davis spring break vacation. Their family treated me as their own after my mom's passing. I still have my dad, but nowadays he seems to be more concerned with business trips and my future career than with me.

In high school I was alone at home more than half the time, and when Ethan discovered that, he urged me to stay with them when my dad was away, so I did. Maddie's parents, Richard and Mary, never questioned me staying at their house more than mine. After all, my mom and Mary were best friends, so Mary took me in with open arms. Although she's never *said* she disapproves of my father's decisions, I still see her look of disappointment whenever I talk about him.

Sadie giggles when her hand brushes my hard cock, bringing me back to the present. "Is that really all it took? Some neck kisses?"

Little does she know that she is *not* the reason for my case of blue balls. The person responsible for that has left the window, leaving me a view of boring white blinds.

I refuse to think about Maddie Davis. Her family is like my own. I consider Ethan to be my *brother*. Having dirty thoughts about her isn't going to make the annual vacation next weekend any easier.

I clear my throat to gain Ethan's attention, and we know each other well enough by now to understand what the other is saying without having to say anything at all. He jerks his head to the sliding door and says, "Guest bedroom."

Thank fuck.

Rising from the chair, I hold my hand out to Sadie, unsurprised when she takes it without hesitation. She's been in my DMs for a month now, asking when I'll be home from college, and the pictures she's sent me haven't been innocent by any means. She knew what I wanted the second I invited her here, and she isn't complaining.

When we get to the correct room Sadie tugs me in by the hem of my T-shirt and presses her lips to mine. I don't bother turning on the lights, and I can try to reassure myself it's just because I'm lazy, but that's not the case at all. The darkness allows me to imagine blond curls when I tug on Sadie's red ones. It allows me to fantasize soft, supple curves rather than Sadie's thin frame. The girl I'm hooking up with right now is beautiful, but she's not *her*.

When I'm away at college I don't have this issue. I'm able to forget about Maddie for a while. I don't picture her leaving my living room bawling when I told her to get out. She was trying to comfort me after my mother's death, and I pushed her away for good. I didn't want to get close to *anyone*, and Maddie . . . I was already close to teetering over the line with her. If she stuck around and witnessed the hurt I went through, I would have used her as a distraction to forget the pain and break her heart. I was too self-aware to make that mistake, so I said things I didn't mean when she visited, and I don't know why I was disappointed it worked.

Vodka and strawberries cloud my senses as Sadie's tongue entwines with mine, but it's vanilla and honey that I'm craving. I skim my hands down her sides until I reach the hem of her dress and shove it up to sit around her waist as we fall back onto the mattress together. We're a mess of teeth and tongue while we rid ourselves of our clothes, and when she's finally naked, I put my skills to work.

I swipe my thumb delicately across her clit and don't let up until her head is thrown back and she's practically screaming. I've always loved how wet women get for me. I'm a man who craves to be the best at everything, and over my years of sleeping around I've studied a woman's pleasure as much as possible. I know not to rub too hard, and when my finger plunges into Sadie's wet heat, I keep my strokes slow and precise, listening to her breathing, and her gasps let me know when to speed up or slow down.

"Oh my god, *Cameron!*" she moans.

Just as I'm about to grab a condom from the pocket of my sweatpants on the floor, loud bangs sound against the door.

"You've got to be *kidding* me." Sadie is seething. Rising from the bed, she wraps the sheet around her now-naked body and throws open the door to reveal Maddie on the other side. I can almost see the steam blowing out of her ears.

"Are you fucking joking?" Maddie shouts. "In our *house*? In our *guest room*? Do you not have any respect at *all* for our parents?"

I'm still in my briefs when I move to stand in front of Sadie, and now isn't the time to be thinking this, but Maddie looks hot as hell when she's pissed. Her arms are crossed underneath those heavenly tits, and her eyebrows are scrunched together, forming a tiny *v* in the crease.

I've practiced keeping her at arm's length for years, and now is no different. Putting on my best asshole facade, I say, "We were kind of in the middle of something." I glance down at my hard-on for emphasis, and the instant pleasure I get from noticing the redness of her cheeks is different for me. Whereas most girls would have to touch me to turn me on, Maddie seems to elicit the same response by simply standing here.

"Well, finish it elsewhere," she grumbles. "It's not happening here."

Sadie pokes her head out from around my shoulder. "Why are you such a fucking *bitch*? You have a goddamn stick shoved so far up your ass. Just let people have some fun! *Christ.* You act as if—"

"That's enough." I don't realize I've said it until the sentence leaves my mouth, but Maddie's glassy eyes instantly meet mine in confusion. I've known her long enough to realize she's seconds away from breaking down, and while Sadie might be right about Maddie never having fun, she took it too far.

Plus, I can't allow myself to be the reason Maddie bawls her eyes out for the second time.

I just *can't.*

Maddie spins around and stalks off down the hallway. I should let her walk away from me, but I don't know if this incessant fucking need I feel to check on her will ever disappear. Maybe it stems from the guilt of not following her the last time

I made her cry, but whatever the reason, I can't stand by and do nothing.

"I'm going to talk to her," I tell Sadie before I can change my mind.

Sadie's eyebrows shoot to her hairline. "*What? I'm naked,* Cameron!"

I live up to my reputation when I slam the door behind me and chase Maddie down the hall. Unfortunately, this isn't the first time I've left a one-night stand without an explanation, and I'm afraid to admit it probably won't be the last either.

"Maddie!" I call. At the sound of my voice, she whirls to face me, nothing but pure, unfiltered rage staring back at me. "Look, I didn't mean to offend you, okay? We needed a place to go, and Ethan said—"

"I don't give a *shit* what Ethan said! What is wrong with you? Can you not keep your dick in your pants for more than twenty-four hours? You have a whole house to yourself, and yet you choose to fuck someone under *our* roof. I don't get it."

"It's a *party*, Maddie. People fuck at parties. It happens."

"Well, I don't want to hear you—" Her mouth snaps shut.

Now *that* grabs my attention.

"You don't want to hear me what?" I ask, taking a step closer. Despite how much she tries to fight it, her eyes dip to my exposed torso, where my abs are on full display to her. My cock twitches in response. "You don't want to hear me *fuck*?"

I watch her gulp before she averts her eyes.

"Why would it bother you to hear me fuck, Mads?"

"Don't call me that," she says, seething.

I ignore the crushing sensation in my chest and continue to push her. Being out here in the hallway with her is dangerous, especially when I barely have any clothes on and she's in a tank top so thin I can see her nipples, begging to be released, but I can't ignore the force of attraction that draws us together. If I'm a magnet, she's steel, and there's nowhere else I'd rather be.

Now that I'm standing directly in front of her, I tower over her. She has to tilt her head up to look me in the eyes. One more step and I'll be able to feel her nipples against my chest. One more step and I'll inhale the scent of vanilla and honey that seems to give me more of a hit than weed ever will.

"You want to know what *I* think?" I breathe onto her lips.

She continues to hold my stare with her chin held high like a soldier heading into battle. I'm fighting the urge to shove her against this wall and do what we've *both* wanted to do for years. If things were different and Ethan wasn't her brother, we'd have fucked each other senseless a billion times already, and that's saying something considering I never have sex with the same girl twice. However, if I had an exception to that rule, Maddie Davis would be it.

"No," she replies in a choked whisper. "I *don't* want to know, but if you decide to fuck that girl in the guest room, at least have the decency to throw the sheets in the wash before our parents return from their trip."

All I can do is watch in disbelief when she walks away from me and closes her bedroom door behind her.

Three

CAMERON

The morning after the party reminds me why I don't drink anymore.

My dad taught me that alcohol compromises my motor skills, and with me playing quarterback, I *need* my motor skills. Reaction time, hand-eye coordination—all of it matters, and I didn't want to risk getting dropped from the team when I worked so hard to get into West Bridge in the first place. As soon as I started training, alcohol and drugs were off the table.

The light shining through the windows is blinding, and my back is fucked-up from sleeping on the couch. I can feel my heartbeat thumping against my temples as I slowly sit up, wincing from the pain.

I used to think my dad was spewing bullshit at first, but now I fully believe him. I don't know what I'd do if I had to work out this morning.

What time is it?

Falling back onto the couch, I smack my hand around on

the coffee table until I find my phone. There are two voicemails from Sadie—no doubt both of them consist of her cussing me out—and that's all I need for last night's memories to hit me like a train.

I almost made a move on Maddie. For a split second I thought about giving in to the temptation and just getting it out of the way so it wouldn't hang over our heads like a fucking storm cloud all the time.

What a *mistake* that would have been.

The sounds of pots and pans clattering in the kitchen make me groan, but I sit up regardless and peek over the top of the couch. Maddie is cooking breakfast, and there are three plates on the island with eggs and toast on them. She's busy plating the bacon when I join her in the kitchen, and the delicious smell makes my stomach growl.

Maddie has never had to try to be beautiful. It just comes to her naturally. Even now with her hair piled up messily into a bun on top of her head and wearing only a T-shirt and a pair of pajama bottoms with fuzzy socks on her feet, she's stunning.

Her face gives no indication of how she might be feeling after last night. I wouldn't blame her if she was pissed, but she doesn't seem like she wants to chop my balls off. After all, she made me breakfast, so she can't hate me *that* much, right?

Unless it's poisoned . . .

I inspect the plate carefully, not putting it past her. "Is this for me?"

I hold my breath for the sharp reply, but it never comes. Instead, she nods and sits down on one of the bar stools and digs in to her food. She's giving me the silent treatment, and somehow, that's even worse. I'd much rather she got in my face and fought with me because it would mean she cares. Her indifference isn't something I'm used to. I don't like it at all.

We eat our breakfast together in silence, and when I'm finished, I wash my plate so she doesn't have to. Not that it makes a difference considering the countless plastic cups and other trash sprawled across the counter and littering the floor. "It was really good," I say. "Thank you."

"You're welcome," she replies in a monotone voice.

"Mads—" I freeze at the nickname and grasp her wrist to stop her from going upstairs. It used to come naturally to me, but things are different now. They have been for years. *"Maddie,"* I correct. "I'm sorry for what I said last night, I—" *Am I really sorry, though?* As much as I say it would have been a mistake to kiss her, I know it wouldn't have been.

"It's fine." She pulls her hand back, rubbing the spot on her wrist where my fingers were. "You were drinking and didn't mean it. I don't fault you for it. Ethan said you could use the guest room, and I shouldn't have intervened. Hopefully I didn't ruin your night."

Ruin my night?

How could she think that? I mean, yeah, she stopped me from following through on my plans with Sadie, but if it meant I'd get to stand that close to her again, regardless of whether or not she was pissed at me, I wouldn't change a thing. We've spoken to each other more in the past twenty-four hours than we have in years. I didn't realize how much I missed her until last night. How much of an *idiot* I was for pushing her out of my life for good.

"Maddie, I—"

"I'm so fucking hungover." Ethan enters the kitchen and plops down on the empty bar stool, tugging his plate closer without telling his sister thank you. He begins to inhale his bacon, and whatever I was about to tell Maddie dies on my tongue.

"That's what happens when you drink." Maddie chastises him. "Consequences."

"Please, shut *up*," he grunts. "I'm not in the mood today, Maddie."

She takes that as her cue to leave, and it bothers me that I feel like whatever happened last night isn't resolved between us. The need to apologize to her is stronger than usual, but why? I've been a dick to her since I started high school, but I've always been able to keep the urge to apologize for my behavior at bay because I knew it was for the best. What's the difference now?

"How was Sadie?" Ethan asks.

Since I can't exactly share the run-in I had with his little sister, I do what I do best and change the subject. "Fine, but I'm more interested to know about how you hit things off with Jennifer."

Jennifer was the other girl at the party last night. Someone I invited to set Ethan up with. My best friend's been off his game lately, so I thought I'd help him out. "She was all over you last night, so I'm assuming you got lucky."

Ethan drags a hand through his shaggy blond hair and gives me a sheepish grin. "Before we talk about me, let's talk about *you*. Sadie texted Jennifer that you left her alone in the guest room last night."

Because your sister was more intriguing.

"I wasn't in the mood."

"Dude." He narrows his eyes and lets out a scoff. "She was naked, and you just left her there?"

I'm unsure why he's surprised when he should be accustomed to my ways, which haven't changed since we got into high school.

That knowledge doesn't tamper the growing disgust I have for myself, though. "She was too desperate," I lie. "It was a turnoff."

"Have I ever mentioned how much of a fucking asshole you are to girls?"

"And you aren't?" I counter.

Before he can reply, the front door opens, and we share terrified expressions. If his parents are home early with the house looking like *this*? We're dead.

Thankfully, Maya, Maddie's best friend enters the kitchen instead. She sets her purse on top of the island before she analyzes the mess we made last night. "Damn. You guys are fucked. Why haven't you started cleaning yet?"

I point at Ethan with a cheesy grin. "Just swapping sex stories before we get to it."

Ethan whips his head to mine with the promise of *death* in his eyes. *What the hell?*

Maya casts a lingering stare at Ethan before she props a hand on her hip and asks, "Where's Maddie?"

I'm still trying to decipher why Ethan gave me that look, but when I realize he's incapable of replying, I answer for him. "She's upstairs in her room. Would you care to help us with this disaster of a house first?"

"Hm . . ." She ponders, tapping a finger to her chin. "Help clean up after a party I wasn't invited to? I think I'll pass. You guys have fun, though!" Tossing her long black ponytail over her shoulder, she disappears from the kitchen, my best friend's eyes glued to her ass the entire way.

"You've got to be kidding," I deadpan. "*Maya*? Dude, that's a recipe for disaster. You realize Maddie would kill you, right? Like, shred you to pieces and feed them to the wolves."

"It's not like I'd even have a chance." He's seething. "Why'd you have to say something to her about swapping *sex stories*? She's going to think I'm a perv."

I cock my head to the side. "Aren't you? We're one and the same, Ethan. Always have been."

His jaw sets into a firm line but eventually he releases an exaggerated sigh and reaches beneath the sink to grab a garbage bag. "It doesn't matter. Like I said, I don't have a shot in hell."

"What makes you think that?"

"Oh come *on*. Maya probably goes for guys who look like you. I'm not over six foot, I don't have an eight pack, and I damn sure don't have your ability to flirt. I wouldn't have a shot, and that's not me trying to be self-deprecating. It's just the truth."

I hate that he has such a low opinion of himself. Ethan is the funniest guy I know, and while he might not be a gym rat, he has one of the biggest hearts. Any girl would be *lucky* to have him.

Together, we pick up the house, but about ten minutes in, I ask, "Why don't you take a chance with her? You might get lucky."

He scoffs as he shoves a cup into the bag. "Maya isn't the hit it and quit it type. If I were to hit it, I don't think I'd be able to quit it. Not that *you'd* understand that."

Oh, but I do.

All too well, actually.

"Maybe Maddie would understand if you told her how you feel. If she knew you felt *that* strongly about Maya, then—"

"Ha!" He tosses his head back and laughs. "This is Maddie we're talking about. Besides, there are just some things you don't do to a sibling, like fuck their best friend. It'd be like *her* making a move on *you*." He shudders at the thought.

Just for a moment, I'm glad Maddie thinks our conversation

last night was a mistake. Letting her know my true feelings and the desire I feel for her would only result in catastrophe. It's clear Ethan wouldn't be okay with it if I were to make a move, so leaving that fleeting moment between us forgotten is for the best. I'll let Maddie chalk it up to me being drunk and rambling if she wants. It's better this way.

Safer.

"I guess you're right," I reply, and even though I want to say so much more, I decide to keep my mouth shut instead.

It's better this way.

Safer.

I just need to keep repeating that mantra until I believe it.

Four

MADDIE

"And he *apologized*?" Maya, holding a bottle of red nail polish, glances up from the foot of my bed. "Cameron *Holden*? Are we talking about the same person?"

I still can't believe it either. Six years ago he told me he didn't want anything to do with me, and now we've interacted more than we have in ages. It's like whiplash the way he goes from hot to cold. When I caught him in the guest bedroom with that girl—she did an *exceptional* job of expressing herself—he went from being a dick saying he was in the middle of something to chasing me down the hall and asking for my forgiveness. He's an anomaly I have yet to figure out.

And I could have sworn he had wanted to. Well, I'm not going to make any assumptions, but the way he looked at me was *breathtaking*. I've never seen his eyes get so dark and serious.

But he was drunk, and I interrupted his night of fun. Of course he was horny. He probably would have made a move on *anyone* standing there. Not that he did make a move, but when he stepped closer to me in the hallway and was towering over me, I thought . . .

"Stop fidgeting!" Maya scolds. Her grip becomes firmer on my foot and she dips the brush back into the polish. "You're being a horrible test subject."

Right. Maya's in the cosmetology program at the local community college, and I never complain when she wants to practice on me. But I can't focus with thoughts of Cameron on my mind.

"Sorry," I grumble. "Anyway, I was in shock too. Believe me. The whole night was strange."

"It is weird," Maya admits. "But I hope you're not stuck on the whole 'bore' comment they made. Cameron and Ethan think anyone who doesn't party is boring, you know? Don't apologize for trying to get out of this desert-ass town and make something of yourself."

"I would never apologize for that, but sometimes I wonder if I'm missing out. Is partying *really* that much fun? The ones I've been to at college weren't like the movies. They seemed pointless, but maybe something is wrong with me because I think that? I should enjoy partying, right? I'm nineteen. This is the time in my life when I'm supposed to let loose and have fun. Am I a loser?"

Maya scoffs and switches to my other foot. "You're far from a loser, Maddie. You're a loner. There's a difference."

If she wasn't so focused on painting my nails, I would have chucked a pillow at her face. "Because that is *so* much better. *Thanks.*"

Maya never pressured me to go out in high school, which is why we were so close to each other. Her parents were strict, and I had no interest in getting high and drunk every weekend, so we spent our nights watching corny movies while she practiced braiding my hair and painting my nails, like she's doing to me now. She's the type of friend I can go months without seeing, but as soon as I'm back home, it's like I never left. We pick back up right where we left off.

"It's not a *bad* thing." Maya reassures me. "You'd rather stay in and read a book than go out. There's nothing wrong with that. It's your preference."

"But to everyone else it seems like a bad thing."

"Everyone as in *Cameron Holden*?" She gives me a knowing look, and it's no use hiding my feelings for him from her. If anyone would understand, it would be her. She was with me through my years of hard-core crushing on him. I never admitted it to her, but anyone could see it whenever Cameron was around. I followed him like a lost puppy when he came over to the house. And Maya was by my side after he told me he didn't want me in his life. She held me while I cried, and we stayed up eating pints of ice cream until three in the morning.

"Maybe," I admit in defeat. "I don't know."

Maya screws the cap back on the nail polish and says, "What will make you feel better? If you want to go to a party and try to dip your toe in again, let's go. Mark is throwing one at his place tonight, and your lover boy will be in attendance too."

"He's *not* my lover boy," I snap. "How do you even know he's going?"

She scoffs. "Maddie, Cameron is a shoo-in for the NFL. The minute he comes back to this rinky-dink town, people talk. His whereabouts are *always* on everyone's radar."

I don't know how I feel about Cameron being famous around here. I'm used to the nerdy kid who ran through sprinklers with me and walked me to the ice-cream shop on scorching summer days. He was shy back then, and even though he's more outgoing now, I can't imagine he enjoys all this attention. I'd like to think I still know him, but maybe the personality changes over the years have become permanent.

Maya is still staring at me as she awaits my answer.

"I don't want to be *that* girl."

Maya scrunches her brows together. "What girl?"

"Like, the girl who's not used to partying and suddenly shows up to try to fit in. This is a small town. People will talk."

"And since when have you given a shit about what anyone thinks?" she asks. "Look, I'm not trying to persuade you to go if you're not comfortable with it, but if you want to go, we can, and I'll make you look superhot."

I arch a brow. "Hair included?"

She almost looks offended. "Um, of *course*. I need all the practice I can get."

I slump back into my pillows, and she swats my foot to get me to be still before she starts on the clear coat.

I don't know what the hell I'm thinking. Am I really considering going to this party? I've always been confident in who I am, and I've never regretted my decision to focus on studying rather than getting shit-faced like everyone else, but I'm not *Maya*. She radiates sexiness everywhere she goes. With her deep-tan skin, glossy hair, and features that models would kill for, she stands out in any room she walks into. I can't say the same for me.

Still, I can't shake the memory of Cameron's expression last night. I felt like we were close to a breakthrough, but I had to leave him alone in that hallway because if he'd been drinking, anything he said could have been a lie. If he wants to apologize for that day six years ago, I need him to be completely sober so I know he means it.

"Fine," I relent. "I'll go."

"Perfect, but if you want to get there on time, I suggest you *stop* fidgeting! God, you're the worst!"

I lift my head from the pillows. "Word of advice? You *really* need to work on your customer service."

"*Voy a matarte*," she mutters as a grin tugs at her lips.

Five

CAMERON

After my fifth shot, I'm beginning to feel good. *Really* good.

It's hard to believe I woke up so hungover this morning. I guess it's true that to cure a hangover, all you need is to drink more, because I feel fucking fantastic.

Mark's party is vastly different from the one Ethan and I threw last night. Where ours was low-key with fewer than twenty people, the large house Mark lives in is packed. I stopped counting after the last shot, but I didn't think we even *had* more than fifty people in this town.

I feel like I'm in a can of sardines with the number of people brushing against my shoulder as they pass. The bass is thumping loudly from a nearby speaker, drowning out the conversations around me, and it's so damn hot that my leather jacket is sticking to my skin. I would take it off if Ethan and I weren't seconds away from winning our fourth round of beer pong in a row.

"Oh shit. Here." Ethan passes me the blunt he's been harboring. "Sorry. I didn't even realize I was holding it."

I shake my head as I take my aim for the center cup. "You know I can't smoke. Not with football."

"It's spring break," Ethan says. "It'll be out of your system before then."

"Not risking it." I let the ball fly, earning a round of cheers when it makes a wet *plop* in my target. "My dad went to college with the Arizona coach. Thinks he can get him to come watch one of my games this season." Although I could have been selected for the NFL after my first year of school, I opted to get my degree first before entering myself for the draft. It's what my mom would have wanted, but it doesn't hurt to have NFL teams keeping track of my stats or flying out to my games to watch me play in the meantime.

Ethan blows out a whistle when he takes his turn. "Shit. Really?"

"Yeah, which means staying *away* from drugs and training as hard as I fucking can. This weekend has been fun, but come tomorrow, it's grind time. No more bullshit. My dad would murder me if he found out I'd been drinking."

Ethan fakes a gasp. "A twenty-one-year-old consuming *alcohol*? The horror."

Before I can reply, Sadie saunters up next to me at the table with a red Solo cup clenched in her manicured nails. She flicks her eyes up to mine flirtatiously and says, "I didn't know you were coming tonight."

My next ball hits its target again, making Ethan and me the champions of the night. He claps me on the back before I bend down to Sadie's ear and shout over the music, "I'm surprised you're even talking to me!"

After all, I left her naked and alone last night, but if there's anything I've learned the past few years, it's that the better looking a person is, the more they can get away with. I'm not proud of it, but it's the truth.

It's why I'm unsurprised when Sadie drags a hand down my chest and smiles, a set of dimples coming alive on her cheeks. "I guess you're going to have to beg for my forgiveness then, hm?"

Like I did with Maddie last night?

Maddie is the only girl I've chased out of fear that she was mad at me. Hell, she wrote me off six years ago, so I don't know what made me follow her down that hallway, but I can't shake the interaction between us no matter how hard I try. Maybe that's why I agreed to come tonight.

To forget.

And Sadie is offering me the chance to do just that.

"I'm glad you came," she adds.

My grin kicks up a notch. "How glad?"

Her hand passes over the crotch of my jeans, but my cock doesn't react at all. Not even a twitch. I've never had a problem getting hard for a girl. Normally the slightest brush of someone's fingers will set it off, which is why I should already be half-hard right now.

What the fuck?

"Meet me in one of the bedrooms upstairs in five and find out," Sadie says. "Third door on the left."

I watch her weave through the crowd of people, but even the view of her ass doesn't get me going. Maybe I need her lips around my cock to start things up, or maybe I need to find someone new. Maybe Sadie isn't doing it for me.

I scan the swarms of options for anyone who might give me a reaction. There are two girls making out by the kitchen island, but again, nothing. A half-naked girl smoking in the corner, a set of twins grinding in the middle of the living room to a seductive song. Nothing works, and I'm starting to believe something is *seriously* wrong with me until—

There.

My gaze homes in on a perfectly round ass hugged tightly by a black leather miniskirt hardly covering the girl's underwear. A blond ponytail hangs down to the middle of her spine, and fantasies of me wrapping that hair around my fist while I—

"I can't believe she came," Ethan scoffs, taking another drag of the blunt. "I've truly seen *everything* now."

"Who?" I ask, unable to drag my eyes away from the girl. Mark seems to have already laid claim on her, whoever *she* is. He's laughing at something she says, and although I can't see her face, her body language seems to indicate she's enjoying her time with him.

"Maddie," Ethan says, pointing in the same direction I'm staring.

No.

No way in hell.

There's no way that's Maddie, but as soon as I get ready to tell Ethan he's too stoned, she spins around. Maya joins them a second later, passing a drink to Maddie, and I seriously can't comprehend what I'm seeing.

The girl who spent all her summer days with me and Ethan growing up looks *nothing* like the girl in the red bodysuit across the room. I'm used to curly pigtails and missing front teeth. Sure, I've seen her over the years mature into the woman she is today, but never like this.

Her curly blond ringlets are straightened to perfection, and her makeup is heavier than normal, with eyeliner and red lipstick, but that *bodysuit*. It cuts to the middle of her chest, outlining the breasts I've tried desperately to ignore for the past six years. I've never wanted to pull a piece of fabric apart as badly as I do now. Do the dirty images floating throughout my head make me a worthless sack of shit? Completely, but I can't stop them.

She isn't wearing a bra, so I can see her hardened nipples. What I wouldn't give to shove her right against that wall and release those tits so I can lap over them with my tongue and—

Well, it's nice to know my cock isn't broken.

It's suddenly giving a standing fucking *ovation* for Maddie Davis.

And now is *not* the time for this when I'm standing next to her brother.

My knuckles grow white on my cup. "Are you going to stop her from talking to Mark, or . . . ?"

He shrugs. "Why? She's a grown adult who can make her own decisions. I'm tired of babysitting her. Maddie knows right from wrong. Plus, it could be worse. Mark is a decent guy. If she wants to go for him then so be it."

"And is the reason you're telling her not to get lost because of the *friend* she brought with her?" Maya takes another sip of her drink, and despite how much she tries to hide it, her eyes slide to Ethan. She's in a pair of high-waisted ripped jean shorts and a white tube top that showcases a glistening belly ring. Ethan's mouth is practically watering at the sight.

"Partly," he admits. "Fuck, I need another blunt. I'm going to find Jackson and see if he has one. Be back in a few."

I don't notice him leaving. How could I when Mark places a hand on Maddie's waist and bends down to whisper into her ear? Granted, I don't really know the guy. He was on the football team with us in high school, but we were never close.

Are his intentions good when it comes to her?

My eyes narrow as he dips his gaze to her breasts when she isn't looking. Not that I have room to judge when I've been doing the same fucking thing since I laid eyes on her. I have no right to be protective. She isn't mine, nor can she *ever* be mine. I ruined my chances when I pushed her away; and aside from that, there's Ethan.

But even with the knowledge of how wrong it is, my legs still carry me across the room.

Maya eyes me skeptically before she shares a look with Maddie that I can't decipher. "I'm going to get a refill," she blurts, disappearing.

Maddie takes a slow sip of her drink, eyeing me over the rim. "What are you doing here?"

"I could ask you the same question." My eyes flick to Mark, who raises his hand to fist bump me—the same hand he placed on her waist a few seconds ago. I fight the urge to ignore him and instead reciprocate the gesture.

"How's it going, man?" he asks with a wide grin. "I haven't seen you in years. Heard you're doing big things in Pennsylvania. NFL bound, right?"

"Those are the rumors," I reply, keeping my eyes locked on Maddie. "Can you give us a minute alone, Mark?"

He glances between us, sensing the tension. "Uh, *sure*. I'll circle back in a few minutes."

When it's finally just the two of us in the corner of the room, I take my time studying her. Her glassy eyes and rosy cheeks tell me she's had too much to drink. She rarely parties, so one or two drinks is more than enough for her.

Her pulse is thrumming rapidly against her throat, and it makes me wonder if it's because of me, or Mark.

"If you came over to reprimand me, it isn't going to work. I can talk to whoever I want."

"I wasn't going to reprimand you."

"Then why did you come over here?" She hiccups, and fuck it's cuter than it should be. I fight the smile threatening to appear when she wobbles in her heels and takes a step closer to me. She sticks a finger into my chest and says, "You don't get to do this, Cam."

Cam.

She hasn't called me that in years.

A simple nickname puts my heart into overdrive.

"Do what?"

"Start speaking to me again as if we're suddenly close. I don't *deserve* the whiplash you give me. I don't deserve for you to cut me out of your life and then hop back in years later like nothing happened."

She's right, as always, but now isn't the time to have this conversation. Not when she's plastered and vulnerable.

"You have nothing to say?" she asks.

"I think we should discuss this when you're sober."

She scoffs. "Whatever. Just go enjoy the party elsewhere. In case you hadn't noticed, I was in the middle of something."

I cock my head to the side. "In the middle of *what* exactly?"

"I'm trying to *fuck*, Cameron, and if you hadn't interrupted, I would already be upstairs."

Christ. That word on her tongue . . .

This isn't Maddie. We haven't known each other in years, but I know her well enough to call her bluff. She would never fuck someone. *Fuck* isn't in her vocabulary. Maddie needs an emotional connection, not a one-night stand.

"And you want to fuck Mark?"

She huffs and crosses her arms over her chest, and dammit, I'm not strong enough to look away. Her tits are on full display, and I take my fill knowing she can tell I'm checking her out. The tiny inhale of breath she gives in response travels straight to my cock.

"Have any other suggestions?" she asks breathlessly.

Fuck me.

I refuse to be the bastard who takes advantage of her when she's drunk. I'd never stoop that low with a girl, especially not with her. But damn if I don't drink in the expression she's giving me and save it to memory. It intoxicates me more than whiskey ever could.

Lust, want, and desire all wrapped into one. Her sky-blue eyes have gone as deep as the ocean, and it takes everything I have to take a step away from her.

I may not want to, but I have to.

This is *Maddie Davis*. Ethan's little sister and someone I used to consider one of my best friends. Nothing will ever happen between us. Isn't that why I pushed her away in the first place? After that night in Myrtle Beach, before my mom's passing, I had been about to make a move and holy fuck did that scare me.

Even if I *had* made a move that night, it wouldn't have gone anywhere. Maddie has always been off limits, and I've had to fight this attraction toward her tooth and nail ever since that night on the beach.

I try to tell myself I can fight it for another night, no matter how difficult it might be, but my cock isn't listening to my brain. It's painfully hard against my jeans, and the liquor is coursing through me.

When Mark reappears at her side, there's a devil sitting on my shoulder persuading me to tell him to get lost, and as much as I want to act on those urges, Maddie is right. I did this to myself. Despite how wrong it feels for her to be flirting with someone aside from me, I don't have the right to stop her. It's not fair to her when I ruined everything, so I turn on my heel and leave them alone, ignoring the ton of bricks landing on my chest and carrying an overwhelming amount of regret.

I have a beautiful girl waiting for me upstairs, and although Sadie isn't *her*, she's going to have to do. With my use of alcohol and weed limited, I'll resort to sex like I always do. Even if it's only an hour, it'll numb my pain, and right now, I need a hell of a lot of numbness.

I *refuse* to be stuck in this never-ending torment of wanting someone I can't have.

Six

MADDIE

As soon as Mark returns Cameron walks away, leaving me in a daze.

What the hell is he playing at? I swear he knows the effect he has on me. Despite how much he tries to deny it, he was *jealous*. Why else would he have come over here without an explanation?

He had to know that coming over here would distract me from Mark. He knew he'd be the only thing on my mind as soon as he disappeared back into the crowd and went upstairs. Is he meeting that girl who was in the guest bedroom again? Is *he* fucking someone?

Oh my god.

This is exactly *what he wants!*

I'm so caught up in what he's doing that I'm no longer focusing on the attractive man right in front of me. Mark wants to get to know me. He's been nothing but a gentleman since he approached, and I'm not going to let Cameron Holden win whatever game he's playing.

He thinks he distracted me, but I'm about to flip the tables on him. He has no right to be jealous. *He's* the one who almost kissed me on that beach and then tossed me to the side a week later like I meant nothing. Ever since that day in his living room I've been unsure if Cameron was attracted to me or if it was all in my head, but he proved it to me tonight without having to say anything at all.

And if he can't grow a pair of balls and come to terms with that then *he* can live with the consequences.

I'm done putting myself on hold for him.

I've done it for longer than I care to admit.

"Can we get some fresh air?" I ask. The room is stifling hot and the music is so loud I can hardly hear my thoughts.

Mark pulls a set of keys out of his pocket and jingles them in the air. "I've got something better to show you. Come on."

He takes my hand in his, and his large, bulky figure easily cuts a path through the crowd to the front door. I'm hit with a rare breeze when we step onto his driveway, grateful for the reprieve it brings. A shiny red Mustang sits pristinely in the driveway as if it's never been touched, and Mark opens the passenger door, ushering me to get in.

"Have you been drinking?" I ask.

"No. I always stay sober during parties at my place. I learned the hard way after too many incidents. If someone pukes on the carpet or a vase shatters, I want to be fully alert to take care of it." He runs a hand through his shoulder-length blond hair while he waits for my answer, and although I feel Mark is someone I can trust, I can't be certain that he's had nothing to drink, and I don't feel confident driving somewhere with someone I barely know when I'm tipsy myself.

"Can we just talk out here? Is that okay?"

He nods and tucks the keys back into his pocket. "We can do whatever you want, Maddie. Truthfully, I'm surprised you came tonight. You've never been the type to party."

"That's because I'm not. I was trying to branch out, but parties are just . . . not my thing."

He chuckles. "Trust me, I know. I used to see you in the stands reading a book at our games in high school. Ethan said your parents forced you to go."

Now I'm the one laughing. "Yeah, football isn't my thing either. I'm most comfortable staying inside watching a movie instead of *this*."

"Well, maybe I can take you on a date sometime. An introverted one, of course."

Oh god.

His suggestion should give me butterflies or that giddy feeling I used to feel with Cameron. A person should be happy they're being asked out, not utterly petrified. I shouldn't have tears welling up, and my stomach shouldn't be wrapped in a knot.

But I've spent the majority of my life lusting over a man who is probably hooking up with another girl right now. Even when he told me he wanted me out of his life, I never truly left. I was always in the background listening to anything my brother shared about Cameron's time away at college. I kept up with him even when my brain screamed at me to let him go.

I had boys at college and even in high school who showed interest, but it never worked out. After Cameron broke my heart in the seventh grade, I let myself grieve for a few years before I started dating this boy, Michael Collins, for a couple of months in high school. He was nice enough and treated me well until he discovered

I wasn't ready to do anything more than kiss. I was fifteen at the time, and thrilled to be going out with a junior, but no matter how hard he tried, I couldn't bring myself to take the next step. And that resulted in me finding out a week later that he was cheating on me with a girl named Penelope, captain of the cheerleading squad. I can still picture the black eye Ethan gave him.

Regardless, the boys I tried to move on with would kiss me and I'd feel nothing. Their lips didn't bring me the spark that a brush of Cameron's fingers against mine elicited. All the little moments with Cameron over the years made my body feel as if it was on *fire*. The brushing of his knee against mine on car trips with my family. How we would always seek each other out no matter what room we were in. How he knew me. The *real* me.

What has holding out for him gotten me, though? I'm a nineteen-year-old virgin because whenever another boy touches me it doesn't feel right. I'm tainted by someone who will never be mine. Someone who has been dealt too much pain to understand how to push through it.

I can't keep waiting for him when there are handsome, genuine guys out there like Mark, who are mature and emotionally ready for a relationship. Going on a date with Mark would be uncomplicated and easy. It's about time I start choosing what will make *me* happy.

"I'll think about it," I reply.

His grin grows wider. "Cool. I won't pressure you to do the number exchange. If you want to reach out, Ethan has my number. Just ask him for it."

Mark has a way of settling my nerves. He makes me feel at ease, and honestly, he doesn't understand how much I needed that tonight.

I jerk my head toward his Mustang. "So, what's the sound system on this thing like?"

He arches a brow. "Wanna find out?"

What the hell, right?

I've already gone out of my comfort zone by coming to this party tonight. What's a ride in a car with a hot guy going to change? Screw my reservations. For once, I want to be a daredevil.

"Lead the way," I reply with a bright smile.

Whether it's out of excitement or fear, I can't be certain, but when Mark opens the passenger door for me again, a shot of adrenaline courses through my veins. The feeling is foreign, but it's one I'm going to welcome with open arms tonight.

Take that, Holden.

Try all you like, but you'll never win this game you started.

Seven

CAMERON

Five years earlier

We're gathered around the table at lunch—Mallory and Jackie sit beside me while Ethan, Penelope, and Jack, another member of the team, sit opposite us. Mallory is raving about the cheerleaders' new routine for their upcoming competition, twirling a brown ringlet around her finger while she chomps on a piece of gum. She's on a liquid diet, and the only reason I know this is because as soon as she sat down she bragged about how she's already lost three pounds.

I couldn't care less about their routine or what diet Mallory is on. The twins have taken a liking to me, and they've insinuated having a threesome at Jack's upcoming party this weekend, so if I have to pretend to care about liquid diets and routines for the next few days, then so be it.

"Are you guys ready for the game this weekend?" Penelope shuffles closer to Ethan on the bench, flashing him a flirtatious grin that Ethan seems oblivious to.

"Yeah," he replies, shoving another bite of fiestada pizza into his mouth. "This team will be easy to beat. No sweat."

Jack rubs his hands together and wiggles his brows. "My cousin is bringing a keg for us for the after-party at my place. He goes to State."

"Oooh," Jackie drawls. "A college boy. Is he hot?"

I chuckle low and deep, watching as Jackie squirms on the bench. "Trust me, baby. You've got the hottest man sitting beside you."

Ethan rolls his eyes. "Stop being a douchebag, Cameron."

"What? It's the truth."

"Will Michael be there?" Penelope interrupts.

Maddie's boyfriend? He's in the same grade as us, but I avoid him like the plague for reasons I have yet to understand. There's nothing wrong with the guy. He's funny, smart, and he's a great teammate. Maddie seems to be happy, and yet that doesn't make me feel relieved in the least. I expected her to move on eventually and forget what happened between us on that beach, but I didn't expect to feel so annoyed by Michael's face whenever I see him.

"I think so. Yeah," Jack replies.

"Good." Penelope sits up straighter, satisfied by his answer. "I call an upstairs bedroom for us."

Mine and Ethan's gaze both shoot to hers. "Don't bet on it," Ethan says. "My sister is dating him."

Penelope furrows her brows. "Who's your sister?"

"Maddie Davis."

She throws her back with laughter, and Mallory and Jackie join in, and irritation prickles along my skin. "The freshman? Yeah, he's not having fun with her. At least that's what he told me beneath the bleachers yesterday when we—" Her face turns red, and I haven't noticed my grip on the table is damn near making a dent in it, but my knuckles are white, and all I can see is red.

Michael cheated on Maddie with Penelope?

Is he an idiot?

Ethan's face more than likely is a reflection of mine. "He cheated on my sister?"

Realizing the ramifications of what she just revealed, Penelope's face pales. "I—I mean, I thought he was ending things with her. He said he was going to before we—"

Ethan shoves back from the table, his tray slamming into mine. "I'm going to kill him," *he says, seething.*

Anger is boiling beneath the surface, but unlike Ethan, it would be odd if I became outraged like he is. He's Maddie's older brother. He has a reason to be pissed. Michael is a junior trying to take advantage of a freshman, and although this information shouldn't bother me as much as it does, I can't help it.

I already broke her heart once.

She doesn't need it broken again.

And that fucker Michael?

I'll be damned if he lays another hand on her.

"As soon as I talk to Maddie, I'm cussing him the fuck out," *Ethan sneers.*

But me? I'm already rising from the table, muttering an excuse about using the bathroom before I stalk off into the hallway like a lion searching for his prey.

>> <<

"Hey." Ethan joins me at my locker three periods later, eyeing the bandage wrapped around my fist. "I'm guessing that's where Michael got his shiner from? I saw him in history. Everyone's asking about it, but he won't say who did it."

I found that fucker in the parking lot coming back from lunch, and I don't feel sorry about the punch I threw. My anger got the best of me, and looking back, maybe I could have handled things differently, but I was in the heat of the moment, picturing Maddie bawling her eyes out like she did in my living room after my mom passed. I threatened to make his life a living hell if he told a soul it was me. I'm the captain of the football team, after all. I have the authority to exile him from every party and all the girls in school if I want.

It infuriated me that Michael cheated on Maddie of all people. It's ironic, really, considering I've cheated on plenty of girls. I'm not going to claim that I'm a saint because I'd be lying. Who am I to judge Michael when I'm a fucking clone of him? Ethan has covered for me plenty of times when girls become suspicious. I never date them, but I have claimed to be exclusive only to turn around and fuck the next girl who asks.

But Maddie?

I'd never cheat on her.

Never in a million years.

And we may not be on speaking terms ever since our fight two years ago, but that doesn't mean I won't look out for her and protect her as much as I can.

"He deserved it," I mutter. "Don't say anything, all right? If anyone asks, just . . ."

"I'll say I did it," he says. "Unless I get called into the office or something. Then you're fucked."

"You don't have to cover for me."

"Yes, I do. It should have been me who punched him anyway. I'm her brother, you know? But I know you're her older brother, too, in a way, so thank you. For looking out for her."

Right.
That's what I'm doing.
Looking out for her like an older brother.

>> <<

The revving of Mark's car pulling onto the street stayed with me long after Ethan and I got back to his house. I had no reason to wait for her to return. I haven't been her friend in years, but that didn't stop my heart from racing as my mind wandered to what the hell she was doing with Mark until two in the morning. My feelings toward Mark are growing dangerously close to how I felt about Michael, and I don't like it one bit. I'm used to feeling nothing. Being emotionless. But when it comes to Maddie, I feel everything *too* much.

Is she still drunk?

It's pitch black in the living room. Only the gentle ticking of the grandfather clock in the dining room fills the silence. Ethan went to bed when we got home, but it's not unusual for me to sleep on the couch. I'm pretty sure the cushions are indented from how many times I've slept here.

Finally, fifteen minutes later, I hear the jangling of keys and the front door opening. The hardwood floor creaks beneath her feet, and then the fridge opens, casting a golden glow in the living room.

I should leave her alone, but the longer we go without speaking, the more it upsets me. I've been trying to pinpoint why the silence between us has been troubling me so much since I returned. We've ignored each other for the past six years, and I was fine with that because it was the right thing to do, but this is the first time I've come home from college where it *doesn't* feel like the right thing to do. Why is that? Because I'm at a place in my life where I don't hate the world? Because maybe a minuscule part of me believes I could be healed enough to let her back into my life?

Whatever the reason, I can't stop thinking about her, and rather than sit back and let myself be miserable about it, I'm going to *do* something.

When I stand up from the couch, Maddie notices me and jumps back with a hand placed over her heart. "Jesus," she breathes. "I didn't realize you were sleeping here. What are you still doing up?"

I point to the freezer rather than answer her question. "The pizza is behind the frozen lasagna."

"I wasn't looking for pizza," she replies.

"No? Has your late-night snack craving changed in the past six years?"

I inch closer until I can clearly see her face. The red lipstick hasn't moved out of place, and her hair is still pin straight. She doesn't *look* like she's been messing around in the back of a car, and the hope that fills my chest because of that observation is pathetic. Thankfully, the glassy look in her eyes has faded, too, which means she's not drunk anymore. At least I hope not.

"Fine." Her shoulders slump in defeat when she tugs out the pizza. "But this doesn't mean you still know me. I've changed a lot since—"

Since the night she left my house bawling her eyes out. She doesn't have to remind me. The image replays in my head on a constant loop.

"What's new about you, then? Aside from the fact you've become a bore."

She gasps. "I have *not* become a bore! I've always been like this."

"Have you?" I cock my head to the side and study her as she slides the pizza into the preheating oven. I'm pushing her on this only to get under her skin. I know she's been a bookworm since the moment she could read, but that night in Myrtle Beach was different. She showed a side of herself I didn't realize existed.

It's a version I miss intensely.

One I saw a glimpse of tonight when she sped off in that car with Mark.

"I remember a much different version of you in middle school," I continue, knowing she's seconds away from packing a beautiful punch to my face. "You were always convincing me to do dangerous things. Like sneaking out, for example."

It's a low blow considering that the night I'm talking about was the night I almost made a move on her, but I'm desperate to know if she still remembers it.

Does it still haunt her the way it does me?

When she spins to face me, hands balled into fists at her sides, I have my answer.

"I wonder *why* I tried to become a daredevil in the first place, Cameron. Do you have any idea as to why I'd try to convince you to sneak out that night? Being outgoing isn't my thing, but whenever you're involved I seem to—" She clears her throat to stop herself.

"Look, Maddie, I don't want to fight with you. I'm tired of fighting. All I'm trying to say is that seeing you leave with Mark was the first time I caught a glimpse of the *old* you, and I guess I didn't realize how much I missed that version of you until tonight." The speech comes out rushed. I don't sound like myself at all, and Maddie is standing in the middle of the kitchen with her feet rooted to the floor, seemingly in shock.

"We have your family's annual spring break trip to the Grand Canyon next weekend, and I don't want things to be awkward between us anymore, so I'm proposing a truce of sorts."

"A truce," she repeats slowly.

"Yeah. I want us to go back to how things used to be between us. At least until we head back to school. It'll be easier for everyone that way. Plus think about how happy it'd make your parents. You know they've been devastated since we had our falling out."

"*I'm* not the one who caused that," she mutters.

"No, it was me. *All* me. What happened to our friendship was one hundred percent my fault. My mom had just passed, and after sneaking out onto the beach with you only a week prior, I—" *Fuck, I'm not going to get into that now.* "I was messed up, Maddie. I hated life and resented everything, and I couldn't bear for you to become one of those things."

Maddie shifts her gaze to the floor as I try desperately to blink back my tears.

"I wasn't mature enough to admit I was wrong then, but I am now. You deserve to know how fucking sorry I am, and if you'll let me, I'll make it up to you. I'll rebuild our friendship."

Her eyes lift to mine, tears streaming down her cheeks. "Our *friendship*?"

The word sounds thick on her tongue. We both know it's because *friendship* is the furthest thing to describe what we had with each other, but I don't know what else to call it. When break is over, we'll be heading back to separate schools. A relationship has never been in the cards for us.

But for the next twelve days, I'm going to do whatever possible to fix things. Maybe if we go back to being friends the desire to kiss her lips won't be as strong. Maybe if we stop ignoring each other I won't want to grab her wrist and pull her against my chest to get her attention.

I don't know if mending our friendship is the right thing to do, but what I was doing before isn't working anymore, so it's time for a change.

"A friendship that is *extremely* special to me," I clarify.

She smiles softly, and damn if it doesn't make my heart skip a beat. "I miss the old version of you too. The nerdy boy with glasses and braces who could never stop showing me his Pokémon card collection. I'd be lying if I said I didn't miss you, too, and I appreciate your apology, Cam. It means the world to me. I—*what*? Why do you have that look on your face?"

"Because you called me *Cam*. Does that mean we're on a nickname basis now? You're agreeing to the truce?"

She opens a drawer and pulls out a set of oven mitts. "The pizza should be done in a few minutes if you want some, and if you wish to be on a nickname basis again, I'll agree to that. The *truce*, however . . ."

I step behind her to grab either side of the counter, caging her back against my chest. Vanilla and honey floods my senses and *damn* I didn't realize how much the scent of her is like a drug to me.

The way her body relaxes against my chest almost makes me groan in pleasure. We're standing too close. I need to step back, but now that I've got her in this position, it's useless to try to escape.

I dip my mouth down to her ear and whisper, "You already gave me my answer about the truce, Mads."

She twists her head to the side to meet my stare, and our lips are mere inches apart. If I leaned down just a fraction, I'd finally kiss her.

Temptation has never been so unfair.

"What makes you think that?" she asks.

"Because I know you, and you would *never* share your pizza with someone you don't consider a friend."

Her laugh, which is so foreign yet also familiar, tugs at my heartstrings with enough force to bring me to my knees. It's a song I thought I forgot the lyrics to, but her laugh seems to be a tune I've subconsciously stored in the files of my memory, hoping one day I'd eventually get to dust it off again.

I was right.

"You're right about the pizza," she admits. "But to gain my friendship back you're going to have to put in a lot of work."

I chuckle against her skin. "Are you playing hard to get?"

"Maybe. Is that going to be a problem?" She steps back to check on the pizza, but when she does, her ass brushes against the front of my sweatpants. I'm fully hard from being this close to her, and when she feels my cock prodding against her ass, she makes no effort to move. Her body stills, and her breathing becomes erratic. My knuckles grow white on either side of her, and my hands are gripping the granite with so much force that I'm afraid it might crack at any given second.

This would be all too easy. Ethan is upstairs sleeping, and their parents don't get back from their trip for another two days. All I'd have to do is hike this skirt up around her waist, bend her over the counter, and then I would rail her so hard that we'd rattle the dishes in the sink.

Tick.

Tick.

Tick.

The grandfather clock in the next room waits for either of us to make a choice, but we don't move a muscle. Whatever decision we make next will determine our future, and I don't know if we're ready for that.

Thankfully, an outside factor chooses for us. The oven dings, and we shoot apart before we do something we won't be able to come back from. Maddie's cheeks are flushed, and the rise and fall of her chest seems to be at the same rhythmic pace as mine.

Becoming friends again is going to be difficult if we keep finding ourselves in predicaments like these, but the hope is that this feeling of lust will fade if we rekindle our friendship.

Even thinking that sounds insane, but it's worth a shot.

Maddie slides on the oven mitts and grabs the pizza before she asks, "Still want to have a truce?"

I keep my eyes trained on hers while she cuts the pie with lethal precision. "Now more than ever, *Mads*. Pass me a plate."

Eight

MADDIE

Last night felt like a lucid dream.

There's no way Cameron apologized, suggested a truce so we could become friends again, *and* had his hard cock pressed against my ass all in the same night. How can he think becoming friends is something we'll ever be able to maintain? When I backed into his thick length while he had me caged against the island, it confirmed my suspicions about his feelings for me. Well, maybe not *feelings*. I'm almost certain Cameron doesn't know what genuine feelings are. The man is a certified player through and through, but one thing I did become keenly aware of last night? The attraction is mutual, and that's a danger in itself.

Ever since I went to bed, I've tried to convince myself it was a fluke. Maybe he drank too much last night at the party. Maybe that's why we stayed up until five in the morning eating pizza while we laughed and talked about irrelevant things, avoiding the elephant in the room about *why* we put distance between us in the first place. I thought he'd wake up this morning convinced the truce had been a mistake.

But what I *didn't* expect?

Cameron Holden showing up on my doorstep at three in the afternoon with a bike propped against his hip.

I blink at least a dozen times before I finally grasp that this is definitely not a dream. My heart racing a mile a minute is real. My palms slicked with sweat are real. His smile that could rival the sun is *real*.

"What are you doing here?" I ask. "Are you looking for Ethan?"

Christ. Cameron must have ridden his bike here. Droplets of sweat trickle down his tanned skin and run into the band of his shorts, disappearing beneath the indented v-line to—

"Ethan's working a shift at Perry's. He got called in since the weather is nice today. There's nothing like a good ice-cream cone when it's sweltering." He flicks his eyes over my bare legs, and I don't notice until now that I'm only wearing a large T-shirt that hardly lands past my upper thighs. "I'm here for you."

"To what, ride *bikes*? I haven't ridden one since—"

"Your fall in the third grade. I know. I was there." He points to the picnic basket slung around the handlebar. "I wanted to see if you'll get over your fears and ride with me at Papago Park." He waits expectantly for my answer, but I can't seem to get past the fact that he remembered that fall off my bike all those years ago. It was the day my crush on him first developed, and the memory slams into me like a freight train.

"Ethan, you're going too fast! Wait up!" Cameron pedals frantically ahead of me to catch up to my brother, and I'm working double-time to keep up with both of them. They both had growth

spurts this past summer, and now anywhere *we go that involves physical activity is a hard-core workout for me.*

The greenery and pavement whip by me in a blur as I pedal faster. Ethan is long gone now, but it isn't the first time he's left us in the dust. He makes everything *between us a competition.*

Papago Park is my favorite place to ride. It's the only spot where I don't feel like I'm surrounded by desert. Here, there's a pond in the center of trails surrounded by palm trees. I'm used to cactuses and sand that comes with the year round dry heat, but this is the one place where water sometimes kisses my skin when other kids skip rocks a little too hard or the fishermen catch a big one.

When I'm older, I want to live close to the ocean.

Cameron glances over his shoulder a few feet in front of me. "Do you need me to slow down?"

"No, I—"

Before the sentence can leave my lips, my tire catches on a rock and I go flying from my bike. I brace for the impact and hold my breath, which is knocked from my lungs when my elbows connect with scorching hot asphalt.

I don't know if it's from the adrenaline or the pain I know I'll soon feel, but big salty tears stream down my cheeks like an endless river. Cameron, who's stopped trailing after Ethan, tosses his bike to the side and jogs over to me.

My entire body is shaking, and although the fall wasn't that bad, it was still terrifying. I've never fallen from my bike before, and I don't plan on it ever happening again.

"Hey, you're okay." He soothes me in a voice akin to honey. He grabs my arm and twists it to inspect the wound on my elbow. Blood is trickling down my forearm and dribbling onto the asphalt below. "Mads, you're okay. Look at me."

I lift my gaze to his, and my sobs turn into whimpers at the sympathetic grin on his face. His teeth are all braces, and his glasses are slightly crooked, but the mere presence of him beside me causes my terror to recede.

With our eyes locked, Cameron's smile fades, and the breath catches in my lungs when he brings a hand up to my face. At this moment, nothing else matters. The kids playing a few yards away don't exist anymore, and the chirping of the birds is drowned out by the thumping of my heart. My thoughts are jumbled as his thumb strokes my cheek to wipe away the tears, lingering longer than he should before he drops it back down to his side.

"I've got you," he reassures me. "Always."

Cameron stares at me in that deciphering way of his. I've always felt like he could see through every wall I've put up around myself, but at this moment I'm convinced he has a telepathic ability to read my thoughts.

His eyes soften as if he's remembering that moment between us, too, and the lump in my throat becomes practically unbearable.

"If I fall . . ." I warn.

The smile he gives me in return makes my stomach bottom out. It's *devastatingly* handsome, and one I'm sure he uses frequently on his conquest of the week.

"You won't," he replies. "I'll make sure of it."

>> <<

We end up driving my car since the trunk is big and we can stow our bikes in it. My family hasn't taken a ride together since my crash, so the bikes have been collecting dust and cobwebs in the garage ever since, which also meant we had to stop at a store along the way to buy a pump for the tires because they were flat.

But finally, we made it to Papago Park. March is the best time of year to visit Arizona, as the temperature is nearly perfect. It's in the low eighties today, foreshadowing the first glimpse of summer, and although the pond and palm trees haven't changed a bit and look as beautiful as ever, they're not the sight I'm focused on.

Cameron kneels beside my bike as he pumps the last wisps of air I'll need into the tires. His chest is glorious, and his biceps flex with every stroke of the pump. The man could be on any magazine cover in the world, and if he *does* make it to the NFL like others are predicting, his face will be the most sought-after one on the market for advertisements. I have no doubt.

"Fuck." He swipes at his forehead to push back the curls stuck there. "I was expecting a leisurely bike ride, not wearing out my already-tired muscles from arm day at the gym."

I stare pointedly at his chest while he isn't looking and sneak some graham crackers out of the picnic basket perched beside me on the hood of my car. "It'd be a lot easier to dry your sweat if you wore a *shirt.*"

He lifts his eyes to mine, and the heat of his gaze almost makes me choke on the cracker. "*You* want to lecture *me* on my outfit of choice today? Have you looked in the mirror?"

I glance down at what I chose to change into, trying but failing to hide my smile. He showed up for a bike ride without a shirt knowing the effect it would have on me, so I decided to play the game right back. I changed into the shortest and tightest athletic shorts I own along with a sports bra that leaves little to the imagination.

Now that I know he's attracted to me, it's difficult not to tease him about it. He'd never make a move, but the image of him thinking about me in that way late at night while he . . .

Nope!

Change of subject.

Now.

I shrug and pick at an invisible speck of lint on my shorts. "It's hot outside."

"Mm-hm. I'm sure." He rises from the asphalt and pats the seat of my bike. "She's all yours."

Riding a bike shouldn't be as terrifying as it is, but all I can remember is flying midair and the smack of pavement against my skin. I agreed to go bike riding with him, but now that it's actually *happening*?

"What if I don't remember how to ride anymore?" I ask. "It's been forever since I fell."

"Riding a bike is one of those skills you never lose. Trust me. As soon as you pedal a couple of feet it'll come back to you."

Sliding off the hood of my car, I cautiously approach the bike and throw one of my legs over. The sun is beating down on my back, and the leather is practically boiling against my ass.

Cameron steps behind me and places his hands over mine on the handlebars. I can feel his bare skin against my lower back, and I pull my lip between my teeth in response to the *zing* of electricity. I want things to go back to the way they used to be between us, but after that night at Myrtle Beach I don't know how they could. He almost kissed me, and even though he didn't follow through with it, it changed *everything*.

He dips his head until his lips are pressed against my ear. "We'll take it slow, okay?"

Time comes to a pause, the earth stops moving, and the only

thing on my mind, the only thing that makes *sense* is for me to turn my head and—

"Oh my god, *Cameron*?"

The moment dissipates as quickly as it appeared. Cameron takes a step back to look at a girl around my age, maybe a few years older. She's flawless, with a perfect tiny figure. I've never felt self-conscious about the curves I have, but I don't have a workout regimen, and the abs glistening on her body make me feel stupid for wearing these shorts where a tiny roll of mine shows over the top.

"It's been a while," she says. Her eyes slide to mine in a calculating, snarky way when she adds, "Jessica, remember?"

The silence from him is telling. He doesn't remember her, but she doesn't seem offended. Instead, she giggles softly and places a hand on his arm. "High school? We spent time together in the gym after cheer practice . . ."

His body stiffens, a forced smile appearing. "Oh right. Jessica. How are you?"

Dark hair to my blond. Skinny to my curvy. Hazel eyes to my ocean blues. We're complete opposites, and that seems to be the trend for him. The girls he's into are the complete opposite of me. Sadie with her red hair and freckles, *Jessica* with brunet locks. Then again, maybe Cameron is the kind of guy who doesn't have a type. He sleeps around a lot.

"Are you going to Jamie's party tonight? Becca thought you might come."

Is this what spring break consists of? Partying every other day and getting shit-faced? Granted, with no school or finals to study for, what else is there to do around here? The desert doesn't have much else to offer.

"Probably not. I train during the week, so all my focus has to be on that."

She glances between us again. "Is that what you're doing? Training?"

After a moment of contemplation, he dips his chin in acknowledgment. "Cardio is part of my training, so sometimes I like to bike instead of run."

Is that what this is?

Training?

Am I just a placeholder to keep him company while he gets in shape for football?

No.

If that was the case, he wouldn't have packed a picnic basket for us. He can't tell Jessica we're here as friends because, since she went to high school with him, she more than likely knows Ethan too. I've never seen her before, but I also wasn't in their class. If Jessica was to go back and say she saw us together alone with a picnic basket, it would undoubtedly raise questions.

"Well, if you change your mind, I'll see you later tonight." Her hand stays far too long on his forearm, and the bitter taste it leaves in my mouth lingers long after she jogs off to complete her workout.

I'd rather crash this bike than deal with the aftermath of that conversation, so I take off without his help.

Just as he suspected, the motion comes back to me within the first minute, and then I'm pedaling at a leisurely pace, keeping my eyes trained on the road in front of me while I search for any rocks in my way.

Cameron catches up to me in less than thirty seconds, keeping pace beside me. "Are you all right?"

"I'm fine," I reply, the words short and clipped.

"Really? Because it seems like you have something to say."

Twisting my head to glance at him briefly, I snap my eyes back to the path in front of us and say, "Other than the fact you're a total dick? Not really."

He tosses his head back with laughter. "Ah, there's the Maddie I missed. Tell me, how am I dick?"

"You didn't even remember her name. Have you slept with *that* many girls?"

"I didn't realize this bike ride would result in me opening up about my sexual history." It's meant to be a joke, but he seems to sense the brewing anger inside me because he adds, "Honestly? Yeah. I've slept around. However, the girls I sleep with know it won't turn into anything serious. I'm a fan of getting laid, not breaking hearts."

Just mine, then?

The sentence is on the tip of my tongue, and I bite down so hard on it I fear it might bleed.

"Consensual sex isn't a bad thing," he continues. "I'm not going to feel guilty or ashamed of my body count. I'm safe, and that's what matters."

"I'm not saying you should feel *ashamed*, but don't you want to reserve some of that intimacy for the person you end up with for the rest of your life?"

Trees and blue sky whiz by us in a blur. Cameron pedals until he's slightly ahead of me, but after a minute or so he says, "I think fucking and making love are two different things, and with the right person, I'll be able to enjoy both. There hasn't been a girl I've fucked yet where I've wanted to do both, so until then, I'll wait."

Right. Because that girl will never be me. It's a constant reminder every second I'm around him, and regardless of if *I* want it, he'll never go against my brother. He may find me attractive, but it's not enough. It'll never be enough.

"On the bright side, I think the girl I marry will appreciate all the practice I've had," he says with a laugh, oblivious to the pain searing my heart. "All of the skills I've honed over the years will be for her and only her, you know?"

I can only nod in agreement because I don't trust myself to speak.

It makes me feel like an utter idiot for pushing other guys away for him. He's been having the time of his life gathering *skills* for the girl he ends up with, which clearly isn't going to be me, and I've been what? Reading books? Doing homework? Isolating myself and waiting to see if he'll make a move?

What a useless way to spend my time.

It makes me want to act irrationally. It makes me want to ask Ethan for Mark's number and take him up on his offer to take me on a date. Maybe he'll be at that party tonight. I'm sure Maya knows. Maybe I'll shock the entire town of Wickenburg and attend back-to-back parties like I actually enjoy it and know what I'm doing. Maybe I'll go live my best life and hone my *own* skills.

"Want to stop here and eat?" Cameron jerks his head to a clearing overlooking the pond, and while I prop my bike against a tree next to his, he grabs the picnic basket and walks us over to a bench.

I ignore how right it feels as my thigh brushes against his, along with the pitter-pattering of my heart when he pulls out a slew of my favorite foods. The graham crackers I snuck a few bites of earlier, Doritos, a turkey sandwich with mayo and—specifically—American cheese.

I'm moving to take a bite of my sandwich when I hear the sound of a Tupperware lid opening. Cameron has a salad rather than a sandwich. It's piled high with chicken, avocado, and a boiled egg, from what I can see.

"Looks delicious," I say dryly.

He shrugs and takes a bite. Then, with a mouthful of food, he says, "Training. I have to eat clean and get as much protein as possible. My dad came up with the diet plan, and it's helped me build a lot of muscle this year."

I purse my lips, trying to hide my frown. "It's amazing how involved he is with your future career even from thousands of miles away. I mean, if you want to eat boiled eggs for eternity then by all means, be my guest. However, I know you love pizza almost as much as I do."

He gives me a knowing look. "Come on, Mads. You know why I'm taking my dad's advice."

Unfortunately, I do, and I think Cameron's father puts way too much pressure on him to make it to the big leagues. Stacy, Cameron's mother, was the biggest football fan of all time. She was born and raised in Pennsylvania, and when she was diagnosed with stage four ovarian cancer Cameron made it his mission to become the greatest player at West Bridge, smack dab in the middle of Pennsylvania, to become closer to her.

His dad was already heavily involved in Cameron's football endeavors, but after Stacy's passing, it became obsessive. They're two men going through an insurmountable loss, and it seems the only way they can handle the grief is to live vicariously through Stacy's love of football.

I'd never bring Stacy up since I know how sensitive a subject it is to Cameron. I haven't discussed his mother since the day after she passed, and with the way that conversation went, I don't ever want to bring her up again.

However, if I did have the courage, I'd ask what happens if he *does* make it to the NFL? What happens to all that pent-up grief when he realizes making it to the big leagues doesn't heal him in the way he assumes it would? Stacy was the sweetest soul. She was the type of woman who would take the shirt off her back for anyone. I know it would kill her to see Cameron scarfing down boiled eggs to achieve an expectation she never had for him.

But Cameron isn't the only one who lost a role model. Since Stacy and my mom were best friends, she used to babysit me frequently, and some of my favorite memories are of her allowing me to be her hairdresser and do her makeup. She'd look ridiculous in hair curlers, and her face looked like a clown, but she claimed to love it. She'd always tell me she wanted a daughter, too, so she was more than willing to be my test subject on all things girl related. She was someone I looked up to, and although I wasn't her biological daughter, the empty space in my heart sure as hell felt like it.

Stacy only wanted us to be happy, yet we're both killing ourselves to try to fill the space she left.

Dammit.

The anger I felt earlier toward him vanishes.

Cameron is still grieving, and although I'm concerned about him fucking his way through life and using girls to numb his emotions, at the end of the day, he's not mine to care about.

He never was.

He never *will be*.

And it's about time I start living like it.

Nine

CAMERON

I promised myself when I came home for break that I would stick to my strict routine. Weekends I allow myself to relax and hang out with friends, or sometimes I'll spend it bingeing a new show that's popular. But the weekdays are for heavy training and schoolwork. That's it. Nothing more, nothing less. I knew coming home, there would be distractions around me, but so far, none of them have worked.

Until tonight.

Until I received a text that *Maddie Davis* was at Jamie Foster's party.

What the hell has gotten into her?

This isn't her. She's a homebody who would much rather be curled up with a book than surrounded by people she doesn't know, and I'm not responsible for her, but I can't help but wonder why she's having this change of personality all of a sudden.

Did she hit things off with Mark? It was too damn tempting to ask her about it earlier on our bike ride—a bike ride I should have been more careful about planning. Papago Park is about an hour away from Wickenburg, so I thought it'd be a safe spot where we wouldn't be discovered. Jessica popping up was a surprise, and not a good one. She could easily go back and tell Ethan I was there with his sister, but hopefully she didn't recognize Maddie.

The fear of the what-if propelled me to this stupid party. I've already had my fill of drinking this past weekend, but with it being spring break, even the weekdays are considered a free-for-all to everyone else.

This party isn't much different from Mark's. It's the same vibe—beer pong, smoking, dance floor. I haven't spotted Maddie yet, and the gut-twisting sensation that brings me is enough to make me want to take a shot.

No.

This is training week.

I'm here to find her, make sure she's okay, and then I'll be on my way. If I'm lucky, I can still be in bed by ten.

Finally, I spot Mark in the kitchen making himself a drink. Or is he making *Maddie* a drink? I don't want to think about what they did in his car, or if she's waiting upstairs in a room for him to return, but isn't that why I came here tonight? Maddie isn't a partier, and if she's changing herself due to some guy convincing her it's cooler . . .

I step up to Mark's side and glance around the kitchen. "Hey. Have you seen Maddie?"

He nods and takes a swig of his beer. "Yeah, she had to use the bathroom. Should be back any minute now." Tilting his head to the side, he studies me longer than I'd like for him to. "Why do you ask?"

Because the thought of your lips on her skin makes me physically ill.

"Ethan asked me to check. He stayed back tonight." *Lies.* Well, Ethan did stay back, which is odd considering he never misses a party, but he didn't ask me to check on his little sister. That concern is all stemming from me.

"Ah, okay. Well, you can tell him not to worry. I've got her."

My jaw ticks at his statement. He's not her boyfriend. He doesn't *own* her. She belongs to no one but herself, which is ironic considering I'm here acting like a territorial caveman when I have no right to be.

"Can I ask you something, though?"

I nod even though the only thing I want to do is go home and crawl back into bed. It was a mistake coming here. A *huge* mistake.

"I know you're more experienced than I am, and I just have to ask . . . have you been with a virgin before?"

My blood instantly runs cold. "No," I reply tightly. "Why?"

Virgins mean attachment. I don't *do* attachment. Every woman I've been with has had experience, too, but the only reason Mark would be asking me that is because . . .

"Maddie told me she's a virgin," he says, running a hand through his blond hair. "I figured you already knew this considering you've known her for so long, and I . . . well, I need advice on how to go about it. I don't want to fuck this up if I get a shot with her, you know? I want to make it pleasurable for her, too, and—"

Grabbing a shot off the counter beside me, I don't ask what's in it as I throw it back, enjoying the burn it brings.

No fucking way.

Maddie is fucking stunning. Of course, it's her choice when

to lose her virginity, but I assumed she already had. I assumed thousands of guys have begged to sleep with her, so why would she hold out? Or more importantly, for *whom*?

My heart hammers inside my chest with a mix of anticipation and hope.

This can't possibly mean what I think it does.

And if my suspicions are correct? I'm utterly *fucked*.

"I can't help you," I reply. "If you'll excuse me, I've got an early morning with training and everything."

I have to get out of here. My lungs feel constricted, my vision is hazy from the smoke, and if I see Maddie in this crowd before I find the exit, I'm going to do something really fucking stupid like kiss the hell out of her.

Keeping my head down, I won't even let myself look at the people surrounding me for fear of seeing her. Instead, I focus on the littered cups on the hardwood floor and the different feet of strangers.

I'm in the home stretch when suddenly, a hand grasps my elbow.

Fuck. If it's—

Jeremy, another former teammate, slaps me on the back before he pulls me in for a hug. "I didn't think you'd be coming home this year!" he exclaims. Judging by his red face, I'd say he's already three sheets to the wind. "Come on, come on. I'm nominating you."

"Nominating me for—" I inwardly groan, the pieces clicking together. "The blindfolded seven minutes shit? We're too old for that now. We're adults."

He snickers and pushes me toward the coat closet. "Which makes it even better. Now that we're older, we're more experienced, and that means what happens in the closet is dirtier than before."

The blindfolded version of seven minutes of heaven—a childish game where the girls select a female of their choosing and the guys select a male. The two nominees are blindfolded and shoved into a closet without knowing who they're paired up with. It's a stupid-ass game I don't have the time for tonight, but if I don't agree, I know what the consequence will be, and I *really* can't afford to get shit-faced tonight.

My dad will kill me if he finds out.

Rolling my eyes, I wave for him to put the blindfold on. "This is only because there's no way in hell I'm taking three shots. I won't be able to drive home."

"Whatever you say," he sings. "Your lucky lady is already waiting for you. Good luck."

When my vision is black, I'm shoved into the tiny coat closet that can hardly fit me comfortably, let alone another person. It's stiflingly hot, and the silence echoing between me and the girl is awkward to say the least.

I've never failed at this game. Getting a girl to kiss me has never been difficult. Whoever the girl is, she's breathing heavily, like she's nervous, and I can't help but wonder if this is her first time getting roped into playing this game.

That's fine. I'll just put on the charm like I always do.

"You're shy," I note. "Is this your first time doing this?"

Is that a sharp *inhale* I hear?

The girl doesn't speak, and I swear it's another thirty seconds before she puts a hand on my chest. I don't know why she isn't speaking, but oddly it's *hotter* this way. My cock seems to like it, and since he's been out of commission as of late for reasons I'd rather not dwell on, I'll gladly take what I can get if he's excited.

"You can take it off if you prefer," I say, relaxing my head back against the closet. Even though our time is dwindling, she takes her time running her fingers over every indent between my abs. It's as if she knows exactly where each one lies beneath my shirt.

I'm growing impatient, but I hold still until she completes her examination and finally tugs the shirt over my head, leaving my chest exposed.

The second her fingers land on my bare skin, my body is on fire for her.

Every section she touches feels *hot*.

So hot.

Since she seems to like exploring my body, I explore hers. I start at her waist, testing to see how far she'll allow me to go. Just at the mere touch of my fingers on her stomach, she bucks her hips toward me, already ready. She's incredibly responsive, and that makes my *cock* incredibly happy.

She's curvy in all the right places. As I trail inch by inch underneath her shirt I hear her breathing become more intense. Quicker. Unsteady. She's practically panting when I reach what I'm looking for, and as soon as my hand wraps around an—obscenely—overly developed breast, I feel her nipple hard and erect against her bra.

Christ.

Who the hell is this?

I'm too turned-on to care. I'll discover her identity when the timer comes to an end and the people outside rip this closet door open.

For now, it's a secret, and it's *hot*.

I lean in to close the distance between us, mere inches from her face when it finally hits me.

Vanilla.

Sweet, raw hunger fills my veins as I recognize the all-too-familiar scent. My hand is cupping her breast, my other squeezing her hip, and suddenly, everything makes sense. The reason she isn't speaking. Why my cock is raging hard.

It's Maddie.

Oh *fuck*.

Testing my theory even further, I reach up to brush a strand of hair away from her face, unsurprised when a ringlet wraps around my fingers.

I should stop this.

I should pull our blindfolds off and walk right out of this closet.

But this is the perfect excuse. I *technically* don't know it's her. If Ethan finds out, I'll just tell him we unknowingly got paired up for this stupid game, which is the truth. He can't get pissed at me if I didn't know I'd be kissing his sister, right?

Everything has led up to this moment, and suddenly, all the practice I've had seems nonexistent. The girl in my arms isn't just any girl. She's *Maddie*, my very first crush. The girl I almost kissed, something I've regretted changing my mind about ever since.

This is my chance to correct that mistake, and even though it could be the biggest error I'll ever make, she's right in front of me, and that damn scent of vanilla is as intoxicating as ever.

When her fingers land on my chest again, searching and teasing, I inwardly groan and send a silent apology for the sin I'm about to make.

I do something really fucking stupid and kiss the living hell out of her, and as soon as I do, I wish I hadn't.

Her lips are soft, and meld perfectly with mine. I'm trying hard to keep it slow, but I've waited *years* for this. I've waited so long to kiss her that I don't know what to do with myself. Rationality is gone. My gentlemanly nature is out the window. If this is the only kiss I'll share with her, I sure as hell want to make it worthwhile.

Dipping my tongue into her mouth, I get a soft little moan in response. My cock thickens against my jeans, nearly bursting at the seams to be released. I'm hard as a rock pressed against her. Never in my life have I been concerned about coming in my pants, but tonight may unlock a new fear.

I push my fingers into her hair and press her firmly against the wall of the closet. It's hard enough not to make noise for others to hear, but a few coats fall off the hangers and land at our feet. This kiss is filled with so much passion, so many *emotions* behind it, that I find myself melting into her.

It's getting hotter in this small place. We're a clash of teeth and tongue, little beads of sweat traveling down my chest. She doesn't seem to care, though, as her hands move down my biceps, squeezing firmly as if to get out her aggression.

Good *god* this is the best kiss I've ever had.

I want to kiss her harder, *deeper*, until she can somehow understand how much I want her right now—how much space she's taken up in my heart and mind over the years. How I will probably never be able to stop doing this.

"Wait. Cam." She breaks away from the kiss, panting breathlessly. "It's me. Um, Maddie. I—I don't want you to regret this. I heard your voice, so I know it's you. I'm sorry. I should have told you sooner, I just—"

"I know it's you," I pant against her lips. "I know it's you, Mads."

"And you don't want to stop?"

I can't take it anymore.

I remove both our blindfolds, and although it's dark in here, I can still make out her features. She's absolutely *breathtaking* right now. Her lips are parted, and her eyes are wide as she awaits my answer. Her cheeks are a bright red from the heat, and I find myself completely and utterly lost in her.

"Not the least bit," I reply, attempting to catch my breath. "Do *you* want to stop?"

She shakes her head and wraps her fingers in my curls to bring me back to her lips.

We have about five minutes left in here, and I'm going to make the most of it. I don't know when—or if—we'll be able to do this again.

I put my fingers back on her bra, tentatively seeking if she still wants me to go further. Mark revealed to me that she's a virgin, and I was being truthful when I said I've never hooked up with one before. I don't do attachments, but with Maddie . . .

The thought of Mark possibly being the one to give her those experiences makes me pull her bra back, still giving her the ability to tell me to stop. If she didn't want me to do this, she wouldn't allow me to. If I know one thing about Maddie? She always speaks her mind.

In response, Maddie's hips buck up to fully press against my groin.

I'll take that as a yes.

Finally, thank—fucking—*finally* I'm able to move her bra to the side and feel what I've wanted to for years. Her tits are warm and soft, her nipples hard against my fingertips. I've always been a weak, weak man for her, and now is no different. I bend my head down and wrap my tongue around her nipple, licking and sucking and *worshipping* her.

I want to show her how good I am at this.

I'm sure she's given herself plenty of orgasms before, but I want to give her one she doesn't have control over. She has no idea how much pleasure can be felt when another person brings you to the brink of ecstasy.

"*Cam*," she pants. "Oh my *god*."

I'm battling a case of blue balls, groaning at the sound of my name rolling off her tongue in such a seductive way. I've imagined her moaning it in my dreams but hearing it in person brings a whole new level of desire.

I continue to suck, gently rolling her nipple with my teeth before I ease the sting with my tongue. Her breasts are incredible, and given the opportunity, I'd please her just like this for hours.

Unfortunately, we aren't granted eternity, so while I continue to lap her nipple, I press my hand between her legs, over her leggings, until her pussy is placed perfectly—

Fucking hell.

"You're already soaked," I groan, strumming my fingers along the fabric.

She's biting on her lip in pure agony. This is the part where we should probably talk about the repercussions of this and should stop while we're ahead, but her pussy has a heartbeat against my palm, and I'm too weak to pull away.

I put pressure with the heel of my hand against her clit, and my heart skips a beat at the fluttering of her lashes. She hooks her arms around my neck, growing limp in my arms aside from the occasional grinding she's doing to gain friction.

"You need to come before this door opens and we're caught," I whisper gently into her ear. "Can you do that for me?"

She nods frantically, her pretty pussy rubbing against my palm.

So responsive.

So beautiful.

"That's it," I coax as her eyebrows scrunch together. I've never been disappointed that I can't sink to my knees and taste a woman's bare pussy with my tongue, but I have a *craving* to taste Maddie. It's a fucking tease to feel this much wetness and not have the ability to bury myself in it. "Let go for me, Mads."

She clutches my biceps and throws her head back as she falls apart in my arms, and while she does, I log every feature of her face to memory. Her eyes have fluttered shut. Her jaw's dropped slightly open. Her cheeks are rosy and her hair is wild from my hands raking through it.

One of my hands covers her mouth to muffle her moans while my other continues to rub circles on her pussy to gather the wetness. I know she's sensitive, but I'm too much of a selfish bastard to pull away from her.

I want to drown in her.

I want to dive inside her ocean and never climb out.

"What did we just do?" she asks. When I take a small step back, she reaches up to fix her bra and smooth down her hair while I tug my shirt back on.

I don't know what to reply. For the first time in my life, I'm utterly speechless as we both pant heavily, attempting to cool ourselves down. We don't have the luxury to discuss what happened. Not when I know the others outside this door will soon throw it open to try to catch us in the act.

"Maddie—" I start, but I'm caught off guard by the door flying open.

My thoughts are jumbled. I'm too infatuated with the images in my head of Maddie as I made her shatter in my arms a few seconds ago. Everyone stares, disappointed that we aren't naked or in a state of debauchery.

Maddie straightens her shoulders and props a hand on her hip as if I didn't just give her the best orgasm of her life. "Did you all really think I wouldn't know it was *Cameron* in there? Come on, we grew up together."

I blink absently at how well she's able to hide her feelings.

Even if I wanted to say something, I don't think I'm capable of speaking. I don't trust my voice not to falter. As much as *she* can pretend nothing happened, I can't. Not when she just rocked my fucking world and almost made me finish by hardly even touching me. I gave all the pleasure to *her*, and yet it was one of the best sexual experiences I've ever had.

When the lack of entertainment has everyone going their separate ways, Maddie locks eyes with me, and we seem to have a silent conversation. Now isn't the time to discuss it with so many gossips and familiar faces around. If one word got back to Ethan that we actually enjoyed our time together, he'd kill us both.

"I'm going to see if I can sleep at your house. See if Ethan is still up."

We'll talk later?

An unspoken comment, but one she seems to understand.

With a jerk of her chin, she leaves me in the hallway alone, and I'm annoyed I can't explain to her how incredible that moment between us was. I want to give her the reassurance I know she's seeking, that she has no need to worry.

Our kiss was perfect.

It was better than I thought it would be.

But there's *nothing* I can say as I stare after her retreating back.

All I'm left with is the unwavering fear that another opportunity to do that with her may never happen again.

Ten

CAMERON

"Go long!"

With dust trailing behind me, I push myself faster as I watch the ball soar in the air, heading straight toward me. The arm my dad has is impressive. I'm surprised he never tried to pursue a football career himself.

I'm laughing when I dive to catch it, missing it by only a few inches. I begged and pleaded with him to practice with me. It's Thanksgiving, and after watching the big game, it inspired me to come out here to try to get ready for varsity tryouts next year. I need all the time I can get.

Mom is sitting in a patio chair with a lemonade in her hand, laughing with me when I tumble to the ground. She's more tired than usual, but despite my concern, she tells me it's just the cold weather. "So close!" she shouts across the yard.

Dust covers my jeans as I lie on my back, and soon enough, my dad's shadow hovers above me, sporting a grin of his own. "You almost had that one," he says.

"I'm better at throwing," I say.

"Trust me," he replies, "I know you are. I have no doubt you'll make the team."

I take his hand, allowing him to help me up. "What if I don't make the team? What happens then?"

He shrugs and pats me on the shoulder. "Then you try again. If this is something you really want, I'll practice with you. And if it's something you don't want to do anymore, we'll find another sport or activity you're interested in. Your mom and I will support you whatever you decide to do."

"Always," my mom adds, joining us in the yard. She bends down to pick up the football, tossing it between her hands. "Well? Think you can handle a few passes from me?"

This is the best Thanksgiving ever.

>> <<

Morning comes too soon.

The sunlight filtering through the curtains of the living room practically blinds me when I peek one eye open, then both as I attempt to adjust to it.

What happened last night?

I remember coming home from Jamie's party and playing video games with Ethan until the early hours of the morning. I had been annoyed because I had wanted to speak to—

FUCK.

One after another, memories slam into my head like bulldozers.

Maddie's head thrown back in ecstasy. My hands and tongue worshipping her breasts. Her fingers wrapped tightly in my curls.

Last night wasn't a fever dream. It was all *real*, and now I have to live with whatever the aftermath will be. I don't regret it. Kissing Maddie has been something I've wanted to do for years, but do I feel guilty? Of course I do. Ethan is my best friend. The minute he gets an inkling that something happened between us, he'll exile me from his life forever. It's been stated on numerous occasions he wants me nowhere near his sister, and for good reason. I don't have the greatest reputation. Ethan and I don't *do* relationships, and if I had a sister, I'd keep Ethan away from her too.

The sound of pots and pans clattering in the kitchen pushes me to sit up on the couch to investigate who's making the noise. Mary is humming a tune as she cracks an egg into a bowl, and Richard is beside her making pancakes.

Throughout high school, this was the normal routine. Mary and Richard would make breakfast and I'd always help them do the dishes afterward. After all, if it wasn't for their delicious home-cooked meals, I'd have lived on takeout with the money my dad gave me while he was away on another business trip. The least I could do was help clean up.

"Cameron!" Mary wipes her hands on her apron and races over to me, enveloping me in a hug filled with a warmth only she is capable of giving. "Oh, I missed you *so* much, honey. I feel awful that we planned our trip right in the middle of your spring break, but thankfully we still have the Grand Canyon this weekend to look forward to." She rambles cheerily. "We can't *wait* to hear about everything that's new and exciting with you."

She looks back at me expectantly. I don't have the ability to say no to her, but the one event that's been the *most* exciting is one I can't tell her. I don't believe Mary would be upset if she found out Maddie and I kissed, but Richard? He's a different story. The man could have been a football player himself back in the day. He's so tall he almost towers over me, and he's got sleeves of tattoos on both heavily muscled arms. Richard saw me and Ethan do some pretty dumb shit in our teenage years. If he found out I kissed his daughter? I don't know what his reaction would be, nor will I risk a fist to the face by attempting to find out.

"I mean—" I rake a hand through my curls while I try to think of something other than Maddie's face as she shattered apart in my arms.

"Breakfast first, then," Mary says, tugging me off the couch. For a small woman, she sure is strong.

I sit on one of the bar stools while they cook breakfast and fill me in on their trip to the Bahamas. She sipped margaritas and laid on the beach during their port stops, but they both seem to have had the time of their lives. Richard, his face still sporting a burn from his time in the sun, tells me about winning a game of cornhole on the cruise ship.

Their marriage makes me wonder if this is the kind of stability my parents would have given me had my mom not passed before high school. Would they still be in love like this? Would I have woken up to breakfasts being made for me every morning? Would they be so eager to hear about my life? And I'm not talking about my football career, which seems to be the only thing my dad cares about, but *me*. Just me.

Mary's face softens as she flips the bacon, seeming to read my thoughts. "Have you heard from your father lately?"

I shake my head.

"He's on another business trip?"

"Yeah. He sent his condolences before I came home. I don't think he'll see me before I go back to school."

Mary *tuts*, annoyance evident in her features. "Well, you're welcome here for the entirety of the break, but you already know that."

This home became my safe haven during high school. When my dad kept leaving, I started staying here every weekend, and every weekend eventually turned into five nights out of the week. Mary and Richard wouldn't have cared if I moved in with them, but a part of me couldn't allow myself to do that. I waited at home those remaining two nights, holding out hope that my dad would come home and stay for good. I thought my living situation was *temporary*.

"I do, Mary. Thank you." My eyes stray over her shoulder as Maddie enters the kitchen, and my sad memories are replaced by pure, unrelenting lust.

She's wearing a pair of tiny pajama shorts that hardly cover her ass and a tank top with no bra on. My mouth dries out at the sight of her, and I've never been more thankful to be sitting down. Otherwise I wouldn't be able to hide the fact that my hard cock is twitching at the memory of what her breasts looked like.

I went from not being able to get it up a few days ago to not being able to put it back down because of her.

Unbelievable.

Mary grabs the plates while Richard finishes the pancakes. Both are completely oblivious to the sexual tension in the kitchen.

"Good morning," Maddie says, giving her mom a side-hug. "What time did you guys get here?"

"Early this morning." Mary claps with excitement. "I can't wait to hear about everyone's year so far!"

Maddie gives her mother a pointed look. "We catch up at least once a week. I have nothing new to tell you."

Since she wanted to fuck with *me* by wearing *that* little ensemble, I'll fuck with her right back.

I clear my throat and ask, "Really? There's nothing exciting you want to share with your parents? I find that doubtful, Mads."

The flush that rises to her cheeks pleases me more than I care to admit, but before I can focus on it further, Mary's eyes dart between the two of us. "Did you just call her *Mads*? I haven't heard that nickname in ages."

I smile from ear to ear. "Indeed I did."

Maddie shoots daggers through her eyes at me before she twists to Mary and says, "Cameron and I are friends again for the time being. We've sorted out our issues for now."

Friends.

What happened in the closet last night didn't seem like friends to me. Then again, what else are we supposed to call this thing between us? We haven't had the chance to talk about it since it happened, and a part of me is thankful for that. Do I want it to continue? Do I want to sneak around with her knowing what's at stake? More importantly, does she?

Maybe she regrets it. Maybe she kissed me and thought I was shit at it. Who knows?

Mary's sniffling drags me from my thoughts, and I smile when she says, "I knew you two would reconnect. It was only a matter of time. Gosh, I am *thrilled* to hear that. Aren't you, Richard?"

"Hmm?" He drags his eyes away from the griddle. "Oh, yeah. It's great the two of you are friends again. It'll certainly make things less awkward this weekend."

Ha.

Don't be so certain about that, Richard.

The smell of bacon must have woken Ethan up because he's next to join us. He kisses his mom on the cheek and nods at his dad before taking a seat on a bar stool beside me. Everyone in this family knows not to talk to Ethan when he first wakes up. He's the devil incarnate until he's had his cup of coffee, which Mary has already started brewing.

"So, what are your plans today?" Mary asks.

"IT'S LAKE TIME, BITCH!" Maya's voice echoes from the high ceiling of the foyer before she races around the corner, her face blanching when she spots Mary and Richard in the kitchen as well. "Oh, I'm . . . I didn't realize you came back today! I'm so sorry, Mr. and Mrs. Davis. I would have knocked, or—"

Mary scoffs and grabs another plate from the cabinet. "You're like my other daughter, Maya, and I've told you a thousand times to call me Mary. Would you like to stay for breakfast before you leave?"

"Um, yes. Please. That'd be great."

Maya takes the last bar stool beside Ethan, and I don't miss the way his eyes flick to the bikini top beneath the sheer cover-up she has on. She arches a brow at him and asks, "Do you work today?"

Ethan shakes his head. "No. I've got the day off. Why?"

Well, it's nice to know that *someone* can speak to him in the morning without him biting their head off. The rest of his family seems to think the same, exchanging confused glances before returning to their food.

"Well, I wanted to rent a boat for the day, but I don't know how to sail. Maddie said you used to take sailing lessons as a kid?"

Ethan shifts in his seat. "I did, yeah."

"Do you still know how to sail? If so, care to tag along for the day and be our captain?"

"Hm . . ." He taps a finger to his chin, contemplating. "That depends. Can I bring Cameron? I don't want to be on a boat with just you two. I'll die from boredom if I have to talk about Justin Bieber and Harry Styles all day."

Oh no.

No.

No.

No.

"I have training," I blurt, desperate to get out of this. I refuse to be stranded on a body of water with Ethan and his little sister, whom I made fucking *come* in a closet last night. It'll be more than obvious, and if Ethan finds out and he's the one driving the boat?

I'll be swimming back to shore.

Maddie tries but fails to hide her grin. "That's a shame. I really wanted to go on the boat. I'm long overdue for a tan, and I have the *cutest* bikini I've been dying to wear."

Maddie.

Bikini.

Oiled up in the sun.

Kill me now.

There's a challenging look in her eyes and dammit. I told myself I'd be strict with my routine. I'm not even supposed to be eating the piece of bacon that tastes like greasy heaven on my tongue right now, but cardio *is* part of my training, right? We could swim for a bit and that can count. I'll just work out in the gym later tonight instead of this afternoon for muscle endurance. Easy fix.

There's no way in hell I'm passing up seeing whatever bikini Maddie purchased. Yes, I'll have to be on my best behavior to ensure Ethan doesn't suspect something happened between us, but from the teasing she's doing, it seems like Maddie doesn't regret last night, either, and that fact alone would make me agree to just about anything if it means the possibility of alone time with her today, even if it's only for a few seconds.

The stakes are high. I could potentially lose not only my best friend but also Mary and Richard. Over the past six years they've become the only real family I have, and by agreeing to this, I risk losing them all.

But when Maddie laughs at something Maya says, I find myself enamored with the sight, and all of those doubts, all of those *risks* don't seem that daunting.

Right now, my future has never been more clear.

Challenge accepted, Maddie.

"I'll move my schedule around," I reply with a cocky grin. "Lake day it is."

Eleven

CAMERON

The late afternoon sun beats down on my back but the wind on the lake makes the heat tolerable. The scent of seaweed and fish clouds my senses, and it takes me back to when I was younger and my parents would take me camping in this very park. We'd go tubing on the lake for hours, and when I couldn't stand the heat anymore we'd go back to our camper, where Dad would grill hot dogs and hamburgers while Mom and I played cards or a board game of my choosing. Those moments feel so distant now that sometimes it's hard to picture my mother's face in those memories. If it wasn't for photos and videos of her, I'm not sure I'd even remember what she looked like anymore.

"Cameron." Ethan elbows me in the side, pulling me back to the present.

"Hm? Sorry, I was thinking."

The sympathetic expression on his face makes me grit my teeth. He used to come with me on those camping trips, so he seems to know where my thoughts have led me. "I said the water is deep enough here for us to anchor. I need to grab the rope."

I give him a curt nod, moving to the side to allow him to reach around me. Maya and Maddie quickly took over the deck of the boat not long after we set sail. Music from the radio plays loudly through their portable speaker, though I wish there wasn't any music at all. I've always loved the sound of waves gently lapping the sides of a boat. It's relaxing. *Calming.*

Maya comes to stand near Ethan and asks, "How do you know which anchor to choose?" At the shocked expression on his face, she adds, "My dad is into sailing and likes to share some knowledge with me, but I never pay enough attention."

Ethan makes a point of looking anywhere *but* at Maya and the bikini she's wearing when he replies, "Well, this is a fluke anchor, which is pretty standard for any sailboat. It works well for sand and mud, but if we were in an area where the current could frequently change, I'm sure the boat would come equipped with a plow anchor, which is more suitable for—" He cringes, staring out at the gleaming water. "Sorry. I could go on forever."

Maya flicks her gaze over him and rests her elbows against the railing. "I never said I was bored."

Leave it to Ethan to win a girl over talking about *sailing*. If he still thinks he doesn't have a shot with her then he's an idiot. I've never seen him nervous around a girl before, so this is new. The Ethan I knew in high school had all the confidence in the world when it came to women. He was my wingman at parties, but with Maya, he seems tongue-tied.

I refuse to become a cock block, so I leave him alone with her and head for the deck where—

Bad idea.

Maddie is applying tanning oil, and her skin is glistening in the sunlight. I avoided looking when she took off her cover-up and shorts earlier, but now that Ethan is distracted and anchoring the boat, I allow myself to take my fill.

Even though she's short, she's always had long legs, and they're showcased beautifully in the scrap of fabric she calls a bikini. It's baby pink with a tiny butterfly charm dangling between the middle of her breasts—the breasts I had the pleasure of enjoying less than twenty-four hours ago.

She's *stunning*. Her blond curls are wild and free, and the coy smile she gives me when she catches me staring makes my heart lurch into my throat. It's a smile I haven't seen since the night we snuck out—a smile both devious and exhilarating.

What is she planning?

Before I can ask, she turns around and bends over to oil the rest of her legs . . . it's a *thong* bikini. It rides so far up her ass I can practically see everything, and in seconds I'm raging hard, fighting the urge to take her right against the railing. It wouldn't be hard. All I'd have to do is pull that thin piece of fabric to the side and—

Ethan.

Same boat.

Snap out of it.

"*Maddie.*" Her name comes out strangled when I finally reach her. My tall frame blocks her from Ethan and Maya's view, but when she stands upright again to spin and face me, it does nothing to stop the thrumming of my pulse. I can feel the heat radiating from her, and I don't know whether it's from the sun or from how much of a physical pull she has over me.

"I thought you'd stay hidden beside Ethan all day." Then,

more seriously, she adds, "I didn't think about what coming here to the lake would do to you. I've seen you staring off into space for the past hour and I'm sorry if you felt I persuaded or teased you into coming."

I'm not sure what bothers me more. The fact she thinks I'd only go on a fun outing with her because I'm being forced into it or the look of pity she's giving me. Getting emotional isn't something I'm comfortable with. Apologizing to her the night of Mark's party is the closest I've gotten since my mom passed, and even *that* felt like it was too much to handle. Discussing how special this place used to be and how different it is now . . .

I need to find a way back to common ground.

Deflection.

"I didn't realize you were paying so much attention to me," I tease. "Thinking about last night?"

She glances down at my tight board shorts before meeting my gaze. "I think that's *you*, not me."

Fuck. I forgot I'm still hard, but I'm relieved to know she isn't going to push me on the subject and force me to open up. She's going along with it and doing exactly what I need her to do. Distract me.

My voice drops low, seductive and charming. "You expect me not to show a reaction when you're parading around in pieces of fabric so thin I could rip them off with just my teeth?"

The little gasp of hers makes me grin.

"You'd like that, wouldn't you?" I take a step closer, ensuring we keep a foot of distance between us in order not to cause any suspicion. Then I do a lazy, agonizingly slow perusal of her from her perfectly pedicured toes to those blazing blue eyes. "If I took you into the cabin and continued what we were doing in the closet last night, I'd have you completely hooked. That is, if you aren't already, of course."

She rolls her eyes, but I can see the pulse drumming rapidly against her throat. "You're *so* arrogant," she whispers.

I shrug. "Or confident. To each their own. You can lie all you'd like, but the thought of last night turns you on, so much so that you felt the need to give me a show just now in the hopes of it happening again."

On the outside I remain the guy who has always won girls over easily. I look like my future doesn't hang in the balance on her reply, but it does. It kills me that we haven't discussed what happened between us yet. It's *infuriating* that I can't tell whether or not she liked it. With other girls, my phone would have been filled with texts about how good our night together was or asking when we could do it again, but Maddie never reached out. She's kept her opinions to herself, and I'm dying to know whether or not she desires a repeat.

"Do *you* want it to happen again?" Those eyes that match the sky overhead reveal nothing as to what she might be thinking, and I can't decipher my feelings enough to give her a genuine answer. There's not a question in my mind that I liked what happened in the closet, but for it to happen again of our own free will, to take the chance of Ethan and her parents finding out? Of losing the people closest to me?

"I—"

"CANNONBALL!"

Ethan flies past us in a blur, somersaulting over the edge of the rail into the lake below. He hits the water with a splash, and Maya grabs Maddie's wrist, whisking her away before I can reply to her question.

"Oh come on! You guys don't want to do a cool flip?" Ethan shouts from below. "The water feels amazing!"

"We'll use the *ladder* like civilized human beings, thank you," Maya replies with a grin.

Now isn't the time to discuss where Maddie and I go from here. With her best friend and her brother around, we have to pick a time when we can be alone, just the two of us.

No distractions.

For now, we'll have a fun-ass time together.

"CANNONBALL!" I echo Ethan and do a somersault of my own. It's something my dad would highly disapprove of, considering there's a risk of getting injured, but this is one day where I get to relax and enjoy time with my friends at a place I thought I'd never return to or enjoy again. I'm not going to pass that up.

The coolness of the water makes the heat and lust I felt moments ago vanish instantly, and I give myself a few seconds to enjoy the quietness of being submerged. It allows me the chance to clear my head and collect my thoughts.

Whenever I'm around Maddie I seem to forget right and wrong. The line is always blurred when it comes to her, but here, beneath the water, it's quiet. I don't have an angel or a devil on my shoulder trying to convince me what to do. I can bask in the silence without any expectations from my father. I can drown out the grief I feel about my mother. I can just *be*.

When I reach the surface, I gasp and shake out my curls.

"What the hell, man?" I blink my eyes open to see Ethan swimming in place directly in front of me. "I almost had to start searching for you."

"Is enjoying being underneath the water a crime?" I'm wearing the smile I've grown accustomed to displaying to appease others, and it seems to work on Ethan, who rolls his eyes and swims over to Maya without an ounce of shyness showing now.

I make a mental note to ask about their conversation later. Clearly, it went well.

Maddie's gaze burns into the side of my face, but not with the type of heat I want. She seems to be the only one the smile didn't placate. Then again, I shouldn't be surprised. Maddie has always paid attention to me more closely than anyone else in my life.

Still, she doesn't ask why I took so long rising to the surface. Instead, she swims closer until her body is inches from mine and says, "You didn't answer my question."

"Because your brother launched himself off the boat."

"Cameron."

I heave a sigh. "I don't have an answer for you, Mads. It's never been cut-and-dried for us, and you know that. What happened last night was complicated, and our next steps can't be based only on the attraction we feel for each other. We need to talk about this and consider all the consequences. *Really* talk."

She glances over her shoulder to where Ethan and Maya are in a splashing war with each other. A part of me feels like asking if she's aware Maya is into Ethan, but I don't want to upset her. Not when I'm so close to getting her to see me tonight.

"And how do you propose we do that?" she asks.

"Come to my house after I get home from the gym tonight. It'll be a place where we'll have no distractions."

She scoffs. "No distractions? We can't seem to be around each other for two minutes without eye-fucking each other."

My lips tilt into a grin. "So, you're admitting to eye-fucking me?"

"How could I not when you're wearing hoochie shorts?"

I glance down at myself in the murky water. "*Hoochie* shorts? I am not wearing *hoochie* shorts."

"Girls from two boats over were staring, Cam. They leave little to the imagination."

"Are you jealous?" I reach a hand beneath the water and place it on her hip, my pupils dilating at the effect my touch has on her. Any doubts I had of her opinion about last night are gone. I can tell when I rub my thumb across her hip bone just how much she's thought about it, and *damn* I'm obsessed at how sexy she looks tugging on her bottom lip.

"How could I be jealous?" She closes her eyes as I skim my fingers right above her bikini bottoms. "I have no reason to be. We hooked up in a closet last night. That doesn't mean we're in a relationship."

"Never said it did." Flicking my eyes over her shoulder, I see Maya and Ethan are still distracted with each other, and with Maddie's back facing them, it allows me to have some fun with her. "Just because we only hooked up once doesn't mean you can't be jealous. For example, if some other guy touched you *here* . . ." She clamps down on a moan when I place my hand between her legs. "I would be very envious of them."

"*Cam,*" she warns, wanting and breathless. "Ethan is—"

"I'm fully aware of where he is," I croon, withdrawing my hand. "I only wanted to know if you've thought about me since last night, and now I have my answer."

She holds my stare, regal and unflinching. "And if you've been wondering all day about my opinion, then I guess that means I have my answer too."

"Maybe you do." A beat and then, "We still need to talk about things, though. Can you be at my house by eight?"

She floats a few feet away, putting distance between us, and it isn't until now that I realize how empty it feels without her nearby.

What is she doing to me?

"I'll think about it," she says, lips twitching. "What? I can't let you become *too* arrogant. If that head of yours gets any bigger it'll burst."

"Looking forward to it!" I shout as she swims over to Maya and Ethan. She gives me a middle finger in response, which causes me to throw my head back and laugh.

Maddie Davis is going to be the death of me.

Twelve

CAMERON

A part of me is surprised to find Maddie sitting on the hood of her car in my driveway with an open textbook in her lap. I thought she'd make me wait at least a day or two before she came around, but it makes me happy to know that being away from each other might be as torturous for her as it is for me.

I grab my duffel bag from the backseat and throw the strap over my shoulder. My muscles ache from going harder than usual in today's training session, but I've been slacking. I had to make up for it.

"Studying?" I ask.

She drags her attention away from the book, and the pencil she was strumming along her lip freezes in place. I soak in how blatantly obvious she's making it that she's checking me out, watching as her eyes drag over me from head to toe.

I'm in a pair of workout shorts, sneakers, and a backward ball cap that's holding back my sweaty curls. I didn't shower after training because I truly didn't expect her to be here.

"Do you even know what a shirt *is*?" She tilts her head to the side, running her eyes over my abs, and my blood instantly heats at the memory of her fingers trailing over them.

I tilt my lips into a grin. "Why would I when I look so much better without one?"

"Have I ever mentioned that you're arrogant?"

I chuckle and inch closer to her. "Once or twice. Do you want to come inside?"

She closes the textbook on her lap when I place my hands on either side of her. The gold chain around my neck dangles between us, and Maddie eyes it as if she's picturing all the ways to grab hold of it. My cock thickens at the sight, but when I dip my head down to—

"I don't think that's the best idea," she whispers.

Oh.

I take a large step back to give her some space while attempting to ignore the bone-crushing, heart-wrenching sensation spreading throughout my body.

Did I get this all wrong?

Did it not mean as much to her as it did for me?

"Look, what we did was great," she starts, "but if Ethan finds out—"

"He'll kill us both. I get it." It still doesn't stop my jaw from clenching. It doesn't stop my heart from shattering. I knew continuing things was a long shot, and I guess I didn't realize how clear my decision was until she suddenly stripped away the option. I don't want this to end between us. I want what happened in the closet to happen again.

And again.

And again.

And again.

"Don't worry," she continues. "I won't tell anyone about what we did. I wouldn't want to tarnish your reputation."

My eyes bore into hers. "My reputation?"

"Oh come on. You know what I'm talking about. If people found out you messed around with me they'd —"

"Don't you *dare* finish that sentence." I clench and unclench my fists at my sides, but it doesn't seem to stop the rage I feel. How could she think I'd be embarrassed for others to know we hooked up? It makes me want to laugh at the absurdity of it all. Doesn't she realize how much I care for her?

Why would she when you've treated her like shit for the past six years?

Pushing the thought out of my head, I grab her hand and relish the smoothness of her palm. How perfectly it fits in mine. "I'd never be ashamed to admit I touched you, Maddie. In fact, when I found you sitting here on your car a few minutes ago, I expected this conversation to go a lot differently."

"You did?" Her hand tightens around mine. "What did you . . . I mean, how did you think it would go?"

"Well, for starters"—I cage her in again on top of her car, my hands on either side of her thighs—"I thought we'd both admit how fucking amazing our time together was last night, and even though it'd be difficult, we'd find a way to continue it. Explore it."

Her eyes dip to my lips. "Explore it?"

I'm trying not to think about it, but I can't. The way she made me feel during that kiss, like I was high when I hadn't even smoked. The way she moaned my name, practically panting from how badly she wanted me. She was *so* wet. She made my hand *soaking* wet.

"If you agreed to, then yes. I'm not ready for a relationship,

Maddie. You know how detached I've become since my mom passed, and with Ethan in the picture it's something I'm not sure would ever be able to happen between us. But what happened in that closet is something I want to experience again, and I'd never forgive myself if I wasn't honest and up front with you about how I'm feeling." *I already made that mistake once* is what I want to add, but I keep that part out. I allowed her to leave my living room bawling her eyes out six years ago knowing I had developed feelings for her, and watching her walk away was the hardest thing I've ever done.

"And what happens if I change my mind?" She eyes the chain again before meeting my stare.

My forehead falls against hers, both of our chests rising and falling in an erratic, frantic rhythm. "Then we explore." My voice is rough and scratchy, seeming to match the desire coursing through me. "We enjoy it until we can't anymore."

Both of her hands caress my cheeks, and I close my eyes to savor the feeling. "Cam?"

"Hm?"

"I changed my mind."

My eyes flutter open to stare into her baby blues. I always knew Maddie was beautiful, but never like this. I fucked up my chance with her before, and I won't let it happen again.

So this time I crash my lips against hers and tug her off the hood of her car until she has to stand on her tiptoes to continue kissing me, wrapping her arms around my neck to hold on tight. My hands run through her curls, getting caught on the ends, but that only elicits a moan from her when it causes her head to jerk back, allowing me to slip my tongue into her mouth.

I've needed her for days.

I've needed her for *years*, I think.

And that terrifies the living shit out of me.

"So what does this mean?" She gasps, breaking the kiss. "Are we friends with benefits, or . . ."

"Can we talk about it after?" I pant. "I know we've got shit to figure out, but right now I just—"

Her fingers wrap around the chain and she tugs me down to her lips again. I thought at first the connection we felt in the closet was because it was so secretive, dark, and *hot*, but now that we're in broad daylight I realize that's not the case at all. If anything, the connection has only intensified.

I pull her into the empty house, my lips never leaving hers as we stumble inside, and I kick the door shut behind me. We left her textbook and pencil on the hood of her car, but I couldn't care less about them. Problems for later.

Maddie breaks away to slip her shoes off, and I swear, I won't ever be able to get enough of her. Her cheeks are flushed, eyes wild, and her curls are unruly from my fingers running through them. She looks like a hot, dirty mess, and my only intention is to get her even dirtier.

Maybe we should have discussed what we're officially doing prior to hooking up again, but her sweatshirt has ridden up from kissing me, and it's showing her skin. Her perfect, soft, silky skin.

"Oh my god, come here," I mutter, pulling her into me once more.

I kick my sneakers off and continue pushing her back toward the couch. She doesn't fight me when I tug the sweatshirt off her and fling it to the floor. We don't even make it to the couch, though. I can't. Her tits are pushed up in a red lace bra, and for a second I think I'll finish right now. I've never been this excited.

I unhook her bra with ease, and when it drops to the floor I can tell she's nervous. She's biting her lip as I stare at her, almost as if she's insecure for me to see her this way now that we're not surrounded by shadows.

"So unbelievably sexy," I say before reattaching my lips to hers.

We make it to the kitchen, her back pressed against the countertop. I bend down and grab a handful of her breast so I can stick my mouth on her nipple, and she's squirming as I suck, lick, and gently bite it. She flings my hat to the floor, cursing from the blissful state she's in.

"Cam, yes." She sighs and throws her head back, and I groan at how badly I want her. How badly I want to please her.

I grab both breasts now and move my tongue back and forth to cover them while her fingers pull on my curls to try to release her frustration. I've never cared about pleasing someone this much, but with Maddie, I want to ensure she's completely satisfied. Watching her is addicting.

I move my lips to her ear as I find the waistband of her sweat-pants. "Can I finish you off properly this time?"

With two fingers, I pull her waistband back and await her permission, and she gasps at whatever the expression is on my face. I'm unsure what it's revealing to her, but I'm all in this moment. There's nowhere else I'd rather be.

"Yes." It comes out as a whisper, but it's all I need.

Finally, I move the lace of her panties to the side, sliding my fingers up and down her soaking wet slit.

Fucking hell.

When I laugh, Maddie shoots me a death glare.

"*What?*" she asks.

I find her clit, and it's practically throbbing for me. From her tits to her soaking wet pussy, I'm in utter disbelief. "You are going to be dangerous as hell for me," I find myself saying. Before she can reply I push a finger inside of her, my cock pulsating when she moans again.

She's still on her feet, and I'm staring down at her while she's pressed against my chest, my finger feeling just how tight she really is.

I've never wanted to be inside of someone more. I want to feel her wrapped around me without any clothing or distractions in our way.

She's a virgin, though. I have to keep reminding myself of that. Foreplay with her is one thing, but taking her virginity is an entirely different story.

"You like that?" I tilt my head to the side as I carefully watch her face. My finger is pumping slowly in and out, and her mouth is parted, her breathing rapid. I want to feel her climax around me. I want to feel all of that wetness she gave me in the closet and then some. I want to do *so* much more.

"Fuck this." I growl and drop to my knees before her, ripping down her sweatpants and underwear.

And what a sight she is to behold.

Seeing her naked and bare before me could rival any oasis, glorious cathedral, or even the *Mona Lisa* herself. Maddie is so fucking pretty, but her pussy is even prettier, just like I knew it would be. It's glistening right before my eyes, so I don't give her the opportunity to question what I plan to do before I stick my tongue directly onto her.

She sucks in a sharp breath and throws her head back, her fingers wrapping into my hair. "Cam. Oh my *god*."

The taste of her is sweet. Vanilla and honey with a pinch of sugar. I look up from between her thighs as I swirl my tongue in circles against her clit. I'm hardly able to see her face because of how big her tits are, and I reach up to grab one, playing with the overly sensitive bud.

"Cam!" she cries out. Her legs are shaking, and she's squirming so much that I finally have to release her nipple and grab her ass with both of my hands to fully engulf myself in her. She's so damn wet.

So fucking *hot*.

"Fuck, I'm going to—"

Yes.

That's right.

Come for me.

I feel myself finish right in my pants as I await her release, my moans muffled and strangled between her legs.

She didn't even touch me.

I didn't even touch *myself*.

A scream of release shatters my thoughts, bringing me back to the present. Maddie's fingertips are clutching the countertop beside her, her eyes rolling to the back of her head as she continues to come on my tongue. My eyes don't leave hers while I gather every last drop, cherishing the sweetness she gave me, and when she flinches from being so sensitive, I pull away, still on my knees before her.

Maddie Davis is naked in my kitchen, so I take my time gazing at her body, wanting to remember every last detail. The way her thighs meet before parting to the opening gates of heaven. The hip indents she always used to complain about as a teenager. The scar from the surgery she had in the fifth grade to get her appendix removed. Every ounce of her. Every *inch* of her is perfection.

"Um, thank you?" Her cheeks are a bright pink when she notices me checking her out. "I didn't get to help you, though." Then her eyes drop to my shorts, and when she notices the stain on them, her cheeks are akin to a sunburn. "Oh. Never mind."

I rise to my feet and grab her chin, planting a gentle kiss on her lips. "If you tell anyone about that . . ."

"That's never happened before?"

Is she serious?

"Maybe when I was thirteen and had just discovered *Playboy* for the first time?" I halfheartedly laugh. "No, Maddie. That's never happened with anyone."

The smile she gives me in return seems like she's proud of herself, and she should be.

"Well, good," she states, putting her sweatpants and under-wear on. "I think we should keep this a secret for now. You aren't ready for a relationship, but that's something I already knew, so it doesn't bother me. I want to explore this, too, but I don't want either of us to have any expectations of each other. It'll only give us a reason to get hurt when we leave for school."

I think back to moments ago when my face was suffocated by her pussy. If Ethan found out, he'd murder me. However, the more we do this, the more the image of Ethan shoving a knife in my chest while he extracts his revenge becomes less and less intimidating.

"Agreed," I reply. "No expectations. We explore this in secret and enjoy it for the rest of break, and that'll be it. We have to head back to school anyway, so it just makes sense." I glance down at my shorts, still in disbelief. "I need to throw these in the wash."

"Oh. Right." She clears her throat and grabs her bra, hooking it closed expertly.

Why is she in a rush?

"Are you okay?" I ask.

She slides the sweatshirt over her head and stares at me as if I'm losing it. "Um, I'm leaving?"

"Why?" I blurt.

When she continues to look at me as if I've lost my mind, the pieces of the puzzle click into place. I never stick around after I finish. I'm notorious for not sleeping with the same girl twice and skipping out in the aftermath of sex. Maddie isn't like those girls, though. I've known Maddie forever, and the truce I suggested was to make sure we mended our friendship. The intimacy is an added bonus.

"I don't know how we're going to become friends again if you leave."

"You want me to stay?" A smile tugs on her lips, and truthfully, it might just be my kryptonite.

"Yes, I want you to stay. I'll go grab the textbook you left on your car and you can study while I shower. Then maybe we can watch a movie and order some food. Unless you've already eaten?"

She shakes her head. It's almost comical the pure shock etched on her features. It's as if I have six snakes spurting out of my head or something.

"Okay, then we can order your favorite. Pizza?"

"Uh, sure," she says, with that smile still plastered to her face.

For the first time in six years I'm the reason for putting it there, and to know she's happy because of *me* makes me want to continue doing whatever the hell I have to to keep it there.

After retrieving her textbook and making sure she's settled on the couch, I order the pizza. My dad may be a shitty father in the emotional department, but at least he provides for me. He doesn't want me to have to work a job while in college, so he pays my tuition and gives me whatever money it takes to provide me with the proper nutrition I need.

When I'm done with my shower, I come back downstairs in just a pair of sweatpants with no shirt on. I could have worn one, but why would I do that when she likes staring at me so much without one?

The textbook is still open on her lap, that damn pencil eraser strumming her bottom lip. She's thrown her hair up into a messy bun on top of her head, and to see her so focused and concentrated is such a turn-on that suddenly my heart leaps into my chest.

What the hell?

She glances up, furrowing her eyebrows together. "Are you good?"

"Uh, yeah." I scratch the back of my head and continue to stare at the textbook in her lap. "Do you have a test or something?"

"Kind of . . ." She trails off, wincing before she adds, "It's not until next year. The MCATs."

"Oh, okay. So, you're still being diligent about being a bore, I see?"

She grabs the pillow closest to her and chucks it at me. "Shut up!" She laughs. "I'm not a bore. Planning my future and setting myself up for success is far cooler than partying every weekend."

I collapse beside her and push the textbook on the floor. Studying is important to her, I can respect that, but it's not like her test is tomorrow. I want to spend time with her, and we agreed after I took a shower that we'd watch a movie.

Tugging on her elbow, I pull her down so her head is in my lap and lean over to grab the remote. I flip to a random movie, my heart faltering when she snuggles deeper into my lap and curls onto her side. I find myself playing with her hair, wrapping the flyaway ringlets from her bun around my finger.

I could get used to this. Normally, I hate being home alone, but with Maddie here I feel comfortable. I feel closer to her than I have to anyone. I can't explain what the increase in the speed of my pulse means, but I'm enjoying it. Enjoying *her*.

"Would you stop?" She rolls onto her back and looks up at me. "You're very distracting."

"Am I?" I run the back of my finger down the column of her neck and circle her collarbone. I trace her soft, perfect skin, utterly infatuated with how it feels on my fingertips. "You know, I used to think you being a *good girl* was an inconvenience, but now . . ." Her breath hitches when I dip my hand beneath her sweatshirt, tracing the lace of her bra. "Now I'm beginning to think it'll work out in both of our favors."

"Why's that?" she whispers.

"Let's think about it. You always follow the rules and you never disobey instructions, always doing as you're told. . . . If I didn't know any better, I'd think you enjoy being praised, Maddie, and luckily for you"—I brush a fingertip over her nipple, smirking when she squirms—"I love *giving* praise."

She gulps hard. "Oh?"

"Yes, *oh*. I think being a good girl is going to become one of my favorite traits of yours."

Before I can continue, loud knocks sound against the door.

Our pizza.

Dammit.

When she scrambles off my lap with a playful grin, I expel a heavy sigh and rise to my feet. "You are *very* lucky for interruptions."

Thirteen

I'm *hot*.

Too hot.

The sweltering heat creates a trail of sweat running down my back, and when I attempt to move, a set of arms tightens around me, holding me captive.

Did I fall asleep?

Sure enough, when I blink my eyes open, sunlight is streaming into Cameron's living room. The last thing I remember last night is me being flabbergasted that Cameron hadn't watched all the *Lord of the Rings* movies, so we proceeded to binge them. We were on the last one when he fell asleep, and that should have been my excuse to leave, but instead I found myself distracted by his snoring. He looked so peaceful. So much like the boy I used to know before he had the weight of the world on his shoulders. Back when his mom was still around and cancer wasn't even a disease he understood yet.

I guess his snoring lulled me to sleep, and now . . .

Well, I need to get out of here and back home before people start questioning where I am. Not that I'm expected to give anyone an answer given I'm a grown adult, but my family and I are close. It would seem odd if I didn't at least notify them about my whereabouts.

Shit. Where did I put my phone?

I attempt to roll onto my side, but Cameron releases a moan that's much hotter than it should be, one of his hands sliding down my back until it finds my ass.

And that's when I feel it.

His hardness prodding against my lower stomach.

"Cam." I nudge him gently but he doesn't budge. He's still sleeping, and even in a dream state he's beautiful. Where I would have an open mouth with drool pooling at the sides, Cameron could be a model with his chiseled jawline and lips so full and perfect it almost isn't fair. I feel the heat rise to my cheeks when I remember those lips all over me yesterday.

He gave me the best orgasm I've ever had, and I never want him to stop.

"Cam." I shake him again, and this time one eye pops open, a smile falling onto his face that makes my heart completely stop.

He doesn't regret it.

"Another first." Both of his eyes are open now, but I'm not sure what he means by that. Am I the first girl he's ever woken up with after hooking up? The first girl who stayed over? The questions are pushed to the back of my mind when he tucks a strand of hair behind my ear. He captures my chin and brings me close to kiss my lips. It's supposed to be quick, but once we start we can't seem to stop.

He sits up and deepens it, his hand squeezing firmly on my

ass. His hard-on is pulsating against my stomach now, and I don't know what comes over me, but my instinct is to grab it, so that's exactly what I do.

The truth is, I don't know how much longer we'll have the opportunity to do this. Another girl could come along and change his mind, or my brother could find out and make him end things with me. We have five days until we leave for the Grand Canyon, and nine days until we head back to school. That means five days to explore as much as possible, considering we'll be around my family for the remaining three.

I'm not going to waste another second.

So, with a leap of faith and a confidence I don't have, I brush a hand over his full, hard length. Cam pulls his lip back between his teeth in response, his eyes a dark, searing emerald as he stares at me. They resemble the darkest of pines. A four-leaf clover cast in shadows. They're an endless pit I hope I never reach the bottom of.

"Take your pants off," I say.

He continues to hold my stare. "Are you sure, Mads? You don't have to do anything."

Can he tell I'm a virgin?

I mean, it's probably obvious since I've let him take the lead on all our sexual encounters thus far. Even now, when I'm trying to be calm, cool, and collected, my hands are shaking, and I'm terrified I won't be good at this. He's slept with girls who've more than likely done this countless times. I don't want it to be bad for him.

"I want to," I finally reply.

After a few seconds of contemplation, he must see the wanting in my eyes, because he pulls his sweatpants and briefs down to spring himself free. Plenty of girls spread rumors in high school about how fully endowed he was, but those rumors didn't do his cock justice.

A thick, long shaft bobs before my mouth, with hard ridges in all the right places. A bead of moisture has already formed at the tip and though anxiety has me worrying about how well I'll perform, he looks too damn good to be thinking of anything other than what he'll taste like.

Pushing the traitorous thoughts to the back of my mind, I take him in my hand, and a full-body shiver races down my spine at the reaction on Cam's face. He's staring at me like I'm the only girl in the world to him, and it makes me want to try my very best for him. I *need* to be the best he's ever had.

So I don't overthink it when I take him into my mouth, letting my tongue swirl around his tip and then down his length. I can't seem to take him all yet, so I focus on the first half, wishing I could smile when Cam hisses through his teeth.

"Holy *fuck*," he pants, already shifting beneath me. "I'm not going to last long."

I bob my head up and down, feeling his fingers sink into my bun so he can pull the stray hairs away from my face. When I flick my eyes up to meet his, liquid heat floods my veins. I squirm with his cock in my mouth, feeling the pressure build between my legs before he sighs and throws his head back against the armrest of the couch.

"Fuck, don't stop," he groans. "Oh *fuck*."

This is my first time pleasing him like this, but I can already tell he's close. It's in the way his hands keep running over his face. The way he's clutching my hair one second and then gripping the side of the couch the next. He's fidgeting too much, but I keep going, keep sucking, knowing I'm close to getting the end result. A volcano close to eruption. A bomb seconds from detonating.

"*Mads,*" he moans. "I'm gonna come."

I don't pull back.

He tasted me, so I want to taste him.

My eyes don't leave his when he lifts his head to stare at me again. He can tell what I'm agreeing to, and just realizing that pushes him over the edge. He calls out my name just before I feel the salty liquid coat my tongue.

It's nothing like I've tasted before, but I don't show Cam any hesitation. Instead, I keep my eyes locked on his while I swipe the remaining liquid from his tip with my finger and suck it greedily, swallowing all of him down and giving him a full-out show.

"Maddie, what the actual *hell*?" He laughs when I sit up on my knees, and stares at me in amazement, as if he's never had that done to him before.

Which I know is a lie.

My stomach twists into knots when I think about the red-headed girl from the party last weekend, Jessica from the park, and all the other girls who have had their mouths wrapped around him.

I'm no different than them.

The mood in the room has shifted, and Cam notices. Before I can get off the couch, he tugs me back against his chest and asks, "What's wrong? Do you regret doing that?"

"What? *No*, it's not that." I shake my head, biting my tongue to stop the truth from spilling out. Telling him I'm insecure after making him come will certainly ruin the mood, and I don't want to be *that* girl. I want to be confident and not worry about his past flings. They were in the past; this is now.

Except what we have going on between us is just exploring. He said himself he's not ready for a relationship, so in nine days when this is all over, he'll go back to college to the girls he's accustomed to, and I'll be flying back to Connecticut with a broken heart.

Because as much as I said there wouldn't be expectations between us, I'll be crumpled like a flimsy sheet of paper once we part ways. This is all I've ever wanted, and soon I'll have to walk away from it.

I don't know why I'm surprised when Cameron grips my chin to tilt my eyes to his and says, "I have *never* finished that quickly before. It's embarrassing as hell, to be honest." He's always been able to read me better than most, and reassurance was exactly what I needed. It may not be the answer to *all* of my problems, but it's helping.

"Between yesterday and this morning you're having a lot of embarrassing moments. Do I really get to you that much?"

"You stayed the night . . ." He trails off, placing a gentle kiss on my neck. "Trust me when I say I wouldn't have allowed that if I didn't find you absolutely addicting, okay?" His hands slide down to my waist, and suddenly I find it hard to breathe from the fluttering sensation in my chest.

"You fell asleep," I counter. "You didn't exactly have a choice about whether or not I slept here."

He arches a brow. "How do you think you got between my legs in the first place? And where do you think that blanket came from?" He points to the fuzzy black lump on the floor. "I woke up around five. It's my usual time for training, but I fell back asleep with you instead."

I blink not once, but twice. "You missed training? For me?"

"Well, it was certainly worth it." With a lazy grin he twirls a stray ringlet of mine, something he seems to enjoy doing a lot.

"But your dad . . ." His training is on a strict regimen, one his dad keeps up with frequently. If Cameron gets off track, I don't want to be the reason for that. Going to the NFL has been both of their dream since his mom passed. "I don't want to be a distraction."

He sits up on the couch to shrug his briefs back on. "Let me handle my dad, all right? Besides, I'm not straying from the regimen. Only switching my gym mornings to nights instead. It's not a big deal. Truthfully, I thought you would be more upset about me distracting *you*, considering you have a big test to study for."

I shrug. "It's not until next year. I was using this time to get a head start, and I know you think that makes me a *bore*, but—"

He cracks a smile, and I can't help but check him out when he rises to his feet. His abs are as glorious as ever, but my eyes stray to the dusting of hair beneath his belly button, which is a trail that leads right to the cock I've now had my mouth on. It's a double-edged sword, really. I'm upset I've seen it because of the rush of desire it brings, but I'm also glad because of the rush of desire it brings.

"You're not a bore," he says, snapping me back to the present. "I only called you that to mess with you. You're studying to become a fucking doctor. It takes a lot of resilience, and there's no one more self-disciplined than you. I can't *wait* to see you graduate at the top of your class, Mads."

His speech carries a sentiment I thought had disappeared from him forever, but maybe the boy I knew six years ago is finding his way out after being hidden for so long. I'm busy blinking through my tears when he drops to his knees on the floor directly in front of me, wearing a devilish grin.

How can I go from crying to panting in the span of five seconds?

"Now I'm assuming you've got places to be since you never reached out to your parents, right?"

I nod, my eyes straying to the gold chain still dangling from his neck. I'm incapable of breathing properly when he taps my hips to lift up, and in seconds he's stripped me of my underwear and sweatpants, eyeing me like a man deprived of food for days.

"Let me finger fuck you like the princess you are before you have to leave then, yeah?"

With an eager *yes*, I throw my head back against the couch and am screaming his name in the matter of minutes while he brings me to a state of total and utter ecstasy. His face buried between my thighs feels *right*, and as much as I try to ignore it, as much as I try to avoid it, one gnawing, lingering thought remains.

In nine days, this is all coming to an end.

Fourteen

CAMERON

"Two more," I instruct. "You can do it."

Ethan's arms are trembling beneath the bar he's holding. A bead of sweat trails down his forehead from the struggle, and when he shakes his head to tap out, I quickly step in to help him lift the bar back into position.

"Fuck, I hate this shit." He's gasping for air as he finds his water bottle and then practically chugs the entire thing.

"You're the one who wanted to tag along to my training session," I remind him.

"Because I need to get back in shape. It's been years since I played football."

I adjust the weights on the bar so that they're heavier and lie down on the bench to start my set. "Are you trying to get into shape for *yourself* or for Maya?"

The silence that follows my question says more than he ever could. "Look, Maya is into you already, in case you haven't figured that out yet. You're a healthy guy, Ethan. You don't need to have a fucking eight pack to score her, she's made that clear, so what's with being all self-conscious? You never used to be like this." Back in high school, Ethan was my twin. We thrived on getting girls, partying, drinking, and doing dumb shit we weren't supposed to do. He was my wingman, and I was his, but then he chose to go to community college rather than pursue football like me, and without that common denominator, we drifted apart. Now, he's nothing like the guy I used to know in high school. It's not that I don't still enjoy hanging out with him, but it's been weird getting to know the *new* him. The version where he prefers video games to going out, smoking weed to relax rather than getting fucked-up drinking, and the version who almost shits his pants over a girl's opinion of him.

"We spoke a bit on the boat, but she didn't come right out and say she was interested." He takes another swig of water before he adds, "I'm uncomfortable because I've seen her exes, and I'm nothing like them. I'm terrified to make the first move until I know for certain she's into me, and I haven't gotten that sign yet."

"You—" I grunt from the weight, starting another rep. "You want *her* to make the first move? Ethan, be serious."

"I'm not saying I want her to make the first move, but I'm not going to confess my feelings if I think there's even a chance she doesn't reciprocate them. If Maddie finds out I tried to hit on her best friend, it won't be good for me."

My chest is dripping with sweat when I lift the bar back into position. I snatch my water bottle from the floor and take a few large gulps, either from tiredness or nerves about the direction of this discussion. Little does he know my head was between his little sister's thighs this morning.

"What if Maya *does* reciprocate your feelings? What then?"

"Then I talk to Maddie about it. I've been crushing on Maya for a while, so if the opportunity to be with her presented itself, I'd take it."

"Even if Maddie disapproved?" I push.

He locks eyes with me, and for a heartbeat I'm afraid he's figured me out. But then the moment vanishes, and he sighs before adjusting the weights for another set. "I don't want to talk about this anymore. Not when my body feels like it's going to fall apart."

Letting out a laugh, I cross my arms over my chest. "That weak, huh? Weren't *you* the one who used to be able to bench more than me?"

"Shut. Up," he hisses through gritted teeth. His arms begin to quiver on his second set, and just when I relieve him of the weight, we hear the sound of the gym doors opening. Our high-school football coach allows me to use the gym here on breaks or during the summer if I visit from school, but it's rare for anyone else to be here.

"Well, isn't this a surprise." Mark strides over to us with a wide grin. "When did you decide to get back in the gym, Ethan?"

"Don't get used to it," Ethan gasps. "Pretty sure this is my last workout in this godforsaken place."

"It's good you're here," he replies, placing his water bottle and phone on a treadmill. "I was going to ask you about Maddie."

"My sister?" Ethan asks. "Why?"

"I tried to ask her out at my party a few days ago, but she seemed nervous to answer, and since I haven't gotten a text from her, I thought I'd reach out. That is, if it's cool with you. I need her number."

My body is tense as I adjust for my final set. Mark asking Maddie out shouldn't bother me at all. I told her I wasn't ready for a relationship, and she doesn't want any expectations between us. I assume that means we're able to see other people, so she *should* go on a date with Mark. He'd be able to give her everything I'm incapable of. Love. Happily ever after. Marriage. Kids.

Even knowing that, it doesn't stop my heart rate from spiking, and it has nothing to do with the weights I'm lifting. It's *jealousy* that has me pushing through this set faster than any of the others. It's bitterness coursing through me that gives me the newfound strength to finish with barely any strain at all.

I hardly know Mark, yet I find myself fantasizing about tackling him to the ground and giving him a black eye for a week for even implying he has an interest in Maddie.

Ethan shrugs. "Sure. I'll text you her number when we're done with our workout."

Mark smiles wider, and the urge to punch him grows stronger. "Thanks, man."

After Mark puts his headphones in and starts his run, I suddenly have no need to finish the rest of my workout. I'm already halfway through it, and Mark's mere presence is distracting me. I'd much rather do my cardio at home and go for a run than be here thinking of his smug grin and all the plans he has for Maddie.

I have no right to be jealous. She and I will never work out, and I know that. She deserves someone who can show her off at any opportunity they get, not hide her. We're just fooling around for the remainder of our break to *explore* things. That's it.

So why does this gut-wrenching, burning sensation lead me to feel otherwise?

"What?" Ethan eyes me shoving things into my duffel bag. "You think I should have told him no?"

"I don't know what you're talking about."

"Really? Because three minutes ago you were joking around with me, and now that Mark's taking Maddie out you're suddenly in a pissy mood and want to leave. Do you know something I don't?"

Too much.

Her hands in my curls.

My lips on her skin.

Her mouth around my—

"No, I just think it should be Maddie's decision whether or not you give him her number. Who knows? Maybe she was wary about saying yes to him because she wanted to say no." Judging by her relaxed body language at his party, that's not likely, but it's worth a shot.

Ethan ponders my response for a moment and then says, "You're right. I'll ask her about it at dinner tonight, which you're coming to as well, I'm assuming?" Mary texted me an hour ago about joining them, and as awkward as things are between Maddie and me, I've missed Mary and Richard. The nights after a long game when we'd all go out for pizza, or when I'd get sick and Mary would whip up a batch of homemade chicken noodle soup for me. I don't get that sense of *family* in college. Even though Mary checks in on me, it's not the same. I've missed being around all of them.

"Yeah, I'll come. I just have to go home and shower first."

"Cool." We step outside into the parking lot and he adds, "Are you sure you don't have any dirt on Mark? I don't want to set my sister up with someone with a bad reputation."

God, I wish I had something to tell him. I *wish* Mark had fucked up in high school and gotten into a fight, was busted for drugs, or had done anything I could use to persuade Ethan to change his mind, but from what I know, Mark is a decent guy. There's no reason for him not to take Maddie out, and there's no reason for me to stand in their way.

"Even if I said yes, are you really going to consider my opinion? I'm not the best person to take advice from on this."

He chuckles, tilting his face toward the sky to catch the sun. "You're right, but I'm asking anyway. After the whole Michael situation, I just don't want her to get heartbroken again, and if Mark has any playboy tendencies, I'm confident you'd be able to fish them out, you know? You excel at being a player. What's the saying? It takes one to know one?"

Stating the obvious has never bothered me before, and here I am acting like a total idiot wanting some sort of acceptance from Ethan, which is pointless. With all the bullshit he's seen me pull? All of the girls I've used for a night only to discard? It'd be impossible to redeem myself in his eyes.

It doesn't matter anyway.

Maddie and I aren't in a relationship.

We never will be.

This is *physical* and nothing more.

"No, he's a good guy." The sentence tastes sour on my tongue, but I swallow the bitterness and force myself to say the next words. "You should set them up."

Fifteen

MADDIE

I half expected Cameron to join us for dinner. The times he's declined have been few and far between, and him coming out with us has never put me on edge before. For the past six years I've avoided him at all costs, sitting on the opposite side of the table, and while I'd listen closely to his and Ethan's conversation, I'd never join in. Instead, I'd speak to my parents about school, or whatever book I'd been reading at the time.

But tonight Cameron doesn't give me the choice to escape. Tonight Cameron sits directly beside me, our thighs pressed together beneath the elaborate tablecloth.

Since we've all been away at school, my parents splurged on a fancy dinner at one of the most expensive Italian restaurants in downtown Phoenix. It's the kind of place where your napkin should be on your lap and you should know the difference between a salad fork and a dinner fork. We don't come here often, but when we do, we all dress up for the occasion. If we *didn't* wear our best, we'd stick out like sore thumbs.

Maybe that's the reason my body feels electrified sitting beside Cam. He's wearing a pair of dress pants that hug his figure just right, with a long-sleeved white button-down shirt left partially open to reveal the tiny bits of chest hair he has. That damn gold chain glistens beneath the dim lights of the restaurant, and I wonder if he wore it on purpose. I'm not going to be able to focus on eating let alone speaking. Not when my thoughts are clouded with the memory of tugging on that chain during our frenzied kiss.

I shift uncomfortably in my seat, and Cameron notices, staring down at me with an amused expression. "Everything okay?"

No. Goose bumps pebble my skin, and it has nothing to do with the temperature. The red satin dress I chose to wear seems like a horrible idea now that the fabric feels like a caress against my nipples—the kind of caress that reminds me of Cameron's fingers.

"I'm fine," I reply, as if the rippling heat from his body isn't utterly distracting.

Thankfully, my father interrupts. "So, what's everyone getting?"

Ethan, who is sitting to my left, rambles about the steak he deserves after his and Cameron's hard-core workout earlier this evening. I do my best to focus on the menu, but then I feel a hand on my knee beneath the table.

Every muscle tenses at his touch. My skin is like *live wire*, waiting and on edge to see where he'll move next. I want him everywhere, and yet I want him nowhere. We're at dinner with my family. Has he lost his mind?

"Their risotto is to *die* for," Mom says.

His fingers create small circles on the inside of my knee,

completely unaffected when he delves into sports with my father, and Ethan indulges my mom about what his favorites on the menu are.

How can he do this and not be suffocated by the need to kiss me? I want him to stop teasing and tackle me on this table. Right here. Right now.

"What about you, Maddie?" Mom asks. "What's your favorite here?"

"Oh, um." I blink down at the menu, suddenly forgetting every fucking dish this place makes when Cameron trails his fingers higher to my inner thigh. I should have worn tights beneath this dress. I should have made it difficult for him, but I didn't. It'll be too easy for him to slide his hand up to feel my silk panties. It'll be too easy for him to slide them to the side and—

The question.

Right.

What was it again?

"She always gets the fettuccine," Ethan supplies, oblivious to what's going on beneath the table. "Basic as hell."

"I'm not—" *Fuck.* His hand is on my pussy now, his middle finger dragging up and down the fabric of my underwear over my slit. I have to clear my throat to try again, and Cameron covers his mouth with his free hand to stifle a laugh.

I'm going to kill him.

Yet here I am, parting my thighs slightly wider to grant him more access.

"I'm not basic," I reply with more confidence. Thankfully, we're interrupted when the waiter brings us our garlic bread, so no one notices my clumsiness. I'm quick to snatch a piece if only to have an excuse not to speak because my mouth is full.

Cameron grabs one, too, eating with one hand while moving my panties to the side and sliding that middle finger of his up and down my soaking wet slit. He shifts subtly in his seat, but it's a dead giveaway to me that he's finding this difficult too. For whatever reason, that excites me.

He's playing with my clit as I stuff my face with garlic bread to tamp down my moans. We must be pretty good at this considering my family hasn't so much as looked in our general direction.

One second I'm in a lust-filled daze, and the next Cameron rips his hand from between my thighs while wearing that cocky grin of his. His eyes flick to mine, and I can see his fingers glistening with my arousal when he brings them to his mouth and *licks them.*

My body is on fire.

"Mmm," he hums. "That garlic bread is delicious."

"Isn't it?" my mom adds. "I swear, I can't find another place like this. It's expensive, but completely worth it. Don't you think so, Richard?"

"Definitely," he agrees. "One of our favorite date spots."

"Speaking of *dates . . .* " Ethan wipes his hands on a napkin and twists toward me. I'm praying my face doesn't look as red as it feels. My brother doesn't react when he adds, "Mark was working out in the gym today, too, with us, and he asked me if I could text him your number. He wants to ask you out."

Cameron stiffens beside me, the lust in the air between us evaporating with my brother's words.

"He does? Did you give him it?"

"Well, I was going to until Cameron suggested I ask you first." I arch a brow in said person's direction. "Oh really?"

"Yeah." Ethan continues. "We think Mark is a stand-up guy,

so if you're cautious about going on a date with him because you're wary of his intentions, don't be. We want you to go for it."

"We?" The question comes out before I can stop it, but what the hell? I thought Cameron and I were exploring things, not messing with other people. I said there'd be no expectations, but that didn't mean we could fool around with whomever we wanted.

Oh god.

Is he messing around with other girls?

Is that why he agreed to exploring things? Because he wants to play the field?

It's clear I didn't express my wants enough if that's how he's viewing things. Obviously, whatever connection I thought we had isn't emotional. Our friendship might be, but anything past that? Purely physical.

Then again, why am I surprised? He told me he doesn't do relationships. They aren't his thing. What was I expecting? Him to become a changed man after we messed around a few times?

I'm an idiot.

An utter idiot.

"Is that the boy who used to play football with you guys?" Mom asks. She takes a sip of wine, and I've never been more jealous of her for being of legal age. If I was twenty-one, I'd down an entire glass in seconds.

Just two more years.

When Ethan nods, she smiles. "Oh, I always liked him. You should let him have your number, honey. He seems like a nice boy."

Cameron hasn't touched another piece of garlic bread. His hands are clenched on the sides of his chair and a muscle is feathering in his jaw, but he has no reason to be upset when he's all but shoving me into Mark's arms. Sure, he was up front and honest about not wanting a relationship, but I thought we'd at least be exclusive while we explored.

He's probably been *exploring* with the redhead and Jessica from the park too.

If this is how he wants it to be, then fine.

Two can play that game, *Cameron*.

Turning to give my brother a dazzling smile, I say, "I was hoping he'd ask you. I'd love for you to give him my number. I'm long overdue for a date."

"Awesome," he replies. "I'll text him after dinner, then."

I continue to force a smile the entirety of our meal, but I can hardly eat. My heart is shattering, and just as I predicted, I'm a crumpled up piece of paper.

I said there'd be no expectations, but I'd be lying if I said there weren't. I thought this was the time Cameron would go back to the boy I used to know, and now that we finally crossed the line of intimacy, I assumed it meant something.

But just like all the times before, I'm left disappointed, and I have no one to blame but myself and the false perception I have of the boy sitting beside me.

And this time, when Cameron goes to put his hand back on my knee, I slap it away.

Sixteen

CAMERON

It's almost nine, and after three rounds of *Call of Duty* with Ethan, I'm tired as hell. During training weeks I'm normally in bed by eight, but even if I tried to sleep right now it wouldn't be possible. Not with my mind racing with thoughts of Maddie and what a fuckup I was at dinner tonight.

I should have told her about Mark the second I left the gym, but even if I had reached out, I don't know what I'd have said. It's not like I can claim her as mine. Everything is so new between us, and we haven't exactly established boundaries. Maybe she wanted to explore with me and *only* me for the remainder of break. Maybe pushing her in Mark's direction was the wrong thing to do.

Maddie is an emotional girl, and while there's nothing wrong with that, it's something I can't offer in return. I haven't been in tune with that side of myself in so long that I honestly don't know whether or not it still exists, so it'd be pointless to try to find that version for her when I know this will never work out with us in the long run.

A pillow smacks me in the face, bringing me back to reality. "What the hell is up with you?" Ethan asks. "You've been acting weird all day. What gives?"

Racking my brain, I try to come up with some sort of excuse for my mood that doesn't include his little sister.

"College," I say with a shrug. "I'm stressed about the pressure on my shoulders. Every time I come home I'm reminded how everyone in this town sees me as their *hometown hero*, and it's a lot to take in. Coach and others claim I'm a shoo-in, but what if I'm not? What if they're wrong?" I'm not necessarily telling a lie. This *has* been weighing on me, I just haven't wanted to admit it.

"Well, if you flunk out and fail at it, we can always open up that burger stand we talked about when we were younger." I roll my eyes, but he gets a grin out of me. "All jokes aside, if you fail, it's not going to be the worst thing in the world. You can move back home and become the best fucking football coach our high school has ever seen, or anywhere else in the country for that matter. You can be a mentor for kids, or you can ditch the football thing completely and do something with your physical education degree? That's what you're majoring in, right?"

I nod when he pauses the game, giving me his full attention. "There are plenty of options, and anyone who's putting pressure on you doesn't deserve to get an ounce of attention if you do make it to the NFL. Win or lose, you'll still have me, and that's what matters, right?"

My throat gets tight as I dip my chin to acknowledge him. "Thanks, man."

Ethan is the brother I never had. He's there for me through thick and thin, and although I know he'll still stick around if this doesn't pan out, what about everyone else? Would my dad still stay in touch if my football career ended? I don't have a clue, and the fact I can't answer that question is its own problem.

"Maybe you need to get laid." He huffs a laugh, thankfully changing the subject. Right as he finishes his sentence, Maddie walks past his open door. "Maddie," he calls. She freezes in the middle of the doorway and turns to face us. "Tell Cameron he needs to get laid so that he'll stop moping around."

Maddie avoids eye contact with me completely, staring at the floor.

"What?" Ethan waves between the two of us. "Are you *both* in shitty-ass moods? What is up with everyone?"

Then Maddie smiles that same grin she had on her face when she blew me this morning, and it takes an enormous amount of effort to avert my gaze. "I'm not in a bad mood, but I don't think Cam needs any help getting laid. Rumor has it he was satisfied this morning, actually."

If I had a drink, I'd be choking on it right about now.

"Oh *really*?" Ethan spins to face me in his swivel chair. "Who? Sadie?"

Maddie raises her eyebrows expectantly, waiting to hear my answer.

Is this her version of payback?

If so, she's got a rude awakening coming.

With a cunning smile in her direction, I say, "I'm not going to kiss and tell."

Maddie rolls her eyes, and I understand she can't stand me right now, but she has to know that I fucked up earlier. I need to tell her how horrible I feel about what happened, and if I could go back and make Ethan tell Mark to get lost, I would, but I didn't know that's what she wanted me to do at the time.

"So it's a *new* girl," Ethan muses. His face is puzzled as he tries to figure out who it is, but he'll never be able to guess. "And you know who it is, Maddie?"

A smile threatens to appear on her lips, but she hides it and says, "I have no idea. I just took a wild guess. His dick seems to be inside a new girl every day."

I flinch.

I actually *flinch*.

Is that what she thinks I'm doing? Sticking my dick in other girls all because I told Ethan he should set Maddie up with Mark?

She has no idea the power she holds over me. She doesn't have a clue that I haven't stuck my dick in anyone since we started messing around. *Before* that, even. I've been exclusive with her since the moment we kissed, but I can't exactly say that with her brother in the same room.

"Who on earth could she be that you're being so secretive about?" Ethan asks.

If I can't tell her, then I'm damn well going to drop hints.

"I'm not saying names because I want her all to myself," I say, flicking my eyes to hers briefly. Her lips part, but she remains silent.

Ethan's eyebrows shoot to his forehead. "She's got you locked down like *that*? Damn. Is she that good in bed?"

I immediately laugh and then laugh even harder because he has *no* idea he's talking about his little sister right now.

"Definitely," I reply, my eyes never leaving Maddie's. "She's the best I've ever had."

Maddie's eyes drop to the floor, her cheeks turning a bright red. She doesn't want Ethan to see, so she quickly spins around and says, "You guys are gross. I've got studying to do."

"As always," Ethan replies when she disappears. "God, she's so lame."

Not always.

Contact with Maddie, whether it's awkward or not, feels good. *So* good. Although she still seemed annoyed with me, she didn't seem pissed, so I'm taking that as a step in the right direction. Then again, she was in the same room with her brother, so she couldn't exactly act pissed in front of me and make the tension between us obvious.

I replay the interaction on a loop when Ethan starts the game back up, my brain overthinking and worrying about her ending this exploring proposition between us before it's even started.

When did I become this type of guy? The type to analyze every word exchanged and try to read between the lines? It's so unlike me.

I'm *not* clingy. I'm not someone who cares if a girl wants to continue things because I've never continued them before. With anyone. If I found a girl who was okay with what I was looking for, we'd have sex, and then we'd chat for a minute or two, and then they were out the door going about their lives.

Maddie is different.

Clearly, my first crush hasn't faded, and now that I've crossed into the realm of intimacy with her, I'm afraid I won't be able to stop. And I *have* to stop. We'll be going back to school, and long distance has never worked out for anyone. How would it be able to work for us when we would have to hide our entire relationship?

It *can't* work, and yet here I am, trying to conjure up ways to make it happen.

Releasing a sigh, I try to focus on the game again but it's no use.

Maddie Davis fucked me up the very second her lips met mine, and now I fear I've got no chance of recovering.

Seventeen

MADDIE

In high school I used to think girls who were obsessed with their boyfriends were annoying. They'd hold hands everywhere they walked, canoodle by the stairs, whisper sweet nothings when I passed them in the halls. It was ridiculous to think someone could be in love that young, but that was before Cameron Holden kissed me.

Now I've become a sex-crazed lunatic, just like everyone else.

Don't get me wrong, I love the idea of spending the rest of my life with someone, but I always imagined it'd come later in life. My career has always been my first priority, and yet I haven't been able to read one sentence of this textbook since my conversation with Cameron and my brother earlier this evening. The words blur together, seeming to become one, and the only thing on my mind is Cameron's hand between my legs underneath the table at dinner.

Even though my heart says I should be angry at him, my brain is the more rational of the two. I have no reason to be angry at Cameron when I didn't specify my wants and needs from the very beginning. It wasn't ever stated that we were going to be exclusive, so he could have very well assumed *no expectations* meant we could see other people. Now that I've had time to think about things and calm down, I realize I could have been more specific about what this was between us. It still didn't give him the right to push me into Mark's arms, though.

Flinging my textbook on the floor, I fall back onto my bed and grab my phone off the nightstand. I shouldn't, I *really* shouldn't, but I can't help myself when I pull up Cameron's Instagram. It's a thirst trap I happily fall into a lot.

The first picture is of him on the football field with athletic shorts and no shirt on. He's holding a football between his hands with his curls held back by a white snapback, and he's caught off guard, laughing at something someone said, his teeth perfectly straight and white. It doesn't help that he's sweating, tiny beads of perspiration traveling down his abs and pooling above the band of his shorts. *Game time*, the caption reads.

Beneath the photo, I see at least twenty girls have commented on how good he looks or attempted to gain his attention. He's liked some of the comments, but he hasn't replied to any of them. His social media is mainly pictures of himself or with his teammates or Ethan. He's never posted one of a girl, and I'm ashamed to admit I've stalked him enough over the years to notice if he deleted pictures or not. He hasn't.

It makes me wonder if he kept the picture we took the night we snuck out at the beach. It was just us, and he wanted to take a picture with me, which shocked me. He was always shy and tentative about things like that, but that night we were different versions of ourselves.

I'd be an idiot to think he still has it. Not when he hasn't posted a photo of a single girl on his social media. Then again, he probably has thousands of pictures saved in his phone from girls that are far more entertaining than us on the beach one night.

What the hell is wrong with me?

Ever since I've gotten home, he's infiltrated my every thought. It's like my brain is chemically wired to want him every second of the day. Or maybe it's because I've never done these sexual things before, and now that I've gotten a taste of it, I want more.

Need more.

Maybe this doesn't have anything to do with Cameron at all.

Doubtful, my brain snickers in response.

I sigh while gazing at the picture of him on the football field. His lips, which are full and wet and so talented when they're between my legs. His grin, which could drive anyone wild—the kind that could make any girl's panties drop at the sight of it.

I trail my fingers to the waistband of the leggings I changed into after dinner and push inside to find the sweet spot that only Cam and I have touched.

I'm already soaked from just staring at this man's picture. All I can think of is his hands on my body and his tongue flicking against my clit.

Why did I put pressure on him?

We aren't together.

Did I ruin things?

My clit is swollen and sensitive to the touch as it seems to remember all the different ways Cameron has made me come. His fingers, his tongue, his hand . . . my fingers are slippery as I try to replicate what he does to finish me off, but no matter what I do, it doesn't feel like him.

I want him.

He's right downstairs.

I can almost hear his voice in my ear. His moans, the way I made him feel, the way he came in his pants just from pleasing me.

Oh fuck it.

With a frustrated huff, I close Instagram and open the messaging app instead.

Are you still here?

I press Send, holding my breath when he replies not even seconds later.

That depends. Are you still upset with me?

Maybe. Come upstairs and find out.

I'm fidgeting on top of my comforter with impatience. I'm craving his touch. His voice. His body. And in less than a minute there are soft taps on my door.

I tiptoe across the floor, carefully avoiding the wooden boards that creak. My parents and Ethan are sleeping, so I have to make sure we keep this as quiet as possible.

But as soon as I open the door, I don't waste time. I'm so horny I don't know what to do with myself when I see him standing in front of me still dressed in his outfit from the restaurant.

I pull him by the arm to come inside, shutting the door quietly behind us.

"Mads, what are you—"

"I'm still pissed at you," I begin, stripping off my shirt and tossing it to the floor. I'm not wearing a bra, so my breasts are fully exposed. "Don't think this is me forgiving you yet, because it isn't."

Cameron stares at me in a daze before that little flirtatious smirk falls onto his face. "Okay," he says.

I take off my leggings, leaving just my underwear, before I continue. "But I'm horny, and I want you to make me come again."

He leans against the door as he watches me, his tall, muscular body looking like candy to me right now. "Is that so?" My eyes are glued to his when he strokes his chin with his index finger and thumb as if deep in thought.

I nod desperately and strip off my panties before tossing them to him. He catches them and runs the lace through his hands, his eyes growing darker. Then he drops them to the floor, still leaning against the door as he tilts his head to the side. "I want us to be okay again if I do this," he tells me firmly. "Can you agree to stop being mad at me in exchange for a mind-blowing orgasm?"

I don't know what's gotten into me, but I feel so confident and comfortable with him. It makes no sense when there's so much doubt surrounding us, but my body is telling me it's right.

It's *so* right.

"That depends . . ." I trail off and lie down on the bed. I support myself on my elbows and slowly open my legs to him, thoroughly enjoying when his gaze turns *feral*. "Maybe you can make me come hard enough I'll forget why I was ever mad in the first place."

Eighteen

CAMERON

This woman will be the utter death of me.

Who is this?

It's the only thought in my head as my eyes zero in on her spread legs and the glistening wetness already waiting. I always thought Maddie was shy and that when it came to sex she'd be a prude, but as always, she never fails to surprise me. She is *far* from a prude. I almost don't recognize her.

My cock throbs against my pants, begging for release. She's fucking stunning, and all I want to do is bury myself in her. I don't know what made her change her mind about continuing this, but if she wants an orgasm, I'll give her one.

When I finally push off the door, I keep my eyes on hers while I take off my belt. From the moonlight seeping in from the window, I can tell how turned on she is, so excited and eager, and I've never been more determined to please her than I am right now. If she wants to forget then that's exactly what I'll do.

I was an ass, after all.

Her teeth tug on her bottom lip as I pull my belt off and fling it to the floor—my dress pants are unbuttoned and barely clinging to my hips. "How would you like to come, Maddie?" I ask her sternly. "However you want it, I'll do it."

"Oh god," she pants, impatient as I shrug off my pants and briefs.

You'd think I'd just unveiled a porterhouse steak the way she's looking at my cock, and I love it. I'm entranced by how wild her eyes look. How into me she seems to be at this moment.

As I climb on top of her, she pulls on the gold chain I have around my neck, tugging me closer, and as soon as our lips touch, I completely lose myself in her.

No longer can I be dominant. No longer can I be in charge. For the first time, I've found a girl who makes me take the backseat. I would give anything to please her and give her exactly what she needs.

I can't kiss her fast enough. Her hands are all over my body and running every which way while we make out so intensely that our teeth are clashing. I'm gripping those heavenly tits, feeling her nipples grow hard against my fingers.

"Oh, Maddie," I moan into her mouth as she tugs on my curls. My fingers slide to her soaking wet pussy, so ready and perfect that I can't take it anymore.

"*Please* eat me out," she gasps.

Maddie Davis, the girl who was so tentative about sucking my dick yesterday, has transformed into a different person. Or maybe she's gotten comfortable with me and is finally showing me her true colors in bed. I'm impressed by how bold she is.

So hot.

"As you wish," I comply and slip between her legs. I place

my lips on her without a second thought, and she's as sweet as always.

I'm lost in her.

I could *drown* in her.

I dip my tongue into her pussy, feeling her legs stiffen. She's already close, but I don't want her to come. Not yet. She wanted to come so hard that she forgets, and that's what I promised her I'd do.

There's a floor-length mirror directly in front of her bed, so I pull her up onto her knees, her back against my chest so she can see us both in the reflection.

"You wanted to come so hard . . ." I whisper into her ear, my fingers finding her clit before I rub slow, torturous circles on it. "I want you to watch me when I do this. Do you see how sexy you are?"

Her heartbeat is rapid beneath my forearm, which is pinning her to my chest. She can't even speak when I use my free hand to grab one of her breasts, never breaking our gaze in the reflection. "Your tits"—I squeeze one and gently kiss her shoulder—"are the best I've ever seen."

I run my fingertips over her nipple, and I'm so hard as I watch myself do this to her.

Moving my hand to her clit again, I push one finger inside of her and soak up the gasp she gives me.

"That's right, baby." The endearment slips, but it doesn't seem to bother her. It doesn't seem to bother me either. It feels right coming off my tongue—like the sentiment has belonged to her long before this moment. "Show me how much I get to you."

"Cam," she chokes out.

I feel her legs begin to shake, nearing the edge, and the sound of her wet pussy is so intoxicating I think I'll combust.

"Were you thinking about me?" I ask. "Is that why you asked me to come up here?"

She nods, catching me off guard.

"You were?"

"Yes. I was touching myself," she pants.

Oh, sweet fuck.

I chuckle against her skin, my eyes not leaving hers in the reflection as I kiss her shoulder again and say, "So, *so* hot. Do you know that I get off to you too?"

She shakes her head, completely clueless as to how addicting she truly is. How much she has taken over my damn mind.

Not being able to hold back any longer, I place my hand over myself and begin to stroke. Her eyes are glued to the motion as I drag my hand along my shaft, and seeing her reaction is so unbearably hot that I almost can't take it.

"I do this all the time . . ." I trail off. "To thoughts of you."

My finger is pushing in and out of her so easily that it slips not once, but twice. I don't know if a girl has ever been this wet for me before.

"What do you think about?" she pleads.

I'm surprised she's able to talk, so I put in another finger, unsurprised when she takes it like a pro. I nod in approval. "Two. Good girl, Maddie."

"What do you think about?" she asks again. I quicken the pace in her and on myself, never losing focus in the mirror. I want her to watch me finger her. Want to feel this tight pussy explode and drench the comforter beneath us. Want to show her how long I've been waiting to do this.

"I think about this wet cunt," I whisper in her ear. "And I think about how fucking good it would feel wrapped around my cock." She whimpers from the dirty talk, and I'm pleasantly surprised by that. Maybe words can push her over the edge too.

"Look at me," I say when her eyes close. They immediately pop back open in a blazing, icy version of ecstasy. "I want to bury myself inside of you, Maddie. I want to be inside of you just like *this*." I press myself against her from behind, feeling the smoothness of her ass and admiring the way it looks like pure silk in the moonlight.

"I wouldn't even wear a condom," I continue. "And I *always* do, but with you . . ." I push in deeper, feeling her tightness around my fingers. "So fucking wet, baby."

"Yes, keep calling me that," she begs.

With other girls, calling them baby was like a pet name. It was just something to call them because I felt like it was what they expected in the moment. Saying it to Maddie feels different. When I say it to her, the term of endearment makes me imagine a world where she could be mine and I could be hers, and the strangest part about it all is that that world doesn't terrify me. Maybe, deep down, I *want* to make her mine.

And I have no idea what the hell to do with that revelation.

"I want—" I run my tongue up the column of her neck. "To—" I bite her earlobe. "Feel you come." I pant against her ear. "*Please*, baby."

I finish before she does, and I feel her hips buck against my fingers as she watches me stroke myself in the mirror and stain the purple comforter she's had for years. Her moan is loud, so I slap my free hand over her mouth while I bite down on her neck to muffle my own cries of pleasure.

Her legs are quivering when I slip my fingers out and collapse onto my back, panting and feeling as if I'm on cloud nine.

I'm in a dream I don't ever want to wake up from.

She's still on her knees, unable to move while she tries to regain control of her breathing. Then she looks over her shoulder at me and smiles, and something inside of my chest tightens at the sight. I don't ever know what to say to her during the moments after. It's always incredible with her, and each time we do this I become a little more addicted than the time before.

It's silent in the room now, just the faint smell of sex floating throughout the air. She lies down beside me, her leg touching mine, and I instinctively pull her closer and tug the comforter over us for privacy.

"Are you still mad?" I finally manage to whisper.

She rests her chin on my chest and traces my tiny patch of chest hair. It seems as if she's debating whether or not to share what's on her mind, so I beat her to it.

"Be honest," I say. To try to coax it out of her and make her feel more relaxed, I rub small circles on her thigh, smiling at the goose bumps that rise on her skin.

"I think I'd be lying to you if I said I was okay with you messing around with other girls," she admits. "And maybe it's partly my fault for not clarifying, so I apologize for that, but while we're exploring during this break, I want to be *exploring* with just each other." She presses her lips together and releases a sigh. "Keeping this a secret is fine, but I don't want to share you."

Does she want a title?

Would she be willing to take the risk and tell Ethan?

My mind whirls with about a billion thoughts going off at once. I'm not ready to commit to anyone, because the very minute I do, I'm going to run. I have attachment issues after losing my mom, and somehow, someway I'd fuck it up with Maddie if I ever got the chance.

"I know you aren't the relationship type," she reassures me, seeming to read my thoughts. "And I'm fine with that, but only if this exploring situation is with me and only me until we go back to school. I don't want to be messing around with you if you're messing around with other girls too."

"I'm not," I blurt. "Messing with other girls, I mean. I haven't since we kissed." The confession seems to surprise her, but she allows me to continue and doesn't interrupt. "However, I don't want to stop you from finding someone who can give you the things I can't, Mads, and I wouldn't be doing you justice if I tried to steer you away from Mark. Trust me when I say I *want* to be selfish as fuck and keep you all to myself, but you deserve more than that. That's why I suggested you give him a chance."

The thought of her with someone else is like a punch to the gut, but I'm not the guy she's going to spend the rest of her life with. I lost the ability to fully love someone the second I found out my mom was no longer with me.

Maddie's eyes meet mine, blurry with tears threatening to spill. "So you want me to go on a date with him?"

No.

Fuck no.

"I want to give you the choice," I say instead. "You deserve to explore things with him to see where things go." The disappointed expression on her face is enough to tempt me to lie to her and give her false promises I'll never be able to follow through with. I want to tell her I could give her the happily ever after she craves because if my life was capable of having one, it'd be with her, but those words die on my tongue as soon as they enter my thoughts. I'm not going to lie only to crush her in the long run. I'm not going to have her walk away from me sobbing her eyes out like she did six years ago.

I refuse.

"Okay," she whispers. "I'll think about it, and if you're allowing me to explore things with Mark then I guess you can see someone else if you—"

"I don't want to see someone else."

Her brows fly to her forehead. *"Really?"*

"Is that so hard to believe?" I counter. "I've explored enough. I'm fine being exclusive with you until we head back to school."

"No other girls," she repeats. "Just me. Are you sure you're okay with that?"

"Mads." I pull her closer. "I'm completely okay with that."

The smile that falls over her face could rival the moonlight glittering through the window. I'm content when she relaxes her head back on my chest, almost as if nothing could go wrong. With her in my arms, suddenly my relationship with my dad doesn't seem to matter. Making it to the NFL isn't as stressful. Keeping my status as the *hometown hero* isn't as important.

When I'm with her, I'm just Cam.

Normally, this would be the part when I'd leave. I'd make up some lame excuse about having to train or call it an early night, but for the second time, I find myself wanting to stay and talk with her.

I've known her my entire life. Until I got to high school she was one of my best friends, and I care so much for her. Now that we've rekindled our friendship, I feel more myself than I have in years, but with this added intimacy, I'm worried it'll change things for us. We agreed to no expectations and to end this when we head back to school, but when that happens, will I lose this rekindled friendship too? I don't know if I'll be able to handle losing all of her again.

"Do you remember when we went to that ice-cream parlor the summer before you guys started high school?" she asks, dragging me from my thoughts. "When you got a slushy and you laughed so hard it came out of your nose?"

I laugh at the memory. It feels so long ago, and yet I can remember it vividly. It was the week before we all went to Myrtle Beach. "Yeah. Ethan was telling that stupid joke about a cow? Cat? I can't remember what it was, but it wasn't even that funny. I don't know how that happened."

"It was a cow," she says, "and that was the first time I realized I was attracted to you."

I sit up in disbelief. "*That* is the first time you thought I was hot? When a fucking *slushy* came out of my nose? Mads, come on."

"What?" She giggles, pushing some stray curls away from my face. "I couldn't help it! Your laugh was obnoxiously cute. It still is."

Her laugh is cute too. I've always been infatuated with the way her nose wrinkles up, or when she's laughing so hard she can't breathe and snorts. Maddie has always held my attention no matter what she does, but there is only one day I can think of when I had been about to spill all my feelings for her—the night I came to terms with the fact that there wasn't a more beautiful human being on the planet than Maddie.

I bend down to give her a kiss and whisper, "Myrtle Beach."

"Hm?" she asks.

"The summer your family took us to Myrtle Beach. You convinced me to sneak out, and I don't think I've ever felt so alive."

At the mention of that night, her body stills. "That was when you were first attracted to me? I probably looked like shit, Cam."

She didn't. I still remember it as if it was yesterday. Her hair was in a messy bun, and she was wearing an oversized sweatshirt and a pair of my sweatpants I'd let her borrow, but that was *her*, and it was breathtaking.

"Well, if you want me to be honest, the first time I was attracted to you was definitely when you wore a bikini to the beach for the first time," I admit. "Same vacation if I'm not mistaken."

She rolls her eyes. "There's the Cam I know."

"What?" My hand drifts to her breasts beneath the comforter, loving the sharp little inhale she gives when I caress them. "I'm a guy. These were *very* distracting."

When she laughs again and swats my hand away, all my worries fade. It's just her and me, and there's nowhere else I'd rather be.

I don't want to get up. I want to stay here with her all night long, but unfortunately, her parents and brother are under the same roof, and if her father caught us in bed together I'd be a dead man walking.

"Ugh, *no*," she whines when I slide off the bed. I ignore the urge to crawl back to her while I slip my dress clothes back on. They're uncomfortable and stiff, and now I'm regretting not asking Ethan to borrow a change of clothes.

When I'm finished, I find her panties and T-shirt scattered on the floor and pass them back to her. "This won't be the last time we do this," I say.

She grins. "I certainly hope not."

I lean over the mattress to give her one last kiss, groaning when her hands rake through my hair. In seconds I'm hard *again*, ready to spring into round two, but I pull myself away before I can get sucked in. It was dangerous enough doing this once tonight, let alone twice. "I need to see you as much as possible before we leave for the Grand Canyon."

"Yes please," she hums in agreement. "Maya can help out. She wouldn't say a word to anyone if I asked her to cover for me. You know, just so I have an explanation for why I'm away from home so much."

"Sounds like a plan to me." I give her a devilish grin and back up toward the door. "I hope you keep your energy up, Maddie Davis, because if we only have eight days left of this? I'm not going to keep my hands off you."

"Looking forward to it, Holden." She relaxes against her pillows, content and happy, and that tightening sensation happens in my chest again—the kind of feeling one gets before bungee jumping off a bridge or heading out to give a speech to a large audience. It's uncomfortable, but it's not foreign. I've gotten it before, and it's fucking terrifying to know that the only other time I've felt it was again with her on that night in Myrtle Beach right before I was about to pour my heart out and stopped myself.

I had been about to tell her that I was in love with her.

Correction: I *am* in love with her.

No matter how hard I tried to distance myself and push her away, the feeling never made it out of my system, and now I'm left to deal with the repercussions after telling her she should go on a date with someone who isn't me.

It's better this way, I tell myself.

Safer.

But the mantra I've repeated for years is starting to fail me.

Nineteen

MADDIE

"I have to tell you something."

I'm sitting next to Maya on my comforter, a bowl of Cheetos between us while we binge some corny Hallmark Christmas movie. And no, it's nowhere near close to the holidays, but Maya has a thing for the clichéd movies. You know, the ones where the heroine who works for a big corporation in the city comes home to a small town during the break and bumps into an old love interest at the annual cookie bake-off. I've held my tongue the entirety of the first half, but before we get to the third-act breakup, I can't fight it any longer.

"Right now?" she whines. "Maddie, Craig is about to head to the bar in town and drink his sorrows away before he realizes he's in love with Maggie! We're almost to the good part."

"Shouldn't the entire movie be good? Not just a quarter of it?"

With a deep sigh, she leans over to my nightstand to grab the remote. After she pauses it and drags her eyes to mine, she seems to realize the conversation is about to get serious. "Oh god. You have that look on your face. What is it?"

"Okay, well . . ." Despite my best efforts, I'm smiling like a kid discovering they're headed to Disney World. "Cameron kissed me. Well, sort of. We were partnered up for that stupid game of the blindfolded version of seven minutes at a party, but that doesn't matter. What matters is it happened, and Maya . . ." I squeal from the memories. "It was so good. Like, out of this *world* good. After we went to the lake we decided to continue things, but no one else knows except you, so you can't tell anyone. It's all really new, and—"

"I fucking knew it!" The bowl tilts onto its side when her hand smacks it by accident, spilling the contents. "He finally made his move!"

I bite on my lip to tamp down my smile. "Yeah, but since everything is new, we kind of need help sneaking around, so . . ."

"You need me to cover," she says slowly, piecing the puzzle together. "You already know I'll do it, Maddie. You've been in love with this guy for years, so if you need me to make up a few excuses while you figure out your relationship, then—"

"Well, it's not a *relationship*," I interject. "We're . . . exploring things."

The joy on my best friend's face fades in an instant. "Exploring," she deadpans. "Explain *exploring*."

I wring my hands together in my lap, trying to determine the best way to explain this when I haven't yet grasped it myself. "Well, you know Cameron isn't the relationship type, so we agreed things won't become serious between us. We're going to see where things go, and when we head back to school, that'll be that."

"Maddie," Maya says, dropping her face into her hands. "Maddie, Maddie, Maddie. What the hell have you gotten yourself into?"

"I don't know what you're talking about. What do you mean?"

"I *mean* you started a friends with benefits with Cameron fucking Holden. You aren't a friends with benefits kind of girl, Maddie. Look at the way you lit up just telling me you guys kissed. Please tell me that's all that's happened, right?"

The silence is very telling, and it only makes her continue her rampage. "This is your first time doing anything, and you chose for it to happen with a guy who's hooked up with more girls than Hugh Hefner?"

Okay, wow.

That was harsh.

"I chose for it to be with the guy I've been waiting for this to happen with. It wasn't some spur of the moment decision, Maya. I've wanted this for a long time."

She shakes her head. "But not like this. Cameron is the boy you've dreamed of marrying and settling down with. He's the guy you want *forever* with, and he's not going to be able to give it to you. You heard the rumors about him in school. You know he couldn't care less about the girls he barrels through without sparing a second glance. When this is all over, you're going to be devastated."

Don't get me wrong, I knew there was a possibility our conversation would go this way. I've had this same back and forth with myself when I lie awake in bed at night—when my thoughts are consumed with nothing but him but I keep telling myself that I'd rather experience these moments with him and be crushed in the end than to have never experienced anything at all.

Maya grabs my hands and squeezes them. "As your best friend, it's my job to look out for you. I'm just stating the possible repercussions of this. That's all."

"And I'm terrified shitless that this will only result in heartbreak,

Maya, but I'll regret it for the rest of my life if I don't at least try to see where things go between us. If I'm a fool in the end then so be it, but I want this, and I could really use your help covering for us until break is over. I don't want my brother becoming suspicious. You know what a lunatic he became after the whole Michael situation, and if things end poorly between Cam and me . . ."

Maya winces as if she, too, is imagining Cameron facing the barrel of a shotgun at Ethan's hand. "I got it. Like I said, I'll do this for you, Maddie. But I wouldn't be your best friend if I didn't warn you to take things slowly. You need to tread carefully with this."

I hold up my hand like one would swearing the oath in court. "Scout's honor."

"And you need to make sure you never do *that* in front of him. Like, ever, if you want an actual shot with him." I fight back a laugh while she begins picking up the spilled cheesies. "So, you've done more than kiss with him? Was it good at least?"

"Everything but sex," I correct. "But, as you previously mentioned, you've heard the rumors in school. What do you think?"

Her lips tilt into a sly grin. "I think that means anyone you experience after him won't even come close."

Boy, is she right, and it's the quick pinch of fear that sparks my gut that makes me shift uncomfortably on my mattress. I don't want to experience anyone else aside from him. He's the guy I've waited my entire life for, but he's also the guy who's trying to shuffle a lot of cards in his life, and a girlfriend isn't a card he intends on keeping in the deck.

The weight of this conversation settles heavier in my chest.

I need to tread carefully.

Twenty

CAMERON

On the night of the Super Bowl my mom is on the edge of her seat with a bowl of popcorn in her lap, eyes glued to the television in front of her. It's the first time in almost a decade that Arizona has made it this far, and the game is close. Too close. They're in the last quarter with only thirty seconds left. It's first and goal, and Arizona is going for a two-point conversion to try to win rather than tie it up. I don't think I've ever seen my mom more nervous than right now.

"Can I sit here?" Maddie points to the empty spot beside me on the couch. I nod, keeping my eyes on the TV when she takes a seat. The crowd is going wild, and my dad, who is unable to sit down, paces behind the couch with his hands on his head, muttering incoherent things under his breath.

"Come on, come on, come on," I mutter, a lump lodged in my throat. They're unlikely to get this opportunity again for a long time, and after learning a few weeks ago my mom has cancer, I want this for her. I have more than enough hope she'll beat it, but just in case she doesn't, well, I want Arizona to win, dammit. She deserves to see them win.

Mary and Richard are on the opposite couch with Ethan, huddled together as if they're thinking the same. Mary doesn't care for sports, but tonight she's on edge like the rest of us.

Maddie's thigh presses against mine, and I glance down at the contact. We're best friends so I should be used to sitting closer than normal with her, but this time, it feels different. I'm maturing, and girls haven't given me the cooties for a while now. I'm starting high school next year, so an influx of hormones must be why I suddenly need to grab a pillow and place it over my lap. It's not the first time this has happened, but it's the first time with Maddie.

She pulls her eyes away from the screen, eyeing the pillow. "Are you okay?"

"Yeah." I stutter, nervous as hell. "I'm just—"

"THEY DID IT!"

Everyone lurches off the couches at the same time and the bucket of popcorn goes flying. Kernels litter the carpet as everyone, including Maddie and me, screams at the top of their lungs. Thankfully, the jump scare has fixed my hormonal situation, so I'm able to leap off the couch with everyone else before we all rush to hug my mom, who is crying tears of joy. Arizona just won the Super Bowl, but it's not the reason both of our families are crying in a huddle around my mom.

We're here mainly in support of her, and although it remains unspoken, I know we all feared that if Arizona didn't win tonight my mom might not live long enough to watch them have a second chance at it.

But they won, and with both of our families together in this little huddle, it's a memory I'm going to cherish for life.

>> <<

Music has always been a way to escape for me. As soon as I put my headphones on, the world doesn't seem so hard, and just like being submerged underwater, music tunes everything out. It's a way to relax and wind my body down, but ever since starting things up with Maddie, it seems to be having the opposite effect.

Now, listening to music while I work out makes me feel energized. I'm going twice as hard on all my sets because I want my stamina to be up for her. Two miles on the treadmill instead of one. An additional ten pounds more than normal. I feel like I've gained superhuman strength since kissing her, and even with sweat pouring down my back, I'm on the verge of *smiling* with thoughts of her naked and sated in her bed last night. Her curls running wild, a lazy grin on her lips . . .

Ethan and her parents could find out at any point that we've messed around, but where I was terrified of that happening a week ago, I'm indifferent now. It's something I want to avoid at all costs, but to experience this with Maddie has been one of the few decisions I don't regret. Every day gets a little bit harder for it not to slip out that I'm happy for the first time in what feels like forever. Having to hide these feelings for Maddie is almost as difficult as sneaking around.

And you told her to go on the date with Mark.

I shake the thought from my head, refusing to let my mood get ruined when my music cuts out and is replaced by my ringtone. Dragging my phone out of my pocket, I frown at the contact on the screen.

Well, *now* my mood is ruined.

"Hey, Dad." I pin my phone between my ear and shoulder as I exit the gym. "What's up?"

There's a long pause before he asks, "You're at the gym? This late?"

"How do you—" *Fuck. I share my location with him.* "Uh, yeah. I've been going to the gym at night rather than in the morning the past few days. It's working out well so far."

"You have to be careful not to mess up your schedule, Cameron. We have a routine in place for a reason. Going to the gym at night is getting your body off its circadian rhythm. You know how important that is."

A muscle feathers in my jaw. "I know, Dad. When I get back to school, I'll get back to it. It'll be fine. I haven't been slacking at all. Everything is still the same except the gym times."

"Really?" he asks. "Is that why there was a charge for pizza the other night in your bank account?"

He loves you in his own way, I remind myself as I unlock my car. He checks my bank account because he wants to make sure I'm not spending money on things I shouldn't. He funds the account, so I don't have any reason to complain, right?

The twinge of annoyance disappears when I throw my duffel bag in the backseat. "I had a friend over."

"A friend," he repeats. "Is this *friend* a girl or a boy?"

"Does it matter? I had pizza *one* night."

"And that one night can throw off your entire diet, Cameron. How many times have we talked about this? If you want to make it to the NFL, you have to be at your best. It's not the time to dick around." He sighs heavily, and I can almost imagine him pinching the bridge of his nose. "Not many kids get these opportunities. You can't afford distractions."

"I'm not distracted." Well, maybe a little, but he doesn't have to know that. Maddie is a distraction in the best of ways. I'm not straying from my routine, but now I've started *enjoying* my routine for once. If anything, being with her has made me a better athlete.

"I'm not trying to harp on you," he says, but his tone doesn't carry a hint of remorse. "You know this is what your mom always wanted for you. What *we* have always wanted for you. I just don't want you to fuck this up."

The weight of the world comes crashing back down like a fucking avalanche. I'm quickly reminded where my priorities need to lie, but it's not like Maddie and I will continue this after we head back to school. I won't be distracted forever. We both agreed to enjoy it while it lasts, which is exactly what we're doing. I have no reason to feel guilty. I'll still make my parents' dreams come true.

"I hear you," I reply. My car rumbles to life, cutting into the silence. "I'll make sure to stick to my diet the remainder of my break, all right?" *The break you aren't even here for*, I want to add.

"I'll keep a close eye too," he reassures me. "I'll be your support system."

Ha. He's the furthest thing from a support system. Since Mom passed, I've never once gone to my father for advice or help for anything. If he was an actual support system, I'd confide in him about Maddie and how conflicted I am about my feelings. I'd tell him that I wish Mom was here to tell me how to sort through my emotions so that maybe, someday, I could be the guy Maddie deserves. Instead, I'm left with a coach.

"Thanks," I respond dryly. "We'll speak next week?"

"Maybe sooner. Bye, son."

When the line goes dead, the silence that wraps around me is practically insufferable. I put the radio on full blast, letting the music consume and numb me until I no longer feel a damn thing.

>> <<

When I pull into my driveway, the ton of bricks that have been sitting on my chest the entirety of the drive vanishes at the sight of Maddie on the hood of her car. I wasn't expecting to see her tonight, but it's a welcome surprise.

"Missing me already?" I tease.

She rolls her eyes and hops off the hood. "I wouldn't go that far. Maya had no plans tonight, so she said she'd cover. I didn't mean to stop by unannounced, but—"

I cut her off with a kiss, my duffel bag landing on the pavement before my hands find their way to her hips. Kissing Maddie gives me the same numbness that music and being underwater can bring. It's like a drug the way her lips meld with mine. I'm an addict who can't seem to get enough, and in a matter of seconds the unbearable pressure in my chest evaporates, the high of *her* overpowering my sadness.

My hands run up her back before sliding into her hair, and I back her up until she's pressed against her car. This kiss between us is slow. *Passionate.* Every move of mine is deliberate, and Maddie caresses my face with her hands, stroking my cheeks with the pads of her thumbs.

She has no idea how much I missed her. Hell, *I* didn't even know how much I missed having her in my life until we became whatever we're labeled as now. *Friends with benefits* sounds too casual and *dating* sounds too permanent. We're . . . well, we're exploring, and I'm okay with that.

For now.

"I missed you." I breathe onto her lips. My forehead is resting against hers as I scan her eyes, and I can almost hear my brain laughing at me for how ridiculous I sound. Exploring will never be enough—not when she brings me this much peace.

"Really?" she asks.

I nod and give her another quick kiss. "Come inside. I have leftover pizza from the other night if you're hungry."

"I already ate," she admits, "but I might be in the mood for something else."

A smug grin pulls at my lips when I open the door and jerk my chin for her to follow me upstairs.

"Ooh, I'm finally going to see the infamous Cameron Holden's room."

I toss a confused glance over my shoulder. "You've never been to my room before? There's no way. We've known each other since we were kids, Mads."

"I haven't," she replies, staying close on my heels. "When we were younger our parents made sure I didn't go in your room. We were never left alone."

I snort. "Not sure how much good it did."

"Me either." She laughs.

I'm not sure what she's expecting to find, but my room is very bland. Carpet, blue walls, and a twin-sized bed my feet hang off. There's a desk on the far side littered with different trinkets I've collected over the years, and shelves filled with football trophies line my walls.

"Hmm." She spins around, taking it all in. "I have to say, I'm slightly disappointed."

"How so?"

"No pornographic magazines? No sexy posters of women in bikinis?"

I send her a devilish grin. "Oh, those are all under my bed."

"Wait, really?"

Giving her a look as if to say, *Seriously?* I add, "*No*, Maddie. I don't have sexy magazines or posters hidden anywhere in this room. Despite what you think, sex isn't all I think about."

"I don't think that's all you think about." She scans my rows of trophies, seeming deep in thought. "Well, I never used to."

"What changed?"

For a heartbeat, her body tenses, and based on that action alone, I know what she's remembering.

My living room six years ago.

"Nothing exactly changed," she lies. "You grew up and we drifted apart. The boy who loved Pokémon became more interested in girls and football, and I accepted that. You made where I stood in your life clear, so I took a step back from it, and as the years went by, I became okay with the fact that you weren't the person you once were. I tried to l—" She clears her throat and starts over. "I tried to like the new version of you instead, but after . . ."

After my mom passed, I became a dick.

I can finish the sentence for her.

Leaning against the door frame, I point to my desk. "Top left drawer," I say.

"Huh?"

"The top left drawer of my desk," I repeat. "I want you to look inside it."

With a wary expression, she peers in the drawer. "A binder? Why do you want me to—" An enormous grin crosses her face when she opens it. "Oh my god. Your Pokémon cards? You kept them?"

My eyes soften as she flips through the endless pages of trading cards, the tightening sensation in my chest—the *love* I have for her—bordering on consuming me whole.

"I didn't change who I was completely. I still take pride in my collection, even if I don't talk about it anymore." Any hobby of mine that actually mattered died as soon as my mom did, but I didn't have the heart to throw away the evidence completely. It sounds stupid, but in my mind, if I got rid of them, it'd erase the memory of my mom, too, so I locked them away in a drawer and thought I'd forget about them for good.

It never worked.

"This is amazing," she continues. "I can't believe you—" Something falls out of the binder and lands on the floor, and Maddie stares at her feet, where the photo lies face up. When I recognize what it is, I can feel the color drain from my face.

"Our—" She shakes her head as if she's dreaming. "That's our photo from Myrtle Beach."

My heart races when she bends down to pick it up, holding it between shaky fingers. The photo has seen better days. It's faded and worn around the edges, and the left corner is ripped. I've looked at that photo too many times to count, and it shows. It's clear how many times I've run my thumb over her face, trying to remember a time when life was better. *Simpler*.

"You kept it," she whispers, blinking back tears. "Why?"

Closing the distance between us, I grab the photo from her hands and stroke my thumb over the faded part that matches my print. It seems so long ago, and yet it feels like yesterday. I can still remember the dryness of my mouth when she climbed into my lap. I can still feel the electricity that sprang through my veins when I wrapped my arms around her waist and held her close for the first time. We were both so young, and yet it's clear what we both wanted.

Each other.

My chin is on her shoulder and my smile is filled with braces, and her smile is brighter than the damn flash on the camera. I knew it back then that she was special, and everything I've ever done, even hurting her, was to protect her. If I went back and had the choice to change it, I wouldn't. I'm not proud of who I became after my mom passed, and if I'd been selfish and kept her close, I would have done something stupid like use her to numb the pain of grieving. As soon as I got into high school, sex became an outlet for me. It *still* is, and Maddie is worth so much more than what I'm capable of giving her.

"Just because I let you go doesn't mean I wanted to," I say softly. It's the first time either of us has spoken about that night six years ago, but it needed to happen at some point, especially if we're trying to rekindle our friendship. "I was in a bad place, and I didn't want to hurt you, Maddie. I still don't."

"But you did hurt me," she replies. "You broke my *heart*, Cameron."

"You don't think I know that? I've regretted it every day since."

The admission hangs in the air between us, fueling the undeniable feelings we both have never let go of. I could spill my guts again and tell her I love her, right here, right now, but what good would that do if I'm not certain I'll be able to follow through with what that entails? Loving someone means being there for them unconditionally, so how on earth can I promise that when there are times I can't even be there for myself?

"Mark asked me out on a date tomorrow night," she admits, keeping her eyes locked on mine. "Tell me not to go, and I won't."

"Maddie—"

"Tell me not to go," she repeats. "Tell me this isn't purely physical between us. Tell me there's more here to uncover, and I'll never speak to Mark again." I'm panting heavily while she awaits my answer. "If you truly don't think there's something more here then we'll continue exploring until we head back to school, and I'll go on the date with Mark and pretend to forget this ever happened between us."

It's not that simple.

It's *never* been that simple.

Achieving and being the best has been ingrained into my head by my father ever since I started high school. *No distractions. No girlfriends. No junk food.* My life has been planned out since I was a teenager, and I was okay with that because I knew my mom would be proud of me for helping Dad take his mind off her death. Football has been the one thing we've shared, and if I fuck up, if I let this dream go, I'm afraid he'll break, and as much as he's been a shit father the past few years, I refuse to lose him too.

But staring into Maddie's teary gaze, it's the first time I've considered whether or not my mom *would* be proud of me. Would she be happy that I'm giving up the girl of my dreams to keep my dad together? Would she be proud of someone who made the girl she used to consider her own daughter bawl her eyes out?

Doubtful.

"All right," she says, taking my silence as an answer. "I'm telling him yes, then."

No. I can't bear the thought of her going on a date with any-one other than me.

It's always been me.

It's always been *us.*

And I'll be damned if I let her walk away from me again.

So I kiss her before I can stop myself, and she doesn't pull away. Instead, she leans into it and doesn't complain when I hoist her onto my desk to part her thighs and stand between them.

I've never been good at explaining my feelings, but I hope I can show her. I hope I can kiss her deeply enough to express how sorry I am that I can't be the man she needs me to be. I hope she can understand how much I love her by *not* saying I love her. I'm fucked-up as it is, and with the added stress of her brother or family finding out? We'd never be able to make it work. As much as we want each other, we've always been bound to crash and burn, so staying silent and keeping that sentiment to ourselves is for the best.

Almost as if she's thinking the same, she breaks away from the kiss, gasping for air.

"*Please,*" I beg.

"Please what?" she urges. "Say the words, Cameron. That's all I need you to do."

"Christ, Maddie. How could you not realize that I—"

A flicker of movement flashes in my peripheral, and I whip my head around to find my father standing in the room. His tall, bulky presence sucks up all the energy, and his brooding stare causes all the hairs on my body to stand on end. I've grown to understand that expression well, and it's only ever had one meaning.

I'm in deep and utter shit.

Twenty-one

CAMERON

"Ethan, that's not fair!" I stomp my foot on the grass as he waves the popsicle he just stole from me in front of my face. "Give it back!"

I go to reach for it but he sticks his tongue out and runs away from me toward the pool in my backyard. It's a summer day in the dead heat of July—the kind of day in Arizona when it's well into the hundreds. The popsicle is steadily melting on the grass while Ethan runs around with it, and I find myself becoming angrier the longer I can't have it.

"Mom!" I whine, blinking away tears. Ethan continues to taunt me from the other side of the pool. "Ethan stole my popsicle!"

She's busy speaking to Mary and sipping a drink she says I'm not allowed to try, and I stomp my foot again when she's not paying attention.

"Honey, what's wrong?" Her emerald eyes identical to mine fill with concern.

"Ethan stole my popsicle," I repeat.

Mary lets out an exaggerated sigh. "Ethan!" she hollers,

watching as his dirty-blond hair blows in the wind. "Get over here this instant!" Then she looks at Mom with her mouth turned into a frown. "I'm sorry."

My mom waves her hand, completely unbothered. "It's just kids," she explains. "Don't apologize."

Suddenly I feel a tap on my shoulder, and when I turn around, Maddie, Ethan's little sister, is holding out a popsicle to me. Her face and hands are covered in blue sticky syrup, and the color matches her daisy-printed sundress.

"You can have mine," her tiny voice says, as she pushes her blond curls behind her ear with her free hand.

I'm about to take it from her when my dad pats me on the back and crouches so that he's eye level with me. "Come with me," he says with a grin. I smile instantly. No matter what, my dad always fixes things. "I think I know where we keep the secret stash."

>> <<

How long has he been standing there?

Long enough, judging by the redness of the tips of his ears.

My father moves his gaze from me to Maddie, almost in disbelief.

"Mr. Holden, I can—"

"*Out*," he replies sharply. "Now."

His clipped tone has my spine straightening, and the sudden urge to protect her makes me take a step toward him. "Anything you have to say to me can be said in front of her."

"Oh?" He crosses his arms over his chest, ready for a fight. "Then I suppose she won't mind if I call her parents right now to tell them what I just witnessed?"

Finding us making out shouldn't be a big deal. We're grown adults who make our own decisions now, but I know Maddie wants to keep this a secret, and if her parents find out, Ethan is bound to find out, too, and it's a conversation I don't want to have yet. Especially when so much was already left unsaid between us.

As it is, I don't even know if there's anything to *tell* anymore.

Judging from our previous conversation, she's going on a date with Mark, and what we had between us is over, because I don't trust myself to tell her how I really feel.

As expected, Maddie steps around me and scurries out of the room before my father can interrogate her further, and it only causes my anger to bubble closer to the surface. *What the hell is he doing here?* He hasn't seen me since Christmas.

When we're finally alone, he releases a frustrated sigh. "*Maddie?* What the hell are you thinking, Cameron? She's too young for you to be screwing around with. She's like family."

"Too young? Dad, she's only two years younger than me." I snap my mouth shut beneath his scrutinizing gaze. It's a look I know not to mess with.

"Does Ethan know about this? How long has this been going on?"

I've played out a thousand scenarios in my head about how Maddie and I could possibly be discovered. Ethan coming over and walking in on us, her parents going through her phone and finding our texts, or Maya slipping up and accidentally spilling our secret. But none of those scenarios have been my *father* being the first one to figure this out.

"No, he doesn't know," I reply honestly, "and it hasn't been long. Just since break started."

He eyes me judgmentally, but I can't say I blame him. All I do is fuck around with women, and he considers Maddie like his own daughter too.

"I like her, though," I say. "I've liked her for years."

"Cameron, does it look like I care about any of that? Maddie isn't someone you should be messing around with. She's the *one girl* who's off limits. Do you think if Mary or Richard find out they'll let this continue? Maddie is someone you've grown up with, son, and your track record speaks volumes. You can't afford to break someone's heart, or worse, get yours broken too."

I stare at him completely dumbfounded. I haven't seen him since Christmas, and now he suddenly pops back into my life to give me life advice? "What are you doing?" I ask.

He tilts his head to the side, studying me. "What do you mean? I saw the credit card charge for the pizza and got concerned that you had fallen off your game, so I was already at the airport to come see you when I called—"

"You think you can come back into my life after months of being gone and have everything be fine between us?" I pace back and forth, growing more infuriated with each step I take. "You can't just waltz in here and start giving me relationship advice. You know *nothing* about my track record. You're part of my life maybe one month out of the year, and that's being generous. You don't know me anymore. You haven't for a long time."

"Now, Cameron—" he starts, but now that I've started, I can't seem to stop.

"No! Since Mom passed, Mary and Richard have been more like parents to me than you have!"

"*Don't* mention your mother," he warns, getting directly in my face. "I've had to work, Cameron. How else do you think the bills are paid? How do you think you can attend one of the most prestigious schools in the country and not have a lick of debt? How does money get deposited into your account every month? I've busted my ass to make sure you're provided for. I'm *still* paying off your mother's medical bills all while putting you through school to make sure you have the best opportunities available, and you want to harp on me about not being here?"

Tears burn in the back of my eyes, threatening to spill, but I hold them at bay. What am I supposed to say? He's right. I'm sounding ungrateful when I've never had to worry about material things, but if given the choice, I'd rather go to community college with Ethan and have my father present than be alone with only football as the common ground between us.

"You're so close to making it to the NFL," he says. "I can feel it. You're talented, and I just don't want you to mess this up for some *girl—*"

"Ah, so that's why you're giving me relationship advice." I shake my head. "Not because you actually care about my happiness, but because it's about football."

My dad is speechless, his chest rising and falling rapidly as he tries to think of something to say. Telling him how I honestly feel would be fruitless. It's not going to change anything. I won't allow myself to let him see the vulnerable thoughts I have—how I stayed home two days every week in high school to see if he'd change his mind and come home. To tell him that I never needed the best shoes or the name brand clothes, I just needed *him*.

At the end of the day, he is who he is, and if he wanted to be here with me, he would be. I have a deep-rooted fear that if I were to express how hurt I am, he wouldn't make any effort to change, so I'd rather keep my true feelings to myself than get hurt even more.

I avert my eyes, choosing a spot on the wall to stare at instead. "I'm assuming you're leaving soon?"

He gulps and glances down at his dress shoes, which are as impeccable as his suit. I've rarely seen him wearing anything else. No matter where he's at, he's always ready for work. "I leave on a red-eye later tonight," he admits.

I scoff. "Thought so. Well, I'm going for a drive. Don't really feel like being here."

"Cameron." He places a hand on my shoulder to stop me. "I'm just looking out for your best interest, okay? You can't continue things with Maddie. You know that, right? It'll screw up everything you've worked so hard for, and you can't allow yourself to become distracted. Not when we're so close to the finish line."

We're.

As if we're a *unit.*

A *team.*

The absurdity of it all doesn't go unnoticed.

When Mom was alive, that's when we were a team. My fondest memories are playing football in the backyard with him until the sun started to set. He was encouraging about it then, but he never forced it on me or pushed it too hard. The option to play football was always there, but when Mom died it became an obsession, and as the years went on, it wasn't an option, but an expectation.

I don't know who this man standing in front of me is anymore.

"Got it," I reply, my tone clipped.

Pushing past him, I fish my keys out of my pocket and fight past the burning in my eyes. I refuse to let a single tear fall for him when he doesn't deserve it, but the empty space in my heart he created only seems to grow bigger every time we have these discussions.

All I want, the only thing I need, is to see my mom again. I wish she was here to tell me how to handle him and how to mend things between us. I wish she could guide me when it comes to Maddie and my feelings for her and my fear of fucking this all up. I wish she could reassure me that although I'm amazing at football, there's more to me than that.

I'll never be able to hear her voice again, or listen to her laugh, but there is one way I can communicate with her, and every time I'm home, I always make sure to stop by.

I just didn't expect it to be so soon.

Twenty-two

CAMERON

"Son, there's someone here to see you."

Blinking at my father, I can't comprehend what he's saying. Every motion for the past twenty-four hours has felt robotic. Lifeless. Foreign. I'm so numb to my pain that I can't tell whether I'm angry or relieved there's someone here to see me. It can't be Ethan since he already stopped by this morning, so it must be—

My father moves to the side and Maddie steps into view. Her blue eyes are puffy and red from the crying she's done on her own, and normally the sight of her emotions would crush me, but not anymore. It doesn't matter when my eyes probably look the same. I sobbed for a straight twelve hours before I popped a blood vessel in my left eye, and then everything just stopped. My feelings. My tears. And if it wasn't for the constant thumping in my chest, I'd think my heart had stopped too.

"I'll give you guys a moment alone," he says before walking down the hall.

Maddie takes a step closer, her sob echoing across the high ceilings. "Cam," she chokes out. "I am so sorry."

I'm sure she is. Everyone else seems to be too. Frozen lasagnas clutter our deep freezer, and handwritten notes and flowers line the kitchen island. When the kind gestures first started appearing last night, I found myself infuriated by them. I don't need pity. I don't need frozen fucking meals or cards or people coming over here to tell me they're sorry. I don't need any of it.

I just want my mom back.

Maddie sits beside me on the couch, her thigh brushing mine, and the scent of vanilla and honey from her hair gives me a brief moment of clarity. For a second I'm reminded how good she smells and how close I'd been to kissing her on that beach.

"I—" She clears her throat, swiping away a tear that's fallen on her cheek. "I brought this for you." Reaching into her pocket, she pulls out some sort of rock that she places in my lap. I grab the object and spin it between my fingers, liking the way the hard edges dig into my skin.

"I'm not really into stones or crystals," she explains. "It's not that I don't believe in them, but I don't know much about the subject. My mom is the one who's crazy knowledgeable about it." When I don't respond, she drums her fingers on her knee and adds, "My mom gave that to me when I had the flu in third grade. Clear quartz is supposed to be good for healing, and I . . . well, I thought you could use it more than me."

I clench the rock in a tight fist, hating how kind she's being. I don't deserve her. I've become an emotionless robot since yesterday, and I have no plans on stopping anytime soon. I don't want to feel, and with her being beside me, in the same room as me, I'm feeling too much. Maddie reminds me of everything good life has to offer, and right now I don't want to see the good. There is no good if my mom isn't here to see it with me.

And with that knowledge, I can't have Maddie around me. I've turned into an empty version of myself, and the thought of her seeing me like this, seeing how evil and dark my thoughts have become, she's going to learn to hate me and eventually leave me too.

Everyone does.

"You should go," I whisper. The sentence doesn't feel right leaving my tongue, but it's the right thing to do.

Maddie glances up from her lap. "What?"

"I said you should go," I repeat. "I'm not in the mood for visitors."

Her eyes linger on mine, filling with tears. "I understand. I'll try to visit tomorrow, then, when you're in a better place maybe."

I shake my head, clenching the rock she gave me with so much force I wouldn't be surprised if it drew blood. "Not then either. I can't be around you, Maddie. Not anymore."

"What are you talking about, Cam? You almost—" Her voice drops lower into a whisper. "You almost kissed me last week."

I turn to look at her, and devastation lines her features when she sees the expression on my face. I've become cold. Lifeless. The kind of human who doesn't give a fuck about what he's about to do to because he doesn't have feelings. "What are you talking about?" I sneer. "You thought I was going to kiss you?"

Her face pales. "I . . . you leaned in. I thought—"

"You thought wrong. I would never kiss you. We're friends and that's all we'll ever be, so get over whatever stupid crush you have on me and leave me alone."

I refuse to make eye contact with her. Instead, I keep my gaze glued on the mosaic carpet. The shock she seems to be in prevents *me from saying anything else, but staying away from me is what will benefit her in the long run. I'm nobody worth fighting for. I'm a broken, shattered mess, and she shouldn't waste time trying to piece me back together.*

"You don't mean that," she says. "You're grieving, and you're hurt, but—"

"But *nothing. Did you not hear me? I said to get out and don't speak to me again.*" The burning sensation forces its way through my chest and into my throat, but I desperately try to push it away, fighting tooth and nail to hold it at bay.

"Cam—"

"Get the fuck out, Maddie."

The tiny gasp of hurt is a sound I'm certain I'll never forget, but the sobs that come after are even worse. They linger long after she disappears down the hall, and when the front door slams shut, I realize I'm a flat-out liar.

Turns out I'm not an emotionless robot after all.

Because the tears I swore vanished for good hit me again like a damn tidal wave.

>> <<

As I sit on the sandy, dusty gravel by my mother's grave I twirl the clear crystal around and around in my fingers. I've kept it ever since Maddie gave it to me, and I bring it whenever I visit the cemetery. It was the only object after her death that seemed to calm me down, and I can't tell if it's because the damn crystal actually works or if it's because it's connected to Maddie.

Releasing a heavy sigh, I glance around the dimly lit grave-yard and frown at the sight. My mother didn't want to be buried here. She always loved farmland, and she'd raved about the smell of fresh grass. We went to her hometown back in Pennsylvania once to visit distant family, and she just seemed *happier*.

Arizona is the opposite of what she loved, and regardless of what it said in her will, she only wanted to be buried here so that my father and I would be able to visit. She'd be devastated to know it's only me who comes. I replace the flowers as often as I can, but my father hasn't had the courage to come here since the funeral.

Resting my elbows on my knees, I hang my head between them and let out another deep breath. Usually this spot brings me peace. I can come here and speak to my mom as if she's here with me, and even though it sounds ridiculous, I think she is. There's a spiritualism about being here. I feel close to her.

Tonight, however, I don't feel like speaking. Memories of Maddie and that day drown my thoughts, and it's something I've never spoken about aloud. I suppose if there *is* an afterlife then my mom is already aware of it, but it doesn't take away the shame or guilt I feel for destroying the girl who means the most to me.

My mother always liked Maddie. She thought she was the sweetest girl, and she'd compliment her whenever she wasn't in the room. A part of me thought she was trying to set us up and could see something before my feelings ever developed.

Maybe I'm an idiot for fooling around with Maddie like my dad claimed, but tonight in my bedroom didn't *feel* like fooling around. Our kiss before we went inside my house felt genuine.

Real.

How can I be so torn about something? I can go back and forth about the pros and cons of being with Maddie, but I'll never make a decision. I've always been conflicted when it comes to her, and it's never been black and white. No matter what I choose, there will always be doubts, and the one person who has the ability to guide me isn't here anymore.

"Fuck," I mutter. "I miss you, Mom." Biting hard on my lip, I try to keep the tears inside but it's no use. They flow freely in a matter of seconds.

The cancer attacked quickly. Too quickly. We found out she had stage four ovarian cancer three months before she passed, and I was too young to understand. Too hopeful. I hadn't seen enough bad in the world to fully grasp what was going to happen, but I wish I had. I wish others hadn't just given me that look of pity when I said she was going to beat it. I wish they had been realistic and warned me she was going to die, and it was only a matter of time.

Maybe then I would have listened to her stories more. I would have made an effort to remember her laugh, and asked her the important questions I needed answers to.

For example, *What do I do now that I'm in love with my best friend's sister?*

Am I ruining my chances of getting into the NFL?

Am I making her proud?

Is Maddie really a distraction?

The last question is useless when I already know the answer. Maddie isn't the type of girl who would let me become distracted. She knows more than anyone how important my future is, and she wouldn't do anything to get in the way of it. My father doesn't know what he's talking about. At the end of the day, I know the truth, and Maddie is the best damn thing to ever happen to my life.

The sentence rings in my head, a terrifying realization dawning on me.

Maddie has *always* been the best thing to happen to me. Even when I was a dick and gaslit her into thinking I felt nothing for her that day in my living room, she still agreed to my proposition to mend our friendship six years later, and I all but told her to go out with fucking Mark tomorrow night because I was too scared to admit my feelings and fuck things up.

Haven't I already fucked things up by *not* confiding in her?

What's the worst thing that could happen? I tell her the truth and she decides to leave? It's my biggest fear, but by choosing the path of not saying anything at all, I'm going to lose her anyway. Maybe not as a friend, but I'll lose her in the way that matters.

I don't want to be friends.

I don't want to explore.

I want *her*.

All of her.

Suddenly, boots crunch on the gravel behind me, and I quickly slip the crystal into the pocket of my sweatshirt before I glance over my shoulder. I'm unsurprised to find Ethan making his way over to me, his truck parked beside mine on the grass.

"Figured you'd be here," he says, plopping down beside me. He places a hand on my shoulder, and it isn't until now that I realize I'm still crying.

Ethan doesn't try to pry, nor does he interrupt.

He sits with me and waits it out.

The gesture only makes me cry harder because what I'm doing to him isn't okay either. I'm keeping secrets that will destroy our friendship if he finds out. The person who, aside from Maddie, has seen me at my ultimate worst and has accepted me regardless of the monster I became after my mother's death. I'm lying to my best friend, my *brother*, after everything he's done for me.

Five minutes pass before my breathing regulates and my sobs turn into sniffles. "I'm sorry," I mutter. "My dad's just a dick."

"No need to apologize," he replies. "Maddie came home and said she saw his car parked in the driveway on her way home from Maya's. You weren't answering your phone, so I pieced two and two together. Mom already said she'd make chicken noodle soup if you need some. Just say the word."

I shake my head, unable to look him in the eyes. "Not tonight. I—" *I can't face your sister after I nearly broke her heart for the second time.* "I want to be alone tonight."

Ethan scoffs. "He's leaving so soon?"

"Red-eye later."

"Prick."

I shift uncomfortably. "I'm sorry you had to come find me," I admit. "You're always there for me when it matters the most and I don't feel like I do the same for you."

"Why do you think that?" he asks. His voice is rushed, so I meet his stare, narrowing my gaze. There's a tiredness in his eyes that hasn't always been there, but when was the last time I truly checked in on him? Really *looked* at him?

"Are you all right?" I ask.

"Dude, I'm fine," he replies, but something about his tone seems off. "Where's all of this coming from? Aren't I the one supposed to be asking *you* these questions?"

I wave my hand, dropping the subject. "You've interrogated me with those questions way too many times, Ethan. You're the type of best friend everyone wishes they could have, and I hope you don't think I take you for granted for putting up with me. My problems are a lot, but you've never made me feel guilty about them, and I'm sorry I haven't been the friend you deserve in return."

Ethan claps me on the shoulder. "You're more than a friend, Cameron. You're a brother. There isn't a side you could show that would make me turn away from you. I understand you've been dealing with a lot over the past few years, and I'd never hold it against you. The best part about friendship is that you can't control whether or not someone accepts your baggage, you know? They just *do*. It's their choice."

It's their choice.

His sentence plays on repeat.

Isn't that what my problems boil down to?

I'm terrified of Maddie leaving if I tell her the truth, and I'm fucking scared out of my mind that I'll hurt her like I did six years ago. I'm not in the best emotional place to be in a relationship, and I've never been a boyfriend to anyone before, but . . .

But isn't it Maddie's choice whether or not she accepts that baggage of mine?

If I lay it all out in the open for her and show her my cards, would she agree and try to figure this out with me one day at a time, or would she choose to walk away and find an easier path with Mark?

I guess there's only one way to find out.

"Thanks, man." Rising from the gravel, I extend a hand to help him up. "And Ethan? I'm really grateful you chose to accept my baggage."

Twenty-three

MADDIE

Holidays at the Davis household wouldn't be complete without the Holdens joining us. We've celebrated Christmas together every year since I was born, and over the years we've created new traditions that always have me itching for December even in the dead heat of July.

My favorite tradition is making cookies with my mom and Stacy. We make my grandmother's sugar cookie recipe, and then we add a batch of Stacy's famous chocolate chip. This year we've added Maya into the mix. We met this year in science class, and my mom insisted she stay to frost the sugar cookies since she could use all the help she could get.

We're seated around my parent's large dining room table, plastic tablecloths beneath jars of frosting and different colored sprinkles. Christmas tunes play softly from a nearby speaker, and Stacy hums along happily. Normally my mom is overjoyed for cookie day, but this year is different. She keeps looking at Stacy with her lips tilted into a frown, worry etched in the lines of her face. She sat me down last week and told me Stacy had cancer and that it didn't look good, but I still don't understand what that means. All I can grasp is that Stacy doesn't have hair any longer, opting for colorful scarves or beanies instead.

"I'm making a dinosaur," Cameron says proudly beside me. I glance down at his sugar cookie, which is in the shape of a bell, not a dinosaur, but Cameron's trying to be creative.

"That's an awful dinosaur," I reply. "It looks nothing like one. Why don't you just make the bell pretty like a normal person?"

He scoffs. "Like yours?" My bell is decorated in edible pearls with baby-blue frosting—a picture-perfect cookie if there ever was one. "Not everything in life has to be pretty, Mads."

"I beg to differ. Pretty things are almost always perfect."

I gasp when he flicks my nose with frosting, sending me a cheesy smile filled with braces. "Not always."

Frosting on my nose should have me outraged, but the only thing my mind seems to be focused on is the assumption that he thinks I'm pretty. It's all I can think about the entirety of frosting, and after we're done cleaning up the mess, all the cookies in their respective Tupperware containers for tomorrow, Stacy taps me on the shoulder, jerking her head toward the hallway. "Can I steal you for a second, sweetheart?"

I nod, following her silently into the foyer, where she grabs her large purse off of the banister and rummages around before pulling out a tiny gift bag. "I wanted to give you this," she says with a watery smile.

"Now?" I ask. "But Christmas is tomorrow."

"I know, and you have a few other gifts coming from us, but I wanted to give you this one myself."

My brows are scrunched as I remove the tissue paper and pull out a velvety blue box. I'm still confused until I open the lid and see the gold necklace lying inside. It's a beautiful locket with diamonds encrusted around the edges, and I open the clasp to reveal an image of Stacy holding me as a baby. A lump forms in my throat as I process this gift and why she'd want to give it to me when it's just the two of us, but she beats me to it before I can ask.

"You need to know how proud I am of you," she whispers, reaching up to wipe a stray tear from my cheek. "You're the daughter I never had, and I am so blessed to have been given the opportunity to watch you transform into a beautiful, kindhearted girl."

"Stacy," I choke out.

"I wanted you to have something to remember me by so that no matter what happens, I'll always be with you."

I hug her so hard I fear I'll knock the wind out of her, and my tears stain her purple sweater. I inhale deeply, wondering how many more of her hugs I'll get to experience. This is her goodbye gift to me, which means . . .

"I'm not ready."

"None of us ever are," she soothes.

"I can't accept this, Stacy. It looks way too expensive." But I also don't want to accept it because if I take this necklace, it means I accept her goodbye, and I don't. I can't. Imagining life without her is impossible.

"Of course you can," she says. Then she swivels her finger for me to turn around. I move my hair for her to clasp the chain, and when the gold heart hits my chest, something final settles in the depths of my soul. "Do you like it?"

"Like it?" I twirl the heart between two fingers, admiring it between sniffles. "I love it, Stacy. It's perfect."

"Good." She laughs. "I can't take all the credit. Cameron helped pick it out."

My eyes snap to hers. "He did?"

"Yep. Took two hours to find the perfect one, but we found it eventually."

Thinking of Cameron in a jewelry store for that long makes a laugh bubble up my throat. "He must have hated that."

Stacy arches a brow, and the next words out of her mouth make my world come to a standstill. "I don't think he did considering it was him *who took two hours debating which one to get you."*

>> <<

As I stare at myself in the full-length mirror in Maya's bedroom, I can't help but let my insecurities take over. Don't get me wrong, my best friend made sure I looked incredible for this date. My hair is curled to perfection rather than its usual mess of tangled ringlets, and my makeup is smoky and date-like, but no matter how hard I try to convince myself I'm good enough, it doesn't seem to work.

Cameron's silence after I came clean and practically begged him to say the three words I needed was very telling. I don't want to go on this date with Mark because my heart is and has always been with Cam, but if he's unwilling to admit this is something more than a hookup between us, I need to see what else is out there. A boy like Mark, who is kind, charming, and treats me well, is worth testing the waters with.

"You look hot." Maya looks up from her phone and nods in approval from where she's sitting on her bed. "I knew that dress would look good on you."

The deep-purple fabric clings to every curve I have and hardly goes past my thighs. Mark had said our date would be introverted, and this dress *screams* a night out on the town. I'm no doubt overdressed, but Maya reassured me it's better to be overdressed than under, so I'm reluctantly taking her advice.

"You think?" I do another twirl to give her a full-body view.

"Totally. Mark is going to be drooling like a dog, and Cameron is going to feel like a fucking ass for messing things up with you."

I had no reason to turn Mark down, so I wish this churning of guilt inside my stomach would stop. Cameron made it clear that this was purely physical between us. He wants to hook up for the remainder of break, and although that hurts me to the very core, I have to accept that. Spilling my guts didn't change anything.

So when Mark picks me up, I'm going to push Cameron to the very back of my mind and put all my focus on someone who deserves my time and attention. If Cameron wants to continue our friendship, then fine, but anything extra is off the table. I can't keep messing around with him if my heart is in it and his isn't. I thought I could do this and commit to no attachments, but I was a fool. I've been in love with him for *years*. Feelings that strong don't just disappear.

"I'm jealous," Maya admits. "I haven't been on a date in forever."

I join her on the zebra-print comforter she hasn't changed since middle school, wincing at how tightly the dress squeezes my ribs. "Go on a date, then."

"Oh, because it's that simple?"

"For you? Completely. You could have any guy you wanted." I begin ticking off on one hand the names of guys I know she's had a history with. "James, Carlos, Micah, Emmanuel, my *brother*."

Her body stills, and I suppress a grin.

"Ethan? Why would you mention him?"

"Do you think I'm an idiot? We've been friends for years, Maya. I know when you're flirting with someone, and that day at the lake made it more than obvious. You asked him about *sailing*."

"I—" She shakes her head, her cheeks tinted pink. "It doesn't matter if I have a crush on him or not. I wouldn't do that to you. To us."

"Truthfully, I don't exactly have room to judge, do I? I'm doing the same thing with his best friend. Or was. I don't know. Regardless, I'm not upset. It'd be more of a relief for you guys to tell each other already so you can be happy."

Maya gnaws on her bottom lip. "You think he feels the same?"

I've had suspicions about them for a while now. There were always stolen glances when she'd come over to visit in high school, but lately my brother has made his feelings clear as day. She seems to be chipping away at his willpower, and with every flip of her hair and innocent smile, he's close to breaking.

"I know he does," I reply confidently.

"And you're sure you won't be upset if I make a move?"

"I swear it. However, you can keep the *details* to yourself if anything happens."

"Why?" she teases. "Afraid your ears will bleed? I might do it anyway just to—"

Knocks echo on her front door, and my heart stills in my chest. Mark isn't supposed to be here for another half hour, but maybe he's early.

Fuck.

I don't know if I'm ready for this.

"Breathe," Maya instructs. "You've got this, Maddie. It's one date. If something goes wrong, I'll have my phone right beside me. I'll come to your rescue and give you an excuse to ditch if you need me to. Just send the emergency word." She disappears out of the room, and it doesn't take long for her to reach the front door. Maya's home is a trailer, and for the longest time she refused for me to see where she lived because she was embarrassed by it. Her parents work long hours every day, but their trailer is well kept and homey. She has no reason to be ashamed of it.

"Uh, what are you doing here?" Maya asks.

"Did she leave yet?"

The voice makes my pulse skyrocket. In seconds my palms are sweating, my ears are ringing, and I don't even notice when Maya strides back into the room with an expression bordering on pissed off.

"It's Cameron. Should I tell him to get lost?"

I shake my head and rise shakily to my feet, regretting letting Maya convince me to wear heels. "No. I'll see what he wants."

She gives me a knowing look. "Okay. I'll stay in here then to give you guys your *privacy*."

With a roll of my eyes, I close her bedroom door behind me and join Cameron outside. His eyes meet mine, and I can see his pupils dilate as he scans me from head to toe. "Jesus," he breathes, shaking his head in disbelief. "You look—"

"Good for my date with Mark?" I finish for him, but his eyes are focused below my chin now, and it takes me a second to figure out why. The locket Stacy gave me glistens in the sunlight, distracting him.

"I wear it on special occasions," I whisper, awkwardly shifting my weight.

His jaw ticks before he shoves his hands into the pockets of his sweatpants. Purple bags line his eyes, and it seems as if he hasn't gotten any sleep. I hate that my first instinct is to ask him if he's all right. He's the one who created this wedge between us, and yet I'm wanting to see if he is okay.

Unbelievable.

"It isn't," he whispers so quietly I almost don't hear him.

"What?"

"Purely physical," he answers. "It isn't."

I'm too stunned to reply, and I'm grateful when he offers me his hand to help me down the steps because otherwise, I fear my knees would give out. Now that I'm on the ground, the top of my head meets his chin, so I have to glance up to stare into his eyes.

"I'm not the best at expressing my emotions since my mom passed, but I—" He drags a hand through his curls. "I'd never forgive myself if I let you walk away from me again, Maddie, so the answer to your question? It's not just physical between us, and I don't think it ever has been."

Tears fill my eyes. *"Cam—"*

"I'll completely understand if it's too late," he continues. "I've gotten more chances with you than I've deserved, but I need you to hear the truth, and honestly? I don't know if I'm ready for a relationship or if I'll be any good at one. I have attachment issues, and I use sex as a form of therapy. I'm terrified of hurting you if we try this and fail. I'm terrified of losing someone else close to me, and because of that, those three words you want me to say will take some time. But if there's anyone worth trying for, it's *you*, and if you're okay with all of these red flags of mine and are still willing to see where this could go, I'd be an idiot if I let you go out with him tonight without putting my name in the ring."

When he's finished, panting and breathless, I can see how difficult being vulnerable truly is for him. His hands are shaking, still holding on to mine, but knowing he's willing to try to over-come this fear shows me how serious he is about this.

About us.

I knew Cameron had attachment issues prior to him bring-ing it up in conversation just now, but I didn't realize how deeply rooted the fear was. If he needs time to adjust to his feelings, if he needs to take this slow, I'm willing to hold his hand through it because he's worth it.

He may not realize that yet, but I do.

Pulling my phone out of my sparkly crossbody, I open the Messages app.

Cameron watches me curiously before he asks, "What are you doing?"

"Canceling my date," I reply casually, flicking my eyes to his. "Unless you'd rather me still go out with him tonight?"

A storm of emotion crosses his face. Shock, confusion, before settling on my favorite of all. He drags his eyes down my body in a slow, calculated perusal combined with that lazy grin and says, "Looking like *this*? Fuck no."

"Then it's settled, Holden." I send the text to Mark that consists of a lame excuse as to why I changed my mind. I feel horrible, but he deserves better than someone who could never fully be invested in him when their heart lies with someone else. I hope he finds the girl who's meant for him because everyone should feel the way I do right now—like each and every spot of skin Cam touches ignites in flames. "What should we do now?"

Tugging me closer, his hands land on my hips. "I could think of a lot of things, Mads."

"Okay," I reply, suddenly out of breath. "Let me rephrase, then. What should we do first?"

"Hm." I'm in heaven when he drags his hands up and down my sides, caressing the bare skin exposed through the cutouts of my dress. "Right now, I really want to kiss you."

"Oh?"

"I *always* want to kiss you," he admits. "Yesterday, today, and also six years ago."

Is he trying to make me cry?

"Don't," he soothes when he notices my tears. He rubs beneath my eyes with his thumbs to swipe them away. "It's the truth, and I'm so fucking sorry I lied to you. That night I had been about to make a move, and you were right. I did lean in. Every single time I was around you I wanted my lips on yours, Maddie Davis, and nothing has changed. Not even now."

The sound I release is a mixture of a sob and a laugh. "Then what are you waiting for?"

Finally, his lips meet mine in a blistering, all-consuming kiss. I stumble backward from the force of it, but Cameron doesn't let me fall. He hoists me into his arms so that my legs are around his waist, which doesn't bode well for my dress. I break away from the kiss to try to pull it down, but it's no use. Cameron's hands have already found the band of my thong.

"You're *mine*." His voice is gravelly as he gives the band a snap. Those words alone would bring me to my knees if he wasn't already holding me. "And all I want to do is take you home and show you how long I've been wanting to say that."

He trails his lips down the column of my neck, my hands in his hair, and if it wasn't for Maya having neighbors I'd suggest he take me in the back of his car right this instant. There's another issue we have to discuss first, though, and it's one I know he isn't going to want to partake in.

"Is your dad going to tell anyone?" I ask. "Was he mad?"

As expected, Cameron's body goes rigid at the mention of his father. Ever since his mom's passing they haven't had a good relationship, and it killed me to watch him go from a kid with loving parents to having none at all. It's made my own resentment toward his dad grow.

"Don't worry about him," he says. "Everything is fine. He took a red-eye last night back to wherever the hell he's doing his business nowadays, and I highly doubt he'll call your parents."

"Are you sure?" I remember the way he looked ready to tackle his son the second he caught us, and he certainly didn't look happy about it, or like he'd be willing to talk things out.

Cameron dips his head to catch my gaze, and fuck, he's perfect. That damn chain hangs between us, and it's completely unfair how good he smells. Between his cologne and the grin he's sporting, he's making it extremely difficult to focus on anything *but* kissing him senseless.

He chuckles deeply, following where my thoughts have gone, and while holding me on his hip with one hand, he tugs his keys out with his free one. "Text Maya that you're not coming back inside," he says while striding for his car. "I've got better plans in store for you."

Twenty-four

CAMERON

I don't waste time turning on the lights.

We stumble inside my house, too entranced with one another to be bothered by the pitch blackness of the living room. I use my memory of the floor plan and guide her toward the stairs, my hands roaming everywhere on her body, but no matter where I touch, it doesn't seem nearly enough.

I don't deserve her.

It's a constant reminder in the back of my head, but she heard me out and still canceled the date with Mark. She wants this just as much as I do, and I'm fucking tired of suppressing the feelings I have for her. I want to take this leap of faith for us. I want to become a man who's worthy of her, and I meant it when I told her I would try.

Maddie moans blissfully when we reach the steps. My lips are kissing down her neck, then across her collarbone, then her—

"Cam." I'm obsessed with how she says my name—like I'm the object of all her desires. "I want this."

It's an effort for me to pause my kisses, but I drag my eyes to hers, hating that I can barely make out her face in the darkness. "I know, Mads. I want this too."

"No." Her breath is shaky when she adds, "I mean, I want you. *All* of you."

If a pin were to drop in the silence thrumming between us, I'm certain I'd be able to hear it. Her virginity hasn't been talked about, but it's something she knows I'm aware of—at least I think. I'd be lying if I said I wasn't ready. Truthfully, I was ready in the closet when we first kissed, and if I hadn't known she was a virgin then, I likely would have taken things much further than I probably should have.

But having these little moments of intimacy are something I've cherished with her. It makes me slow down, enjoy every second, and leaves me wanting for more. I want to take this next step with her, but does *she*? I don't want to rush her.

"Mads . . ." I trail off, releasing a groan when she tugs on my curls. "Are you sure you want to do this? Even after hearing all my red flags? I can't guarantee this will work out between us. Your brother could find out, or I'll find some way to fuck things up." I sigh. "I don't want you to regret this."

She kisses me again, and it's meant to be soft and tender, but we just can't seem to stop. I press her against the wall of the stairs, fully consumed by her.

"I would never regret this," she says. "If it's not you, it's not *anyone*, Cam. You're it for me."

Her words fuel my desire for her. Like kerosene, the lust flares to life—crackling and consuming every thought I have. It's a forest fire burning through me, raging and begging to be released.

And this time, I'm going to let it.

The flame consumes us both when my hands find the zipper of this damn dress. I tear it down with expert precision and hear the fabric fall to the floor, and my hands land on her soft, silky skin. Her perfume, laced with vanilla, is a scent I've memorized.

It's *Maddie*.

And I wouldn't have it any other way.

Finally, we've somehow made it to my bedroom. My lava lamp provides just enough of a red glow as she falls onto my bed, and my mouth grows dry at the sight of her. Breasts spilling out of a black lacy bra and a scrap of silk covering the most intimate part of her will me to pounce on her, but I rein in that primal part of me and focus on those lavish heels decorating her feet instead.

"You're fucking perfect," I mutter, enamored with the way goose bumps rise on her skin from my touch. Her eyes speak more than her mouth ever could as she tracks my movements. She's breathless when I hook her leg over my shoulder, my fingertips fumbling with the strap around her ankle without looking. I'm ashamed to admit I've done this more times than I can count, so it's a skill I've learned, but Maddie is distracting when she tugs on her bottom lip, and the strap that should be easy becomes more difficult than intended.

I'm too impatient to mess with a fucking buckle on a strap. "I guess we're leaving the heels on."

In every fantasy I've created in my head over the years of this moment, the real thing is surpassing any expectation. I'm breathless when she slides her thong off and tosses it to the side. Speechless when she parts her thighs. I'm hypnotized by her after she removes her bra—at her fucking mercy when I sink to my knees on the carpet beside the bed and tug her toward me.

The locket I spent hours picking out for her in the eighth grade is the only thing she's wearing aside from the heels, and it's a reminder of how important she is not just to me, but was to my mom as well. She surprised me that day at the jewelry store by offering to let me pick it out, and I wanted to make sure it was perfect. Something delicate and stunning, just like Maddie.

"*Yes,*" she moans. My head is buried between her thighs, and I'm fighting the urge to throw my morals out the window and fuck her senseless, but I have to remember this is her first time. She doesn't want to be *fucked*, nor is that what I want her to think I'm doing. I don't know if I'll be able to give her what she needs tonight, but I want to try.

I told her I'd try.

So I take it slow while I suck and lick her clit over and over again until she's coming on my tongue. She arches her back, fist in my hair before she throws her head back against my pillows in a sated, messy heap.

"Oh my *god,*" she whispers.

Rising from the carpet, I allow her a few seconds of reprieve and reach over my head to tug my sweatshirt off. She eyes me greedily, her teeth tugging on her—now swollen—bottom lip. Then she takes the time to remove her heels, and when they land on the floor with a loud thud, I'm completely naked before her.

There's a moment of timidness that passes between us. I need the reassurance that she wants this, *needs* this, and thankfully, she gives it.

One second I'm standing, and the next she's tugged me on top of her, my large frame covering hers on the mattress. My leg accidentally hits her knee, and we both laugh at how impatient we are.

My heart is pounding in my chest as I stare into the eyes of a girl who has been in my life for years. The girl I used to ride bikes with. The girl who had her first crush on me. And not the cool, playboy quarterback, but the old me. The nerd with a face full of braces and not a lick of confidence.

Maddie is so special to me, and I've never taken another girl's virginity before. I don't want to hurt her. I want tonight to be memorable for her—one she'll never forget.

So, in an effort to slow things down, I kiss her tenderly.

Passionately.

My fingertips trace her thigh as she grasps both sides of my face to deepen the kiss, and I can't help but entwine my tongue with hers, which only seems to make the kiss grow stronger. I feel her squirm beneath me, desperate for friction, and it's taking everything I have not to get right to it.

I pull away and scan her eyes. Again, searching for reassurance. I need to verbally hear it from her lips. "Are you sure you want to do this?"

"More than anything," she replies, and the steadiness of her tone is enough for me to believe her.

Reaching over to my nightstand, I open up the drawer to grab a condom. Maddie is smiling from ear to ear, and that tightening sensation explodes in my chest, threatening to detonate me into nothing but smithereens. I'm in love with this girl, and I hate that I am. Hate that I'm petrified to tell her. Hate that I'm afraid I'll never be who she needs me to be.

But I'm in too deep to turn back now. Maybe that makes me a selfish bastard, but I can't help myself when I roll the condom on and hover over her. The smile on her face fades, and now she looks nervous—like it just hit her that she's about to lose her virginity.

"Are you—"

"Yes," she whispers. "I want you, Cam."

I didn't realize I was shaking until now, and it makes me feel like a complete and utter idiot. I'm acting like it's *my* first time, but in a way it is. I've never cared about someone this much during sex. I've never—

She grabs my chin to look at her. "Stop overthinking. Please."

A curt nod is all I can give, and while I support myself on one elbow, I move myself to her entrance. Her chest is rising and falling with anticipation, and my breathing is labored when I glance between our bodies and nearly finish at the sight of my cock so close to her.

Don't overthink.

I push inside, sucking in a sharp breath at the tightness. My instincts beg me to go all the way, but I can't. Not when her face is scrunching up from the unfamiliar feeling.

"It's okay," she says, biting on her lip. "I'm fine. Keep going."

I nod and push another inch, my forehead falling into the crook of her neck at the feeling. I never knew how different this would be, and if I had, I would have made my move on Maddie a long time ago. "Oh *shit*," I moan.

Her fingertips scrape down my back when I slide out and try again. This time, she moans, and the sound is like music to my ears. My favorite symphony. A tune that will be stuck in my head like a broken record.

"Keep going?" I ask. My lips are against her ear, so I can't see her face, but I feel her nod. I slide my cock in and out, moving a bit farther each time, and finally, after about a minute, I'm fully hilted inside of her.

And it feels like I'm home.

"Cam," she whispers breathlessly. I pull back to see her eyes are heavy lidded with lust, eyelashes fluttering shut, and I've never seen someone so fucking perfect. She is *mine*. Even if I fuck this up between us, for tonight, she's mine, and I'm not taking it for granted.

Her hips start to move with mine, matching my rhythm. She's

a fast learner, and my mind strays to all the positions I want to show her. I want to be the one she experiences every single one with.

Our bodies are meant for each other. We're perfectly in sync as she rolls her hips with mine, and the feel of her has my jaw dropping open.

I can't speak.

I can't think.

All I can focus on is the mind-shattering experience she's giving me. It's comical, really. I was so stressed about making sure this is a night she'll never forget, and yet she's doing exactly that to me.

"Cam, it feels so good," she pants.

Fuck.

I'm going to come.

As hard as I am, I fight the need to finish, and wait her out, ensuring she gets what she needs from me. Her legs stiffen, and her mouth is parted, so I know she's close.

"Baby, *you* feel so good," I say, my voice muffled in the crook of her neck. I can't look at her again. If I do, I'll come in a heartbeat. "Come for me. Please."

"Faster," she begs. Her fingers wrap into my hair as I pick up speed, and her soft moans turn into screams of pleasure. I drill my hips against hers, my thrusts erratic and frenzied as she nears the edge of her release, but all I can think about is our conversation at the park last week when I told her I'd never met someone I wanted to both fuck and make love to.

I was mistaken.

She was standing in front of me all along.

I'm rewarded by her orgasm and blissful cries of pleasure as her legs wrap around my lower back, holding me hostage, and as soon as that first wave of her wetness hits, I'm a fucking goner.

I come so hard I see stars.

"Oh *fuck*!" I bite down gently on her shoulder, filling up the condom to the rim, I'm certain. We're a heaving, sweaty mess tangled in one another, but I never want to unravel. If it was up to me, I'd stay inside of her like this for eternity, but this is her first time, and I need to make sure she's okay.

Gingerly pulling out, I study her face, noting the hint of pain on her features. "How are you?" I whisper. Every part of me wants to hold her close and revel in the aftermath of how incredible that was, but I need her to feel the same. I can't celebrate anything until I'm certain she didn't regret it.

"I am—" She giggles as she searches for words, and the relief that washes over me allows me to fully feel the effects of cloud nine. "I mean, I thought I knew what it would feel like, but . . ." She shakes her head. "It was a thousand times better than I imagined."

I roll onto my back, sporting a cheesy grin, panting as I try to regain control of my breathing. I'm still reeling from the feel of her beneath me. Her hands scraping down my back, legs trapping me to her, my name spilling from her lips in ecstasy.

"Was it okay?" she asks, looking over at me. "I mean, was I okay?"

Christ. She put me in such a trance I haven't even said anything yet.

I turn my head to the side and shake my head in disbelief. "That was the best sex of my life, Maddie Davis."

Her brows fly to her hairline. "Seriously?"

I nod. "You've set a new bar."

Rising from the bed, I strip the condom off and walk into

the attached bathroom to throw it in the garbage. When I return to the room, I open a dresser drawer and rummage around for clothing we can wear. She still hasn't said anything, and when I glance over my shoulder, her demeanor has shifted completely.

She notices my concerned expression before she gulps loudly and points to my sheets. There's a couple of spots of blood on them, but it's noticeable. "I'm sorry," she says.

"Why are you apologizing?" I turn to face her with an armful of clothes. "It was your first time. It's normal for that to happen."

"I know, but—"

"Here." I place the bundle of clothes in her arms and jerk my head toward the bathroom. "Take these and go shower. It'll help if you're in any discomfort. *Are* you in pain?" I help her stand, noticing when she grimaces and shifts her weight from one foot to the other. "Okay, while you shower, I'll throw the sheets in the wash and grab an ice pack for you."

"Cam." Tears pool in her eyes before a smile tugs at her lips. "Thank you. You're being so sweet, and I know you think you'll break my heart again, but I mean it when I say I wouldn't have wanted to lose my virginity to anyone else, and even if this doesn't work out, I'm not going to regret it. It's not possible."

And when she closes the bathroom door behind her, I can't help but try to swallow past the lump in my throat.

Because things with Maddie just became a lot more serious, and if I had the irrational fear of losing her before?

It's *nothing* compared to the crippling anxiety I have now.

Twenty-five

MADDIE

The following morning I wake up to an empty bed.

I'm wrapped in sheets that smell of Cameron—a mixture of pine and mint—and the comfort of his scent smothers the spike of adrenaline I have when he's not here.

He wouldn't have left me, right?

No. Not when our night together was everything and more. I can still feel the ghost of his lips on my skin. His mouth against the shell of my ear as he whispered filthy things to bring me to release. In seconds, my skin is flushed at the memory, and I roll onto my side to discover a piece of white folded paper with my name on it on the nightstand.

Getting breakfast, he wrote in his chicken scratch handwriting. Beside the note is a glass of water and an ibuprofen, and I smile before I take the pill and chug the entirety of the glass. I can already feel the soreness between my legs with every movement.

I lost my virginity last night to *Cameron Holden*. He said I was his, and while we haven't discussed labeling this or what it means for our future, I allow myself to bask in the sweetness of his note and the kindness of his gesture for thinking of me enough to leave me pain medicine. For one day, I don't want to worry about what this is between us.

Today, I just want to enjoy this.

The smile is still plastered to my face while I make his bed in just his T-shirt, which is so large on me it falls past my knees. I'm humming a tune and swaying my hips without a care in the world when suddenly, the door to his bedroom swings open.

Christ.

I whirl around with a hand placed over my heart, horrified it might be his father again, but it's just Cameron holding two bags from McDonald's. My heart pounds when his eyes drop to my bare legs, and he doesn't hide his perusal while he drags his gaze back up to my face. "Well, good morning to you too," he mutters in a husky tone. "I thought I was hungry for food, but maybe I was wrong."

He makes it so tempting to tug him back to bed. However, after a night of working out with him, I'm famished. I need to eat first. "What'd you get?" I inquire, attempting to steal a peek into the bag.

"Your favorite," he replies. "A number one with a French vanilla, sugar-free iced coffee."

Even after all these years he still knows me so well. My order has changed multiple times, and yet he remembers my new favorite. It seems we've both been paying far more attention to the other than we let on.

He never stopped caring. Even when I thought he did.

Cameron has never been a coffee drinker, so before he even opens his bag, I know his order by heart too. I repeat it silently to myself as he pulls out the items. A big breakfast with an extra pancake, and then he takes a swig of the worst monstrosity of it all—a *Sprite*—before it's even noon. I'm surprised he's eating this given his fancy diet, but I don't comment on it. He works out practically every day of his life. He should be allowed some type of junk food once in a while.

"Thank you," I say when he passes mine over. Tearing the bag open, I fish out the hash browns and groan at the taste of grease.

For the next ten minutes we eat our breakfast on top of his bed, but I don't miss the way his eyes flick to my mouth when I dart my tongue out to collect the syrup on my upper lip, and he doesn't miss when my eyes are drawn to the way he licks his fingers, his gaze never leaving mine.

"Mmm." His lips tug into a grin when he mimics the night we went out to dinner with my family—the night he had licked his fingers wet with my arousal. "Delicious."

"Is it?" I rise from the comforter, a few tricks up my sleeve of my own. "Can I take a shower before I head home?" I don't know what the hell has changed, but with Cameron, a level of confidence I didn't know existed rises to the surface, and when those green eyes of his grow darker, I become someone I don't recognize.

"Sure," he replies, not moving a muscle.

"Perfect." Reaching for the bottom of his T-shirt, I drag it over my head and toss it to the floor, leaving me bare and on full display for him. He tries to take his fill, but I turn for the bathroom before he has the chance to ogle me for too long.

"And if I want to join?" he calls.

The smile on my face grows wider.

"Then I'd say you better hurry the hell up before the door's locked," I say over my shoulder. A squeal escapes me when he springs off the bed, smacking his forearm on the door before I even have the chance to close it. Then again, I wouldn't have locked it anyway. I can play games with him all day, but this one, he'll always win.

I lean over the bathtub to turn on the water, goose bumps peppering my skin when I hear him begin to strip. His belt falls to the floor, then his shoes. My mouth is completely dry when I feel him step behind me. His bare skin meets mine, his hardness prodding my backside, and all sense of rationality leaves in an instant.

His lips meet the spot between my neck and shoulder, and little jolts of electricity travel wherever his tongue decides to land next. "Well?" he hums against my ear. "Are you going to get in?"

"You're cruel." It's a breathless response, and he laughs as I step into the scalding hot water. The burn feels good against my skin. Too good. And now I'm the one laughing when Cameron hisses and jumps to the far side of the tub where the water doesn't fall. "Why is it so *hot*?" he asks. "Do you always get third-degree burns when you shower?"

I sigh, tilting my head back to let the water soak my hair. "It feels good like this." When I open my eyes back up, Cameron is staring at me with an expression I can't decipher. His stare lingers on mine for a beat too long before he snaps out of it and grabs his body wash off the ledge. "Do you mind smelling like me for the day?"

I remember how happy I was waking up enveloped in his scent, and immediately shake my head. "Not at all."

He pours some of the soap into his hands and rubs them together before he twirls his finger to instruct me to turn around.

I'm completely unprepared for how good it feels when his hands meet my shoulders, massaging and lathering my skin with the suds.

"Does that feel good?" His lips are against my ear when he drags his hands lower, cupping and kneading my breasts. He pays extra attention to my nipples, brushing them gently with the back of his hands, and my head falls back against his chest. I'm incapable of speaking.

His hands move farther south, almost reaching the place I'm dying for him to be until he whispers, "I don't think soap is good for that particular area, Mads."

Of course he'd know that. With how many women he's slept with, he's bound to have showered with at least one of them. They probably taught him everything about the subject, and my fear of only becoming a number, becoming another notch on his belt threatens to consume me until—

"My mom made sure I wasn't an idiot," he adds, seeming to read my thoughts.

I'm speechless as he rinses me off, and once the water runs clear, his hand slips between my thighs. "Is this what you wanted?" he asks. "My fingers on your pretty little clit?"

"Oh *god*." I moan when he speeds his fingers up. My body squirms for more friction, desperate, but his forearm is like a band of solid steel around my stomach, holding me captive.

"Is your pussy throbbing for me yet?" he continues. "Your clit is so swollen from what we did yesterday that I'm surprised you're able to handle this."

"I don't care if it hurts," I somehow manage to choke out. "I want you."

"Oh, you do?" His cock slides up and down against my

backside, teasing and taunting while I bite down on my bottom lip.

"*Please,*" I beg.

Despite how hard he's trying to remain calm, cool, and collected, I can tell he's losing patience too. His breathing is labored in my ear, and the circles against my clit aren't as precise as usual. "If I fuck you in this shower, I'm not going to use a condom," he pants.

"I'm on the pill." There's no use going into detail about my heavy periods right now because, ew. What a way to dampen the mood.

Cameron doesn't ask questions. Instead, he plunges a finger inside of me, and my cry of bliss echoes off the wall of the shower. "Still, I've never fucked anyone without a condom, but *you* . . ." He laughs against my neck, the added vibration nearly sending me to the brink of no return. "You're always so wet for me, baby. It'd be such a damn shame if I didn't get to feel you completely, right?"

I nod, at a loss for words. One finger going inside of me is painful enough, and the second he adds two, he peers down at my face, droplets of water bouncing off his curls and trailing down my chest. "I won't be upset if you want to stop," he reassures. "I know it was your first time last night."

"I want you," I pant breathlessly. "*Please.*"

Water keeps getting in my eyes, but I blink the droplets away and spin to face him. His abs are glistening, making him like some sort of Greek god, and after he finds whatever reassurance he needs, he picks me up so that my legs are wrapped around his waist and pushes me against the wall.

The coolness of the tiles does nothing to douse the fire coursing through my veins.

Then he kisses me, and all of my worries disappear. His hands support my ass while he holds me in place, and I'm so distracted and wrapped up in his kiss that I gasp when he suddenly slips inside of me, the burning sensation from yesterday coming back all at once.

"Oh my god." My head falls against the tiles, eyes fluttering shut, but when I blink them open, Cameron's gaze softens over me, that same flicker of emotion he wore moments ago coming out to play again.

"Holy *fuck*." He inhales deeply, attempting to gain control of himself. "Are you okay? Does it hurt?"

"I'm fine," I blurt, desperate for more. I'm filled to the brim, and yet it's not enough. I don't think I'll ever be able to get enough of him.

When he begins to move, I quickly realize this position makes it far deeper than the one last night. I cry out in a mixture of pain and pleasure. Heaven and hell. It hurts but feels *so* damn good.

"You're so vocal," he says with a smirk, but his smile fades when he thrusts his hips again. "Fuck, Maddie. You feel fucking incredible." Picking up his speed, he plunges in and out, each time seeming deeper than the last. Soon enough, the burning sensation fades, and all I feel is him.

His thrusts become harder until his hips are pounding against mine, giving every single inch of himself to me. Water slaps from the movement, spraying off our bodies, and the heat from the steam doesn't come close to what's brewing between us.

"You. Feel. So. Good," he grunts between gritted teeth. I cry out, sinking my nails into the tops of his shoulders as I try to hold on to something—*anything*—while he fucks me into submission.

My orgasm is building, right on the fucking cusp of spiraling out of control, when he says, "*Please* come for me, baby. Fuck, you're beautiful."

His pleading unlocks the dam I've been holding back, and with two more thrusts, I'm screaming his name before the world gets blurry and I see stars. My legs shake against him while he holds me in place, and when I try to wind down from my orgasm, he pulls out and strokes his release into the running water. I'm fascinated at the sight of his one hand placed against the tile, his other stroking his cock while his head is thrown back and his mouth is parted. He's a fucking dream, and he's mine.

All mine.

After he shakes out his wet curls, he laughs and says, "Jesus, Maddie. When I think it can't get better, it does."

"Are you saying that just because it's my first time and you don't want me to feel insecure?"

He tilts his head to the side, studying me. "You think I'd do that?"

"Well, *no*, but you've slept with a lot of girls, Cam. I'm not mad about it, but I'm new at this and inexperienced. You've probably had plenty of girls work their magic on you in ways you'd never imagined. I'm not them."

"No, you're not." He dips his head to catch my eyes. "And that makes you all the more special." Reaching around me to turn off the water, he steps out and grabs a fluffy towel and passes it over to me. "If you really want to know, that was my first time having shower sex."

My eyes practically bug out of my head. "*What?*"

He shrugs and fixes the towel around his waist. "I told you I've never fucked without a condom. Didn't want to take the risk."

"And yet you did with me."

His eyes meet mine in a blazing, ferocious emerald, and I suddenly can't find the air to breathe as the oxygen is seemingly sucked out of the room. "Yes, I did, and now I don't know how the hell I'm ever going to have sex *with* a condom again."

"Was it really that—"

"Cameron! Where the hell are you? I've been calling your phone for the past thirty minutes!"

Time instantly freezes at the realization of who that voice belongs to.

Please, *no*.

Not now.

I'm not sure who panics first, because my body is frozen in shock when Cameron lunges for the bathroom door and twists the lock. A fist knocks heavily against it seconds later, and I slap a hand over my mouth to silence the heaving gasps racking my body.

There's no way in *hell* this is happening.

But I'm proven just how wrong I am when my brother's voice echoes from the other side of the door. "What are you—" His voice falters, and then he laughs. "Ah, *mystery girl* is here. That explains a lot. You're going to have to come out at some point, Cameron, considering her thong and other articles of clothing are out here."

I'm completely naked aside from the towel wrapped around my body, and with no windows in this room, there's no chance of escape. Cameron seems to be thinking the same before he spins to face me and clasps my arms. "Stay here," he says so quietly I can barely hear him. "Don't panic, okay? I'll get rid of him."

"What if he comes in here?" I whisper hiss.

"He won't. Just stay here and don't make a sound, okay?"

I can't breathe when he closes the curtain to hide me in the shower, giving me little sense of security. My body is trembling, and it has nothing to do with the cold. Cameron and I *just* started resolving our problems and figuring out what this could be between us, and is it really going to come crashing down this quickly?

If it wasn't for having to stay quiet, I'd laugh at the unfairness of it.

Releasing a shaky breath, I try to calm my heartbeat when Cameron opens the door, the future of our relationship hanging in the balance of one conversation.

Here goes nothing.

Twenty-six

CAMERON

What a fucking nightmare.

Since Maddie and I began whatever the hell this is between us, my biggest fear aside from hurting her again has been this exact situation. Ethan is standing outside of this door, knowing I have a girl over, but little does he know the girl I'm hiding in my shower is *Maddie*.

If he had shown up less than a minute before he did, he would have heard his sister's voice for sure with the way she was screaming my name, and if I wasn't on fucking edge about this whole thing I'd probably smile at the memory.

With a deep breath, I slip out the bathroom door with just a towel wrapped around my waist, ensuring to close it behind me. Ethan is sitting in the office chair beside my desk with an amused grin.

With both hands behind his head, he leans back in the chair and asks, "Well, who is it?"

I keep my eyes trained on his, refusing to let him see an ounce of the fear coursing through me. "I told you I'm keeping it a secret for now. It's better this way." *Better for my face*, if I'm being honest. I'd prefer not to get a broken nose before going back to school. Coach wouldn't be impressed if I had to sit out during practice.

"Hmm." His hands are folded across his stomach now, as he contemplates my answer. "To be honest, it's a relief you have someone over. When you weren't answering my calls, I assumed you were still hung up on your dad leaving, so I'm glad it was other endeavors keeping your attention instead."

"You used the spare key I gave you?" I guess.

He nods and holds up the key in question. "Although now I'll probably think twice before barging in again. You've never . . . well, I'm not used to you having a girl over here. You never bring them home with you."

He's right. I don't. Bringing a girl back here feels uncomfortable when it's the very place that haunts my dreams at night. My mother passed away two rooms over. Under this roof is where she took her last breath, and in a way, I don't know if she ever left. Bringing a girl home with me has never been ideal, especially when I couldn't see a future with any of them.

But with Maddie, it's different. I admitted it was more than something physical between us, and while we haven't talked thoroughly about what we're labeling this, we're not messing around with anyone else. We're exclusive, and I feel good about that—*really* good, seeing how my morning started with fucking her in the shower.

I want her all to myself.

Mine.

"I changed my mind," I reply. "But, yeah. It's probably best if you call before coming over from now on in case she's here."

"Is it someone I know?" he asks.

My jaw is set in a firm line when I give him a subtle shake of my head. "Don't do this, Ethan. I'm not going to tell you. It's new, and it's going well. That's all you need to know for now."

He nods. "I can tell, you know, that she's good for you."

I arch a brow, waiting for him to continue.

"The past few days you've been—" He sighs and runs a hand over his hair. "I guess you're reminding me of the guy I used to know—the one who laughs and enjoys life. Our day at the lake was the first normal day we've had between us in a long time. Took me back to the days when we were kids and rode bikes and our only fears were scraping our knees rather than all these fucking life problems."

"I didn't realize we hadn't been normal." I narrow my gaze on him, and he shifts uncomfortably before rising from the office chair. Bags line his eyes, and he's fidgeting way too much. Again, I feel the regret seeping in that it's taken me this long to notice that something is definitely off with him. "Are you okay? And I don't mean surface level, Ethan. Are you *really* okay?"

For a moment I think he might break down and confide in me. Tears are in the backs of his eyes, but he glances at the bathroom door behind me before he gives a quick jerk of his head. "I'm good," he lies, clearing his throat. "I'm happy for you is all. If she's bringing out the old you then I'm thrilled. Just don't fuck it up."

Would he still be happy if he knew it was his sister who's responsible for him seeing glimpses of the kid I used to be? The kid who had never experienced death? The kid who loved the sun on his face, loved to laugh, and thought a hard day was when he couldn't have ice cream after dinner? Or would he turn on me knowing it's his sister's heart I'm gambling with?

Even if I wanted to ask, now wouldn't be the time to do it, when Maddie is still hiding in my shower.

"We'll catch up this weekend when we go to the Grand Canyon," I assure him. "Then you can tell me what's going on."

Ethan groans and leans against my doorway. "Don't remind me. Did Maddie tell you my parents said Maya could come too? I'll have to be around her in another bikini again, and I don't think there's any way in hell I'll be able to stay away from her. It was hard enough when we all went to the lake."

"What was?" I tease. "Your dick or the temptation?"

"I fucking hate you," he grumbles, but a grin tugs at his lips. "Both, to answer your question. How are things, by the way? With you and Maddie?"

"What about me and Maddie?" The sentence comes out rushed, and I mentally curse myself for being so nervous.

It's a *question*, not an accusation.

Calm the fuck down.

"You said you were trying to be friends again, right? Is it working? Things seemed to be slightly better at the lake."

Oh.

The lake.

Right.

"Yeah, they're fine. We're figuring things out."

"Good. I didn't want to go away this weekend with you guys at each other's throats. I can't handle another car ride with you both yelling about the radio station choice."

"She wanted to listen to *pop*," I reiterate, knowing Maddie is hearing all of this. "Country is way better, and you know it." We bickered like hell on our last spring break trip to Disneyland. I smacked her hand away from the radio, then she smacked mine, and we did this on and off for a straight thirty minutes trying to switch the stations.

"Whatever. I'm just glad you sorted things out. Maybe this time we can all enjoy each other's company."

Maybe.

If he doesn't find out and break my nose first.

"All right, I'll let you continue your afternoon," he adds with a wicked grin. Then he shouts at the closed bathroom door, "Hoping to meet you soon, mystery girl!"

Christ.

My face is bright red when he shuts the door to my bedroom behind him, and I wait until the front door closes, too, before I finally open the bathroom door. "He's gone," I say. "You can come out now."

The shower curtain is thrown open, and then she steps out with only a towel wrapped around her. Eyeliner from last night is still smudged beneath her eyes, and her curly hair has already started drying. It's frizzy and all over the place, but it's how I like her best.

Mine.

"How *dare* you mock pop music!" Standing in front of me, she jabs a finger into my chest while trying to be intimidating, but it just makes me smile instead, which only seems to irritate her more. "I told you last year, and I'll tell you again: country music makes my ears bleed."

"Funny." I take the finger on my chest and wrap her hand in mine. "You pitched a fit for almost an hour, but as soon as I started singing you dropped the argument."

"That's different," she whispers.

"How so?"

"Because your voice is . . ." She trails off, finding her words. "You were relaxed and content singing those songs, and I hadn't seen you like that in forever, so I allowed it."

Her palm is flat on my chest, mine covering hers, so I know she can feel the rapid beating of my heart. "And what if I told you my mood that day had nothing to do with the music choice, Maddie? What would you do then?"

"I'd—" She gulps, her eyes dipping to my lips for a split second before she says, "I'd say my brother was right, then. I'm good for you."

The steam evaporated from the shower a while ago, and yet my body still feels surrounded by nothing but heat. "And I'd say you're correct." With one hand I tug at the towel around her body and watch it fall to the floor between us. "I'd tell you that I picked a fight with you because I missed you, and fighting with you was better than no contact at all." My chest rises and falls rapidly from speaking about my feelings, and now that I've started, I'm sure as hell not stopping.

"Being with you is like that first gasp of air after being beneath the water for too long, Maddie. You're a reprieve from the negativity that surrounds me. You always have been."

She lets out a shaky breath, but neither of us moves an inch from where we're standing.

Finally, she lifts her eyes to mine and says, "And if I said you were the same reprieve for me, what would you do then?"

I flick my gaze to her mouth before my lips tilt into the flirtatious grin she always claimed to be annoyed by, but I know the truth. She loves this grin, whether she'll admit it or not. "I'd take you back to bed so we can show each other just how much of a *reprieve* we can bring."

The giggle that fills the room makes my cock stir beneath the towel, and it's standing at full attention when she walks into my room and falls back on my comforter, a flirtatious grin of her own teasing her lips. "I only have an hour before I have to leave, so we should probably get started, right?"

With just those words alone, I no longer worry about Ethan figuring things out between us. I don't care about my dad and his opinion about her being a distraction. He's wrong, and I didn't go into depth about our conversation with Maddie because it's not going to change anything between us. My dad isn't going to win on this, and if anything, it makes me want to rebel even more, thus why the McDonald's purchase this morning was made on the same card that I purchased the pizza with, and which got me into trouble.

The bottom line is that for the first time in my life I'm choosing my happiness. Not my friends', my dad's, my mom's, but *mine*.

And I choose Maddie.

The towel falls to the floor beside hers, and it takes me hardly any time at all before I crawl to her on the bed, more than willing to get that hit of reprieve if only for an hour.

Twenty-seven

MADDIE

With only two days left before we leave for the Grand Canyon, time only seems to become more pressing.

In forty-eight hours Cameron and I will be surrounded by my family, and these moments of blissful serenity tangled in his sheets will all come to an end. Granted, Cameron agreed to *try*, but what does that mean? I've been too afraid to ask since he was the one who wanted to take this thing between us slowly. Is putting a label on it too fast? Is speaking of the future too much pressure?

I hate that I don't know what I'm doing when it comes to relationships, but as much as I wish I could regret not having more experience, I don't. Waiting for Cameron was the greatest decision I've ever made, but there are so many insecurities I have about this being my first time with someone, and I don't know how to shake them.

Maybe that's why I decided to have Maya over for a sleepover tonight even knowing this is using up one of only two nights I have left with Cameron before we're thrust back into secrecy.

Well, more secrecy than *usual*, I should say.

It's imperative I talk everything out with someone who *is* experienced and who can lead me in the right direction as to how and when to approach Cameron about what comes after this when we go back to school.

However, I should have known better than to anticipate Maya instantly giving me advice. She seems to be stuck on the losing my virginity part, and I swear she screamed so loud I'm surprised my eardrums didn't burst.

"Oh, this is good! Ah, I've waited for *years* to have this conversation with you! Ugh, and it sounds *so* romantic." She leans forward on my bed, perched on her hands and knees. "Tell me, is he as big as everyone said he was in high school?"

"Maya!" I retort, utterly mortified.

"It's a simple question." She sits back on her knees, awaiting an answer.

"I didn't want to talk to you about this to discuss the size of his *dick*." But even speaking about it brings a flush to my cheeks. Forgetting what his dick looks like is something I'll never have to worry about.

"Right. You're scared of asking him what happens when you head back to school." She sits cross-legged on the bed, seemingly unable to choose a position from excitement. "He said he wanted to try, and to me, that means continuing this after break ends, but all you have to do is *ask* him, Maddie. It's simple."

It's simple to *her*. I've never put myself out on a limb for a guy before. I rarely attend parties, and I can count the number of dates I've been on with one hand. I've put my future career of becoming an oncologist ahead of every social aspect of my life. Cameron doesn't know that's what I'm studying to become, and neither do my parents. It was a decision I made after Stacy passed, after I saw firsthand how much of an impact losing her had on our families. Me included. A cancer specialist seemed daunting at thirteen. It was a faraway dream for me to accomplish, but it's times like these when I feel a twinge of regret because of it.

Maya has piercings along her ear, and various tattoos lining both forearms. I take one glance at her and just *know* she's lived. I've kept my head down because, just like Cameron, I'm trying to make Stacy proud of me, and the only way I know how to accomplish that is by helping others with the same disease she had while I wait for a miracle cure to be found.

Who would I be if I had indulged in more partying and dating? Would I be a less boring version of myself?

Reading books and studying has always been my comfort. I live vicariously through characters, and because of that, I've never felt the urge to live on the wild side or dabble in things that aren't the norm for me. Why risk getting caught by police doing something reckless when I could quite literally put myself in the shoes of a dragon rider who does reckless shit at every turn? Did I mention I can experience this from the safety of my *bed* as well?

But sometimes I feel like something's wrong with me because I don't ever feel the need to drink myself into oblivion like everyone else, but I also don't enjoy the fact that studying seems to be the only personality trait I have. I *want* to come out of my shell once in a while, but it's hard when spending the night curled up with a good book instead is all the more tempting.

"Look." Maya grabs my hands with hers. 'He likes you, Maddie, and he's been honest with you so far, right? If you ask and he feels too pressured, I think he'll tell you."

"Maybe, but do you think I'm an idiot for ignoring all his red flags? For saying to hell with it and continuing this when there's a chance of getting my heart broken?"

Her lips form a thin line as she contemplates her answer. "I think that any relationship you enter can be deceiving. You could assume you have the most loyal guy on the planet only for him to stab you in the back. To me, him being so up front and honest is a good thing. It means he cares. However—" Her eyes soften when they meet mine. "As I said a few days ago, you should keep your guard up until he's completely in this. I don't want to see you get hurt, Maddie."

I nod, my eyes welling with tears as I remember the countless tubs of ice cream and Lifetime movies we went through trying to get me to recuperate from Cameron all but exiling me from his life.

"All I'm trying to say is he's Cameron Holden," she adds softly. "He has a reputation, you know?"

"Yeah," I whisper. "I know."

Maya falls back onto my comforter, her black hair sprawled out on my pillows. "Thanks for inviting me this weekend," she says, thankfully changing the subject. "I'm totally going to make a move on your brother, by the way."

I wrinkle my nose in disgust. "Great. You have fun with that."

"I will. I packed a neon-green bikini that is going to make my tan look *incredible*. The goal is to have him drooling like a dog."

"I have no doubt you're going to look amazing." And it's the truth. Maya is toned in all the right places, and any guy would be lucky to have her. My brother won't last five minutes with her pulling out that ensemble. I know exactly which swimsuit she's referring to, and my brother doesn't have a shot in hell at withstanding her.

"You know . . ." She bats her eyelashes at me in a childish manner. "I have an extra bikini you can borrow if you'd like. It's skimpy and the same purple as the dress Cameron ripped off you the other night. Might give him some *flashbacks*."

Grabbing the pillow off my bed, I chuck it at her face. "You are a menace! The whole point is to keep this a secret. Not make it obvious."

"Teasing isn't making anything obvious," she retorts. "Don't act like you're not going to try to get his godlike cock in you at some point this weekend."

I almost choke on my spit. "*Godlike?* What rumors have you heard?"

"Are you saying it's not?"

Christ. Fighting with Maya is useless. She always gets what she wants eventually, so if I refuse to tell her, she'll annoy me all night until she wears me down.

"It's better than the rumors," I admit with a smug grin.

"I knew it!" she shrieks. "Okay, stop me when I reach the length." She holds up two fingers and begins to stretch them farther apart. Just to mess with her, I allow her to reach an abnormally large size.

Her eyes grow wide. "No way. You're bullshitting."

"Am I?" I ask with a teasing grin. Leaning over to grab the remote and the popcorn bowl, I place both between us and point to the television screen. "Enough about dick sizes. Pick the next movie."

"*I'm* sorry I'm enjoying my nonexistent sex life through you. I haven't gotten laid in months. I'm in a dry spell that's never going to end, I swear."

A laugh bubbles up my throat at the image I have of my brother seeing her in the neon-green bikini. "Something tells me a *vicious* storm is coming your way this weekend, Maya. I suggest you prepare yourself."

Twenty-eight

CAMERON

After an entire hour of sweating my ass off on my run, the sun is beginning to set in the distance as I wind my way around the familiar sidewalks that lead back to the house. Living in Arizona, there are tons of incredible views, but the sunsets would make the top of my list if I had one. Swirls of oranges, reds, and pinks paint the sky like a glorious canvas, and if I look hard enough, Shadow Mountain looms in the distance.

I used to love looking at the sunsets with my mom. We'd make a habit of coming out on the porch swing with blankets and mugs of hot chocolate, and she'd ask me about my day or we'd discuss trivial things that didn't matter.

Now, looking at the porch swing feels lonely. The wood is splintered and cracked, and the chains are rusting. It's been a long time since anyone last sat on it.

Ignoring the heart-wrenching twist of pain, I push through the front door and head upstairs before I let a wave of despair consume me. My T-shirt is damp with sweat and my curls are stuck to my forehead and the back of my neck. All I want to do is shower, but when I open my bedroom door *Maddie* is standing in front of my mirror.

Oh hell.

She jumps when she sees me in the reflection, spinning around while attempting to tug the shirt past her thighs. "I'm sorry," she says. "I took Ethan's spare key and thought I'd surprise you, but I got bored, so I snooped in your closet, and—" She cringes. "I'm sorry. This is stupid."

I put my hand up to stop her, letting my eyes trail over her body in my jersey. The shirt with my number from high school has never looked so right. It grazes her thighs, and I'm more than curious to know if there's anything underneath it.

I tilt my head to the side and lean against the doorway. "I'd prefer you leave it on."

"Really?"

"Yes." I can't look away from her curvy frame wrapped in navy-blue fabric when I add, "Keep it."

"*Keep it?* Cameron, this is your jersey. I can't—"

"You can." I take two steps closer, not trusting myself to get within arm's reach. "It's my old jersey, anyway. One from high school."

A faint blush creeps onto her cheeks. "I know. It's going to sound ridiculous, but I always got jealous of whatever cheerleader wore your jersey for homecoming, and I wondered what I'd look like in it, so I tried it on. I didn't think you'd be back so soon. Normally your workouts take longer."

"It was cardio tonight," I explain, but despite the steadiness of my tone, my heart skips a beat at her words. Maddie has always had a thing for me, and while I already had an inkling about it, it's completely different to hear it from her lips. It makes me wish I had kissed her a long time ago. Maybe I could have told Ethan about us and he wouldn't have wanted to pummel me, and maybe then I could have played those games with *her* wearing my jersey every weekend.

My eyes soften at how beautiful she looks in my number, and if I could go back in time, if I had *known* I could be this happy, I would have changed everything. "Keep it," I repeat. "It looks better on you."

"But it's a keepsake," she whispers, twirling the edge of the jersey with her fingers. My eyes are drawn there next, but I force myself to break away from staring at her thighs and give her the honest truth.

"So are you."

Three words.

Three *words* have the power to shift the energy in the room.

Maddie's eyes glaze over with desire, and then before I can even *blink* she's launching herself into my arms with her lips crashing against mine.

I catch her with ease and stride toward my bed, damn near falling on top of her from lack of control. She rips her lips away from mine and attaches them to my neck instead, and the feeling of her tongue swirling different patterns on my skin is enough to make me combust before we even get started.

Sliding my jersey up around her waist, I'm greeted with bare, smooth skin. The sight has me groaning before I begin to sink between her thighs, but then she shakes her head, panting and breathless as she props herself on her elbows. "Tonight was supposed to be about pleasing *you*," she says. "I surprised you for a reason."

I kiss her shoulder, then her collarbone. "Pleasing you *does* please me, Mads. That's what you don't get."

Taking me by surprise, she flips us over so that she's on top of *me* now, and the expression on her face is breathtaking. "And pleasing you"—she runs her hands down my chest until she finds my cock hard and waiting against my shorts—"pleases *me*."

I can't think of a reply, completely entranced and stunned that she's capable of doing this to me—making me feel like I belong to her and only her. It's a foreign feeling, one I'm not used to, but the more we do this, the more comfortable I'm becoming with it.

And if I had to guess, I'd say the same goes for her. Maddie's confidence is flourishing as well, and I soak all of it up when she strips off my jersey and tosses it to the floor. She's straddling me in nothing but *skin*, and her tits are on full display for me. I can't help but reach up to grab one, giving it a squeeze and becoming obsessed with the way her head falls back in response.

I've imagined her in this position way too many times. I want her to ride my cock just like this with her hands on my chest to support her weight, but Maddie seems to snap out of whatever daze she's in and sinks between my thighs instead, tugging my shorts and briefs down.

Well, that works too.

My cock springs free with a heartbeat of its own when Maddie grabs hold of it and runs a thumb over the tip. The tiny grin she gives me has me groaning in agony for her to go further, but she continues to tease, stroking her hands lightly enough to not bring too much pleasure but enough to make my hands fist the sheets beside me.

"*Maddie*." Her name is a desperate plea. I'm unable to look away from her when she finally puts her mouth on me, and the feeling is indescribable.

"Oh *fuck*." I sigh as she bobs her head up and down, getting adjusted to my length. I put one hand behind my head and hold her hair away from her face with my free one.

That's the *least* I can do.

She sucks at the very tip, flicking her tongue against my crown before she takes all of me. I nearly come off the bed when I reach the back of her throat, and I'm transfixed by the way her eyes remain locked on mine through it all. Seeing those blue eyes so determined is a sight I'm going to store in my memory forever. My cock filling her mouth should be considered a masterpiece.

"Just like that, baby. Fuck, you're gonna make me come."

With watery eyes, she gags finally before coming up to gasp for air. I want to shout in protest from the lack of contact, but then she gets that little grin on her face again, and I'm completely unprepared for what comes next.

She grabs her tits with both hands—the tits I've fantasized about for years—and I'm incapable of *breathing* when she leans over to slip my cock between them.

Holy.

Fucking.

Shit.

I throw my head back against the pillows, but my brain screams at me to watch her. I don't want to miss a second of this, so I lift my head and watch as she slides them up and down my length. Maddie has already brought all my fantasies to life and added new ones to top it off, but *nothing* compares to this.

She watches my face carefully as she does it, and I know it's because I'm the only one she's done this to. My cock grows harder at that revelation, and it seems to have a mind of its own when my hips jut forward to take over for her.

"God *damn*," I pant. My eyebrows knit together as I fight my release. I don't want this to be over too soon. It's our last night together before we leave for the Grand Canyon with her family, but she feels so fucking *good*. I can't stop. Can't drag my eyes away from the sight of them wrapped around my cock. Can't stop—

"Fuuuck." My release bursts out of me like a goddamn firework, painting Maddie's face, chest, and hair. She jumps back in shock at first before she leans into it, fisting me with her hand to get the last drops.

She's *smiling* with my come splattered across her skin, and the thing I said about sunsets being my favorite view in Arizona? *Scratch that.*

Maddie becoming my personal canvas just took the top spot.

Twenty-nine

MADDIE

Our ride to the Grand Canyon is *insufferable*, but this time it isn't because Cameron and I can't decide on a music station.

We're all packed in my parents' minivan. Ethan and Maya took the front seats while Cameron and I took the back. Cameron claimed it was because he'd have more leg room back here, and Ethan and Maya certainly didn't complain that they'd be sitting next to each other.

Even with the AC on full blast the temperature in the car never seems to cool. We're supposed to be keeping this a secret between us, and Cameron and I both agreed last night that we would be cordial. That agreement didn't include stolen glances out of the corner of his eye or his hand brushing against mine when no one is looking, but he doesn't seem to care about our rules. I've squirmed the entire drive, and it's all due to *Cameron Holden* and his tight fucking shorts that outline the exact body part I'm trying desperately to avoid.

I'm addicted. Utterly and completely addicted.

Maybe it's because we've had to cram this situationship of ours into the span of two weeks, and after talking to Maya, I *do* want to confront Cameron and ask him what happens when we head back to school, but that would mean getting him alone, and I'm afraid if we do manage to get a second of alone time this weekend, it's not going to be spent talking.

Finally, we arrive at the Airbnb my parents rented. It's high up on a mountain overlooking the canyon. The late afternoon sun beams down on the vast, seemingly endless expanse of priceless landscape before us.

I never knew the true meaning of the word *breathtaking* before I visited the canyon for the first time. It was a painting come to life when I first saw it, and I had to suck in a sharp breath of air after being so transfixed by the peace that was almost too overwhelming to bear.

Aside from the wind, it's silent here, allowing me the time to truly think and reflect on every stressor and inconvenience going on in my life. It brings a sense of *security* that I didn't realize I needed until now.

Footsteps crunching on stone shift my attention to Cameron, who has come to stand beside me and admire the view too.

The more he stares, the more distant he becomes.

Maybe Cameron needs this moment of peace even more than I do.

There's a deck with a built-in pool, a grill, and even a hot tub attached to the house, and when Maya spots it, she squeals with excitement. "We are *so* hitting the pool! Let's go get changed!"

Cameron snaps out of whatever daze he's in and joins my father and Ethan to lug the bags inside. It might be a coincidence, but it doesn't stop the flurry of butterflies taking flight that he's grabbed only my suitcase along with his own.

My eyes are trained on the way his muscles in his back contract from the weight when Maya scoffs beside me and says, "So far, you're doing a terrible job of not making it obvious."

"It's not my fault," I groan. "Why does he have to look like *that*? He's so tall, and why did he have to wear those shorts that emphasize his calves?" Maya bursts out laughing, and I send her a dirty glare. "I despise being a female with hormones."

"Don't worry, girl." Maya pats me on the shoulder and pushes me in the direction of the Airbnb. "You're not the only one salivating. Now let's go get in our swimsuits and give them a taste of their own medicine."

>> <<

Two hours later, my dad returns from a nearby grocery store with some steaks to grill, and my mom is working on the side dishes in the kitchen. She told us she didn't need help and encouraged us to go have fun in the pool.

I prefer to put all my clothes away on the first day of vacation, but for my best friend who is trying to live this trip to the fullest, I'll sacrifice my routine and join her for a pool day.

When I step outside in the skimpy bikini Maya lent me, a portable radio is blaring as my dad gets the grill ready. Maya is already floating on her back in the water, allowing the sun to tan her skin to perfection, and Ethan's eyes are glued to her from where he sits on a patio chair. A bottle of whiskey sits beside him, a full glass in his hand as he gulps half of it down.

I bite my lip to keep from smiling.

He's got it bad.

"Maddie!" Maya exclaims when she spots me. "Come on, let's play chicken!"

"*Chicken?* With just ourselves?"

She rolls her eyes, waving to Ethan and—

Holy hell.

The breath hitches in my throat when my eyes meet Cameron's. His gaze is already burning a hole in the side of my head, and the look in his eyes is identical to when he's inside of me.

He shifts his gaze to Ethan, who's too focused on what Maya just proposed to care about anything else, so Cameron takes his time checking me out, staring at my breasts for a beat longer than he should.

His hard, muscular body is oiled up and he's wearing another pair of hoochie shorts. One arm is on the back of the patio chair he's sitting in, and his long legs are sprawled out before him. I want to sink to my knees, pull those shorts down, and show him just how good he fucking looks.

Shit.

I'm never going to keep this facade up if I keep thinking dirty.

Cameron takes a slow sip from the whiskey bottle, eyeing me over the rim.

"We have two strong, capable men I'm sure would be more than willing to help us out, no?" Maya bats her eyelashes at Ethan, who gives a curt nod and practically hurls his chair back at the prospect of having her legs around his head, even if it's not in the way he wants.

"Well?" Cameron asks with a teasing grin. "What do you say, Mads?"

"I don't know," I reply with a grin of my own. "Are you as strong as you look?"

A twinkle lights up his eyes. "Stronger than you'd think."

Christ. The images slam into my head all at once. His elbows beside my head as he drilled his hips against mine. Him pinning me against the shower wall as he fucked me senseless, never losing stamina or needing to stop for breaks.

He chuckles and slides his chair back as if he knows where my thoughts have gone. "Well, is that a yes?"

Not wanting him to see the effect he has on me, I stomp into the water until it's at my waist, gulping when he trails in after me with slow, precise strides. In every room he walks into, he takes up the entirety of it. He consumes my thoughts, brings my fantasies to life, and has me in a state of tunnel vision, especially now, when droplets of water cling to his chest and trickle down his abs.

"Who's going on your shoulders?" Cameron asks Ethan, who cuts him a glare.

"Maya," he replies. "You know, for height purposes."

Right, because my *shortness* would be the reason he loses.

"Guess you're with me, then." Cameron spins to face me, but when he does, his hand brushes between my legs under the water, hidden by his large frame. I close my eyes at the feeling, and while Ethan and Maya are distracted, he bends down to my ear to whisper, "How should we celebrate if we win?"

"Fucking hell." I don't realize I've said it out loud, but before Cameron can tease me about it, Maya claps her hands to announce the starting of the game.

Wrapping my thighs around Cameron's head is *not* what I need right now, especially when my body is a raging inferno, but Maya is already on Ethan's shoulders, prepared and ready to strike.

Cameron wears that stupid smirk of his before he spins around again to dip under the water. My thighs wrap around his neck to sit over his shoulders, and when he rises easily to his feet, my hands are clutched in his curls as I attempt to gain my balance.

"Feel at home yet?" he mutters under his breath.

"I hate you," I whisper back.

He laughs while Ethan and Maya draw closer. "Keep telling yourself that, *Mads*."

The second Maya launches herself at me, I go at her with a force of my own, squeezing the sides of Cameron's head with my thighs. He keeps his hands firmly around my knees, his legs holding his ground to create stability for me.

I'm not sure if it's because I've gotten used to keeping Cameron in a headlock, but I hardly put in any effort at all before Maya crashes into the water and takes Ethan with her. The win is instantaneous, and when Maya calls for a rematch, we win again.

And again.

And again.

I've been on Cameron's shoulders for over half an hour and the man hasn't faltered once, a tribute to the training he's so ada-mant about.

"Dude, just call it," Cameron says when Ethan rises to the surface panting and out of breath. "You've got no chance."

"Fuck you and your unnatural athletic ability," Ethan shoots back.

Maya wrings out her hair as she adds, "Don't sweat it, Ethan. I intended on getting wet, anyway."

A coughing fit erupts from my brother at her choice of words, and I would have laughed but Cameron catches me off guard when his hands land on my waist and he *lifts* me over his head like I'm a damn feather before he sets me on my feet in front of him. My ass brushes his cock, and it takes every ounce of will-power for me to put distance between us.

"Honey?" my dad calls from the grill. The steaks are sizzling, the wind carrying over a charred, seasoned aroma that makes my stomach rumble. "Can you bring me out the pan for these steaks, please?"

A heartbeat later the glass door slides open and my mom appears at his side with the pan in hand. She glances at him, and the smile that lights up his face makes my chest tighten. The love between my parents has always been evident, but it's in these small moments that I can really see the adoration they have for one another.

Stolen kisses while she's doing dishes.

Holding every door open despite her refusal.

He gazes at her like she's the only girl in the world to him, and after twenty-three years of marriage, they're happier than ever.

It's a love I hope to have of my own someday.

And it could be another coincidence when Cameron's hand brushes mine beneath the water, but deep down, I'm desperately hoping it isn't.

>> <<

"Oh come on!" Ethan laughs hysterically, doubling over after one too many drinks. "You can't seriously believe he's the best quarterback."

My dad is grinning from ear to ear when he replies, "Give him a few years and you'll be eating those words." Then, after a few seconds he adds, "Unless *Cameron* here gets drafted and shows him up."

We're sitting around the patio dining table with our stomachs full. My skin has a slight sunburn from earlier, and my hair is frizzy and damp from the pool. The first day of vacation didn't disappoint, especially all the stolen moments with Cameron. If it wasn't for my brother being so distracted by Maya, I'm certain he would have noticed something was up between us by now.

However, I'm thankful for the reprieve.

It's allowing Cameron to sit beside me tonight at dinner, his hand on my knee while his thumb rubs slow circles on my inner thigh. He's been constant about it since we sat down, until he hears my dad's question.

The thumb on my thigh stills before he says, "It's not a guarantee I'll be drafted."

My dad chuckles. "Please. Your stats are better than anyone else's, Cameron. If anyone is going to be drafted, it's *you*. I wouldn't be surprised if you're a first round pick."

I glance up to see a tight smile on Cameron's face that seems forced. "Hopefully."

Ethan leans over to whisper something in Maya's ear, which makes her smile into her cup of soda, which is definitely mixed with liquor. My parents won't let us drink since she and I are still underage, but the boys have been stealing our glasses when they go to refill theirs. I'm about to give Cameron an out by asking him to get me a refill when my dad suddenly claps his hands and says, "All right, who wants to help me start this bonfire? The logs I bought earlier are in the trunk of the car."

"I'll do it," Cameron says, seeming desperate to get away from the previous conversation. "Care to help, Ethan?"

If looks could kill, the death glare my brother shoots him would get the job done. It's a look that says, *Don't you see I'm making progress with her?* "Can't Maddie help you? She's more than capable."

Cameron shifts his attention to me, eyes gleaming like he was hoping Ethan would say that, and now I'm wondering if his desperation to get away is more to do with me than the conversation. "Shall we?"

"Sure." I stand and follow him across the patio to where the steps lead down to the gravel. As we walk down the long driveway and away from the tiki torches, it's pitch black and eerily quiet aside from the crunching of stone beneath our shoes.

Finally, when we're far enough away, Cameron reaches over to interlock our fingers and tugs me off the beaten path that is most *certainly* not toward the car.

"What are you—" He spins me around, and suddenly my back is pressed against the bark of a tree before his lips meet mine. It's fast and sloppy and difficult to keep up with, but my hands rake through his hair in an effort to match his pace as his hand slips into the bottoms of my swimsuit.

"We have two minutes before they get suspicious," he pants against my ear. I can't see his face in the dark, but it almost makes it hotter. Secretive.

Wrong.

"Can you come for me in two minutes?" His voice is husky and laced with nothing but desire, and I can do nothing but nod when he circles my clit. "Fuck, I missed you. I'm fucking addicted to you, and today has been torture not being able to touch you the way I want."

"*Cam,*" I whimper.

He shoves two fingers inside, not giving me any time to adjust before he's pumping away and gathering the wetness that's accumulated throughout the day. He groans as his fingers coax my walls, and he moves closer until his hardness is pressed against my stomach. "You're so wet, baby. Does this turn you on? My fingers fucking you when we could be caught any second?"

"*Yes,*" I gasp.

He pumps them faster, the sound of my pussy filling the silence. I'm in heaven when he rubs his cock against me, and we're practically dry humping against this tree to try to make this quick.

I'd like to think him taking me down here to do this was planned, but the fake smile he gave my father at dinner leads me to think this was a spur of the moment decision. He's confessed that sex has always been an outlet for him. A *distraction.*

If this is what he needs to take his mind off everything, I'll be his outlet.

I meant it when I told him I'd hold his hand through this.

"Fuck." He reaches between us to mess with the tie of his swim trunks, and then he's fisting his cock in his hand. It's only his gritty voice and labored breathing in the blanket of darkness covering us, and I can't breathe when he drags his cock along my slit to gather the wetness, using *that* as lubricant to pump himself. "I can't get enough of you. I want you all the fucking time."

His fingers go deeper, curling against the spot that has me gasping. Before I can cry out, he shakes his head and adds, "Don't you *dare* make a sound, Maddie. Put a hand over your mouth."

I do as I'm told, my moans muffled by my own palm, and Cameron chuckles darkly. "See? I knew you being a good girl would work out in my benefit. So fucking *beautiful.*"

My eyes roll to the back of my head when I feel the ghost of his lips brush against my neck. He flicks his tongue on my skin as his pace on himself quickens, and when he grunts into my ear, I'm a detonating mess against his fingers.

There's no saving me from this torture of having to come without making a sound. We should be talking about the future and what this means between us when we leave in a few days, but after years of pent-up sexual frustration, no amount of pleasure he gives seems to be enough.

I want more.

Need more.

But one more minute and my family will start to get concerned, and we can't risk that. At least, it seems *he* doesn't want to risk it. The more I'm falling for him, the less I care about my family's feelings on the matter. I do respect their opinion, but I'm an adult, and if Cameron and I want to date, there shouldn't be a problem with it.

But Cameron wants to take things slow. He isn't ready to say those three words to me, and until he is, I refuse to say them either. I don't want my family knowing about us if it's not going to work out or turn into something serious. I want to wait until Cameron is sure before I tell anyone else.

"You okay?" he whispers as he fixes the tie of his swim trunks. When he's finished, he moves the bottoms of my bikini back into place and interlocks our fingers to tug me back on the gravel path.

"I'm more than okay," I admit. "You have a *filthy* mouth."

I can hear the smile on his face when he says, "Well, judging from your wetness, I'd say you like it, no?"

"Definitely," I admit, a blush creeping onto my cheeks. "Never stop."

After we grab the bags of logs we head back to the patio, where laughter carries from up above, and when we reach my family again, nobody questions us or even casts a glance in our direction. I help Cameron set up the logs correctly in the pit before my dad joins us and lights it up.

The flames crackle to life, casting our faces in an orange glow, and my heart plummets into my stomach at how devastating Cam looks at this moment.

His curls are unruly and wild and his eyes are the brightest emerald that could rival the gems themselves. A smile covers the entire bottom half of his face, probably due to the memories of what we just did in the woods, and seeing him so carefree and happy has me coming to the conclusion that Ethan was right.

I'm *good* for him.

And it's only a matter of time before he realizes that too.

Maya joins us and tosses me a hoodie she grabbed, but when I bring it to my nose, the smell is all too familiar. It's mint with a hint of spice, and my best friend shrugs when she sits down on one of the benches beside the fire pit and says, "I grabbed the first one I could find. I can't help that it's Cameron's." She shifts her attention to him when I slide it over my head. "Do you mind if she wears it?"

Ethan steals the spot beside Maya before I can sit down, his thigh pressed against hers. She's wearing my brother's sweatshirt, and I only know this because it's an old one from high school when he tried soccer for a season and hated it.

Cameron gulps when his eyes run over me. "Not at all. Are you going to sit or stand all night?"

My feet move before my brain can catch up when he pats the spot beside him, but sitting here with my family brings a heavy reminder that there's a possibility we'll *never* be able to work things out. If my brother or parents discover what's been going on and disapprove, Cameron won't go further with me because of how important my family is to him.

Sitting around this fire reignites the fear that I may never know what it feels like to experience my head on his shoulder and his arm wrapped around me, holding me close. He may never be able to love me fully because of the trauma of his past and his fear of facing the reality of his feelings.

I'm sinking into quicksand with him, and the longer I wait, the more difficult it's going to be to pull myself out if he changes his mind.

"Your hair," Cameron mutters under his breath, drawing me from my thoughts.

"Hm?"

"A leaf is in your hair. Left side." The smug grin he's wearing makes me roll my eyes as I discreetly find the leaf and discard it before my parents join us. My mom launches into a story about a romantic picnic my father planned for them tomorrow evening on one of the trails, and Ethan discusses a new restaurant he wants to try for dinner, subtly hinting that Maya should join us.

Everyone seems excited for what's to come, and I want to feel the same, but with so much uncertainty hanging in the air about the future for us, I can't bring myself to get on the same page.

Cameron bumps his knee against mine then lowers his head to whisper, "Have I mentioned before how beautiful you look in my clothes?"

My heart stutters in my chest.

When I lift my eyes to his, Cam scans them, seeming to read all the nerves and doubt. "Give me time," he whispers. *"Please."*

I muster up a weak smile, which even *I* don't believe is convincing. I want to hold his hand through this, and I'm going to, but what does that mean for me? I'm putting my heart on the line, and the reality of the situation is we don't have time to spare.

We leave for school in four days, and if Cameron decides he's not ready to continue things, I'm going to be the one left to pick up the pieces of my heart *again*.

But when those green eyes soften, pleading and communicating everything words can't, I'm incapable of telling him no. I'm incapable of holding myself back out of fear of getting hurt. It's always been all or nothing with him, and the truth is, I'd rather have it all than risk being nothing again.

I'm up to my neck in quicksand, and whether I like it or not, only Cameron's hand can pull me out, and it's up to him whether he chooses to save me or damn me for eternity.

Thirty

CAMERON

"I'm never going to make it," Ethan says, approaching my side at the bar. He signals for the bartender, his shoulders tense. Sweat stains his white button-down dress shirt, and he glances over his shoulder to where Maya and Maddie wait for us at our table, releasing a heavy sigh.

"Come on, man." I clap him on the shoulder and give him a reassuring smile. "It's not that bad."

"Do you even *see* her dress tonight?" Unable to help himself, he casts another look over his shoulder at her, but Maya isn't the girl holding my attention. Maddie is wearing a tight red minidress with a sweetheart-shaped neckline bedazzled with tiny crystals. With her curly hair in a slicked-back ponytail, my eyes are drawn to the elegant slope of her neck—a moth to a flame, a magnet to steel, the list of attraction is endless, but each one applies to us.

While their parents are having their picnic, the rest of us went with Ethan's plan and decided to dine at a fancy restaurant downtown. The food was spectacular, but the view was even better, and I'm not talking about the deep-red undertones of the plush leather booths or the low lighting creating a sultry ambiance. I was able to admire Maddie for an entire sixty minutes without being bothered, so I'm taking that as a win in my book.

"Scotch please," Ethan says to the bartender. I order the same, and while we wait, he seems deep in thought before he adds, "I want to talk to Maddie soon about making a move on Maya. I've been thinking about it a lot, and this trip has proven to me that Maya is more than just a crush. I'm serious about starting something with her, but I don't know how to get that across to my sister without her kicking my ass into next week."

"You think she'd be upset?" I take a long sip of my drink when it lands in front of me.

"I know she would be. What reassurance have I given to make her trust me with Maya's heart? I was a dick in high school, and even though I've matured now, all she's going to care about is who I portrayed myself to be."

I tilt my head to the side. "Portrayed yourself to be? Correct me if I'm wrong, but we were straight up assholes. There was no portraying going on, we just *were*."

"It doesn't matter," he mutters. "I've been wanting to have some alone time with Maya to try to get some sort of confirmation that we both want this before I talk to my sister, but being on a family trip makes it impossible."

I attempt to hide my grin after another sip of scotch. Ethan just placed a gift in my lap without realizing it.

Alone time with Maddie?

"Why don't I steal Maddie away from you for the night? I'll make up an excuse for us to get out of here, that way you and Maya can have the alone time you need to make your decision."

Ethan's eyes light up with hope. "Seriously?"

Guilt crawls through my body but I shove it to the side and offer him a tight smile instead. He has no idea what's going on between Maddie and me, and he's oblivious to the fact that he's so worried about what Maddie will think about him liking Maya when Maddie crossed that boundary with me without a second thought about his opinion.

"Yeah. Take the car and take her somewhere. I'll call an Uber for us."

After some contemplation, Ethan nods and drains the last of his scotch, wincing from the burn. "Thanks, man. I owe you one."

No, you really don't.

When we head back over to the table, I tap Maddie on the shoulder and jerk my head at the doors leading out to the deck. Floor-to-ceiling windows reveal the beginning of the sunset, casting the restaurant in pinks and oranges, but nothing compares to the blue of her eyes.

"Do you want to go for a walk?" I ask.

Her eyes dart to my brother, then to me. "Why would I want to go on a walk with you?"

Ethan reaches his max level of patience when he blurts, "Can you just go on the damn walk?"

Everyone is stunned into silence, especially Maya, who fidgets in her seat, fingers white-knuckled around the edge of the chair.

"Um, okay?" Maddie cautiously rises from her seat, and after exchanging a glance with Maya, she follows me through the maze of tables. It bothers me that I can't place my hand on the small of her back. Every second spent not touching her is pure agony, especially when a few waiters turn their heads to catch a second look after she passes them.

It's getting close to closing time, so there aren't too many people left in the restaurant, and one of the waiters looks like he's going to shoot his shot until I pick up my stride to follow close behind her, casting a looming shadow over her and him.

I dare him to try to flirt with her. I almost wish he would so I can tell him to fuck off because she's mine.

She's *always* been mine.

The guy takes one look at me and spins on his heel to head in the other direction. Maddie looks back at me expectantly, oblivious to what's going on around her.

Does she really not understand the amount of attention she draws just by being her?

I hold the door open for her, and when we step outside, we're hit with a cool breeze. I'm already stripping myself of my suit jacket when she wraps her arms around herself, and she sends me a grateful smile as I drape it over her shoulders. "Thank you," she says. "What was that about in there? Why does my brother seem so upset?"

I laugh. "He's not mad. He wants alone time with Maya but he's worried as hell about what you'll think if he makes a move. He's using this time to be certain about his decision before he talks to you about it."

"What?" She gasps, spinning to look back inside the restaurant until I grab her wrist. "All he had to do was ask! I've already told Maya I'm fine with it."

I arch a brow. "Easier said than done, right?"

"Point taken."

"Let them have this alone time," I whisper, interlocking my fingers with hers. "Besides, I want alone time with you too."

I drag her away from the restaurant windows until we're

far enough that we're out of sight. We find a bench that's empty, smack dab in the middle of the incredible fucking view of the canyon. It goes on for *miles*, the river at the bottom traveling far into the distance until it disappears.

The view leaves me breathless. Maddie sits beside me and pulls my jacket tighter around her, the side of her body pressed against mine. Now that we're alone, I wrap my arm around her shoulder and hold her close like I wanted to do at the bonfire last night. I could tell she wanted me to do it, too, and I'm confident if anyone comes out we'll hear the laughter and chatter from inside the restaurant.

She sighs and rests her head on my shoulder. "This view never fails to make me forget about everything bad in life."

I frown, attempting to swallow past the sudden lump in my throat. "It does the opposite for me. Views like this make me *over*think, and it—" My jaw ticks as the memories rise to the surface. "It makes me remember *everything*."

My mom.

Saying goodbye.

Watching her take her last breath.

"I miss her too," Maddie whispers, knowing where my thoughts have led. "Sometimes I can still hear her laugh. Do you remember when she'd laugh so hard that it was silent? There wasn't any sound, it was just—"

"Her nose would crinkle up." I smile faintly at the memory.

"And her face would get as red as a tomato," she adds, reaching up to hold the hand that's around her shoulder. The gentle strokes of her thumb bring a calming presence, allowing me the space and time to get whatever I need to off my chest.

"Sometimes—" I shake my head, trying to find the words.

"Sometimes I think she'd look at where I am in life and be disappointed. Yeah, I'm playing football, but at what cost? I fucked my way through high school to try to cope with the pain, and my dad and I aren't close anymore. I don't think she'd be proud of who I've become, and the thought of that terrifies the hell out of me." My first time confessing that works its way into the void of the canyon, and I wait for a sign. Anything to see if my mother heard me and agrees or thinks I'm crazy for relying on the fucking wind to give me an answer.

Maddie tips her chin up to study me, and I hate that she's always been able to see right through me. It's useless trying to hide my emotions from her, so I don't bother with the facade. I allow her to see the hurt and despair that's stifled me for years. "Is football something you really want to do, or are you only playing to appease your dad?" She bounces her knee nervously before she adds, "I don't want to overstep, but it's something I've always wondered, and—"

"I'm not mad you asked it. I just . . . well, I haven't been asked that before." Until tonight, no one has ever looked closely enough to care about my answer. "Football has always been something I'm good at, and at first, I played for fun. Then I got into high school and coaches started to notice I was talented, and then offers started coming in and I lost sight of why I started playing in the first place. My dad was on my ass about training, and he still is, but I don't play because it's fun, and I don't play for my dad. I play because it makes me feel closest to my mom, and I wouldn't give that up for anything."

Tears prick the backs of my eyes, but I blink furiously in an effort to clear them. That very same question has been weighing on my chest for months. The pressure has been insufferable, but whether I make it to the NFL or not, I'm not playing for anyone but *me* and the connection it brings me to her memory.

Maddie squeezes my hand, blinking away tears of her own. "Your mom would be *so* proud of the man you are, Cam. Whether you believe it or not, you'd take the shirt off your back for anyone."

I arch a brow. "Is that a sexual innuendo? Because *yes*, I've gotten around."

"What? No." She laughs, and it's a welcome sound given the depressing turn our conversation took. "Before your mom's passing, you loved hard. You were the kindest person I knew, and I don't think that boy went anywhere. He's still inside you. You're still *you*, you've just picked up some cuts and bruises along the way that still need healing. Your mom knows that too."

"You seem to have a lot of confidence in me," I reply. "Hopefully, I don't disappoint."

"You won't. If that boy was long gone, why would you be so worried about changing?"

I tilt my head to the side, contemplating her answer. "I guess I hadn't thought about it that way. Are you sure you don't want to become a therapist instead of a doctor?" Then, after a few beats I ask, "What kind of doctor do you want to be, anyway?"

Those blue eyes of hers lock on mine, and it feels like an eternity before she answers. It's almost like she's hesitant about telling me, but the next words out of her mouth steal the breath from my lungs. "I'm studying to become a cancer doctor."

Of all the things I thought she'd say, that sure as hell wasn't it.

"An oncologist, to be exact. Well, that's if I graduate, of course. I still have a million obstacles to face before I can practice, but—"

"A cancer doctor," I repeat, my voice thick. "*Mads—*"

Why am I surprised? Maddie has been a constant in my life

even when she wasn't in it. Even when I broke her heart, she was determined to find a way to mend me. Given how close she was to my mom, it shouldn't be shocking that she'd try to do the same for her even after she passed. She's always tried to fix things even when they're not capable of being fixed.

I'm terrified of letting her down.

"You don't have to say anything," she whispers, tears tracking down her cheeks. "I saw firsthand what the disease can do. *Who* it can take away in the blink of an eye. I've watched those I lo—" She snaps her mouth shut, but, fuck, I wish she'd say it. It's good of her to keep the sentiment to herself because even though I want to, I'm not ready to say it back. Selfishly, I want to hear it spill from her lips that she loves me.

I've always known it, but it'd be another thing to hear it.

"This is my connection to her too," she says, "so, I get what you mean. You lost your mom, and I lost a woman I looked up to immensely." A mixture between a laugh and a sob escapes her. "She always thought so highly of me. It was a pressure in itself, and although I'll never carry the amount of pain you do, I can understand it. A part of me holds on to who she thought I was. Nothing short of perfect. I don't want to disappoint her, either, so I've tried my best to be perfect in everything I do. And it's stupid, because I know she would be proud of me regardless, but it's a fear I can't shake."

Wiping away her tears, I press my lips to her forehead. It never dawned on me that we'd have the same fear, and if only we had talked about this years ago, we could have been there for one another. "She loved you, Mads, and no matter what you choose to do with your life, I know she's rooting for you every step of the way. A part of me thinks she was trying to set us up a long time ago."

She lifts her watery eyes to mine. "Really?"

"Yeah." I turn to stare off into the distance and clear my throat. "That's why what we're doing makes me nervous. It's not that I haven't always wanted to take this step with us, but if I fuck it up like I do with *everything* good that comes into my life, it's just another reason to make her disappointed in who I've become."

"She could never be disappointed in you, Cam. She loved *you* more than anything."

"Well, she loved you more than anything, too, and if I wind up being the shittiest boyfriend at the end of this, then—"

"Boyfriend?" She cuts me off, staring up at me like a deer in headlights.

"I—" Knitting my brows together, I'm trying to determine what I said wrong. "Is that not what I am to you?"

"I didn't . . . I mean, you didn't specify. I thought—" She giggles, and the sound loosens the ball formed in my chest. "So, you're my boyfriend?"

"Yes? Sorry, I'm confused here. Did you think we weren't together? I called you *mine*, Maddie."

"I know, but you said you wanted to take things slow, so I thought you meant *mine* as in just being exclusive until break ends."

The dark, raspy laugh that fills the silence has her shivering against me. "Christ. Add communication to the things I need to work on." Then I tug her onto my lap and pull her close until her lips hover above mine. "You're mine, in every meaning of the word, Maddie Davis, and I don't want to end this when break ends. I want to see where this goes."

She smiles, that red lipstick of hers tempting me to smear it. "Okay, then, we'll see where this goes."

My eyes dip to her breasts, which are pushed up from the dress and in perfect view for me to admire, but for the first time in my entire existence, sex isn't my top priority. I've never had a girl I'd prefer to sit and talk about life with rather than fool around with in the sheets, but tonight, I don't have the urge to do anything other than enjoy this beautiful night with her.

"Have I ever mentioned how lucky I am?"

She smiles brightly, a faint pink tainting her cheeks. "No, but I like hearing it."

"I'm lucky," I repeat, pressing a kiss to her cheek before I proceed to kiss all over her face, my heart bursting with pride when she erupts into a fit of giggles. "I'm lucky, I'm lucky, I'm lucky."

"Okay!" She gasps. Then, when she calms down, she runs a hand through my hair and says, "Even though you don't think it, you're a catch, Cameron, and I'm the luckiest woman alive to have you by my side. I'll keep telling you that until you believe it, and after this conversation, I think your mom would be proud of both of us. I think she'd be overjoyed we decided to take this step together, and no matter what we choose to do with our lives, she's going to be rooting for us, just like you said."

The sentence is right on the tip of my tongue. Fuck, I want to say it. I want to shout it from the damn rooftops that I'm in love with her, but until our relationship is out in the open, I'm not going to add to her devastation if things can't work once the secret of us being together is out.

As hard as it'll be, I'm going to wait.

"I think so, too, baby."

The cheesy grin she's sporting is a sight I want to store to memory forever. "What?" I ask.

"That's the first time you've called me baby without sex being involved."

Huh.

The sentiment slipped out without me having to think twice about it.

"I guess you're right," I admit. "I like calling you that, though."

She surprises me by twisting in my lap so that she's straddling me. Her dress rides up, but thankfully my jacket hides anything that might be exposed. "I like when you call me that, too, *baby*."

Hearing the nickname has my heart threatening to burst. It's never sounded so right before, and my cock seems to like it too. This was supposed to be an emotional night and nothing more, but with Maddie I'm learning that the emotions are part of the intimacy between us. Having her call me a nickname, and holding her close and talking about life, are all factors that contribute to turning me on now.

It's going to take some getting used to.

"What do you say we get out of here?" She trails her hands down my chest until she reaches my belt. "I recently found out I have a boyfriend, and I'm *desperate* to show him just how much I appreciate him."

I pull my lip back between my teeth when she caresses my hard cock, fighting for its life against the zipper of my pants. "Oh yeah? And who might that lucky guy be?"

With some teasing and all the confidence in the world, she scurries off my lap with a sly grin.

"You wouldn't know him," she says with a laugh. "He collects Pokémon cards. He doesn't play football."

I spring off the bench before she flees for the parking lot, using the restaurant's outdoor porch stairs. She's laughing her head off as I chase after her, and it doesn't take long before my strides beat hers and I toss her over my shoulder.

"Cam!" She's trying to breathe but she's laughing too much. "My underwear is showing!"

"Good," I reply, pinching her ass as a punishment for the teasing. "Easier access."

I pull out my phone with my free hand to call an Uber, but I have two missed text messages from Ethan.

Took her back to the airbnb. Hot tub!!!

Then, an hour later, *Dude, I don't know what to tell Maddie, but we definitely crossed a line we shouldn't have tonight. She's going to hate me.*

I can't hide my grin when I place Maddie back on her feet and pull up the Uber app. I won't reveal anything about his night until he or Maya decide to tell her. It's not my business to share, but I'm really fucking happy for him. He took a leap of faith, and it worked out. He has no reason to worry when Maddie will be more than understanding about it. A part of me wishes she'd put him out of his misery and just tell him it's okay already, but I get her reluctance. Telling Ethan it's okay to date her best friend would persuade her to tell him about us, and I don't know if she's ready for that.

Why can't I be like Ethan and push myself to do the same?

I went out on a limb by deciding to be Maddie's boyfriend, but I'm holding myself back because of my fear of commitment and losing someone close to me again. I'm not who Maddie needs me to be, and I don't know if I ever will be. And whether or not she decides my baggage is worth putting up with, she deserves *better*.

She's *always* deserved better.

"Maya said the date went well!" Maddie squeals while she checks her phone.

Clearly, we got two different texts.

"Is that what you're calling tonight?" I tease. "A *date*?"

She gets flustered before she says, "What? No. I mean, I don't know. I can't determine that."

"Sure you do. Does this beat going to the movies or bowling or any other dates you've been on?"

She shakes her head, shifting her eyes up to mine. "I mean, I can't determine that because I've never been on one."

"A movie date, or bowling?"

"Neither. Well, I've been out to eat a few times with guys at school, but those were always with other friends, so it was never just the two of us. And I've been bowling and to the movies before in group settings, but if you mean a date as in a guy formally asking me out, showing up with flowers, and holding the door open for me? Then no."

The word echoes in the silence, but I still can't grasp that she said it. Maddie has never been on a proper date? What the hell is wrong with people? If Maddie and I were strangers and I saw her at a club, or even out at the mall, or *any* public place, really, I'd hit on her in an instant. She's fucking stunning, and I know I'm not the only one to have this opinion since the waiter earlier tonight was seconds away from doing the same.

"Are you serious?" I ask. "What about Michael? He never picked you up or took you anywhere?"

Her nose wrinkles in disgust. "The few times he picked me up, we didn't *go* anywhere. He'd drive to a deserted spot, make conversation, and then try to make a move on me. He was only interested in the one thing I wouldn't give him."

For so long I've carried the burden of acting irrationally by punching that fucker in the face, but I won't be carrying it anymore. Not after hearing that.

What a piece of garbage.

"Is that so hard to believe?" she continues. "That I've never been on a real date?"

"Uh, *yeah*. I assumed guys would kill for the opportunity to take you out."

She tilts her head to the side, studying me. "You think guys haven't tried to ask me out? I get hit on *plenty*, Cameron, but I'm not someone who goes out with the first guy who asks. Maybe I wanted my first real date to be special, and maybe—"

And maybe I waited for you.

I can finish the sentence for her, and before she can make up some lame excuse to cover the almost slipup, I smile down at her and say, "Well, I guess this means I have to take you on a date then, hm?"

"Tonight wasn't a date?" she asks.

I laugh beneath my breath, my eyes locked on hers. "Maddie, when *I* take you out on your first official date, you aren't going to question whether or not it's a date. You'll know."

"How can you be so sure I'll know?"

A smug grin pulls at my lips, and it has Maddie rolling her eyes. "Trust me, baby. *You'll know.*"

Thirty-one

MADDIE

I am going to *kill* my brother.

With every step up this godforsaken trail, my calves and thighs are on fire. My muscles are strained and tired, and my water bottle was empty after the first hour. Ethan thought it would be a good idea to go on the trail my parents took after they raved about the views, and since he's still doing a terrible job at keeping whatever transpired between Maya and him last night a secret, he invited Cameron and me along for the *group* activity.

Shielding my eyes from the beaming sun, I squint uphill and see the beginning of a clearing at the top. My thighs are pulsating from exertion, trembling and cramping as I try to keep up with the rest of them. I wouldn't classify myself as out of shape, but I don't train every day like Cameron, who hasn't even broken a sweat on this stupid hike. Maya with her morning yoga sessions is sticking close to Ethan, who, although he's sweating, isn't nearly as tired as I am.

I despise them all.

My shirt is sticking to my back, which seems at odds given the wind from the canyon. I should be chilly, but instead I'm a panting, disgusting mess.

Fuck it.

Tugging my shirt over my head, I'm in just a sports bra now and a pair of leggings, glaring at the three people a few feet ahead who are handling this hike like it's a walk in the park.

Ethan glances over his shoulder, laughing when he says, "Keep up, Maddie. Maya is making you look bad."

I narrow my eyes at the two lovebirds who are pretending they aren't lovebirds. Although Maya said the date went well, she refuses to give me any details. From the looks of it, my brother seems even more infatuated with her than usual. They're kicking rocks and dust in their trail, which does nothing but coat my skin in a gritty texture.

Cam slows, and while he was calm, cool, and collected before, he now puts his hands on his hips and begins to breathe heavily. "Damn. It's getting to me now."

Liar.

"Don't try to placate me," I seethe.

His voice drops into a whisper when he says, "I love when you use big words on me." Then, when Ethan and Maya are far enough ahead, he adds, "You're really going to wear just a sports bra in front of me?"

"Your—" I lean over to place my hands on my knees. "Your pickup lines aren't going to work on me today, Cam. I'm fucking exhausted, and I'm not in the mood."

When I glance up at the trail ahead again, it only seems to be getting longer. The more I walk, the farther the distance between me and the clearing seems to be.

"Come on," Cam encourages. "You can do this, Mads."

"I really don't think I can," I admit. "I think I'm going to puke."

Ethan and Maya have reached the top now, and Maya squeals, her voice echoing. "Oh my god, it's *so* pretty up here, Maddie! You have to see this!"

A slew of cuss words works their way up my throat, but Cam squats beside me to catch my gaze with his. "Come on," he reassures me in a whisper. "You've got this, baby. Drink some of my water."

He passes his jug over to me, smiling when I chug most of it down.

I can count on one hand the things that would make me keep trying to climb this fucking trail, but Cameron smiling at me like that ranks in at number one. He seems to realize that too.

Pressing the jug back into his chest, I push past the excruciating pain and walk the remaining few feet to the top.

"Yeah!" Cameron claps behind me as he follows, and I roll my eyes, fighting a smile of my own. Even when I'm about to pass out, he can still find a way to make me happy.

Finally, we reach the clearing. There are a few rocks we have to climb over to get there, and Cam's fingers on my sides bring goose bumps to my already fiery skin.

I thought for certain I'd say the hike wasn't worth it, but the breath is knocked from my lungs at the sight before me.

The canyon is laid out before us, and the sky is a beautiful blue, the sun gleaming down on the rocks and river running below. Here, it feels as if I'm *part* of the canyon, not just admiring it. If I felt like I had seen the canyon before, I was wrong. So wrong.

This is a painting come to life.

It almost doesn't seem real.

"Whoa." I breathe out as I scan the view. I'm too busy taking it all in to notice Cameron step beside me. Ethan is busy helping Maya take a picture for her social media, so the brush of Cameron's fingers against mine is intentional.

"I wish Ethan knew," he says, seeming to read my thoughts, "because then I'd be able to kiss you in front of this incredible ass view."

Is he contemplating telling Ethan?

Telling my brother means the possibility of us having to end this for good, and I don't know if either of us wants to take that risk. He could be unhappy about it, and if he tells Cam to break things off, I have no doubts that Cam will. Ethan is like a brother to him, and aside from me, he's been the one constant Cameron's had his entire life. I want to be mad knowing he could choose Ethan over me, but I understand the importance of their friendship, and I could never come between them.

I love Cam so much that I fear I'm losing myself in the process.

My wants and desires have been placed on the back burner since we made things exclusive between us. He told me about his red flags and that he's fearful of following through with this commitment, and yet I'm *clinging* to the fraying rope of potential for dear life regardless of what it'll do to my heart if it breaks.

I chose this, I remind myself.

"Cameron, come take a picture with Ethan!" Maya shouts.

I follow him over and stand beside my best friend while she snaps a few pictures of them. Cameron's arm is slung around Ethan's shoulder, and both of them wear cheesy grins. My eyes travel down Cameron's six-pack and the way sweat is clinging to them, and I inwardly groan.

It should be a *crime* to be that good looking.

"Ooh!" Maya points to a rock with a flat surface. "I want a photo there, Maddie. Be my photographer."

I take her phone and follow her over to the rock while Ethan and Cameron walk to the opposite side of the clearing. It's silent for a moment before I ask, "When are you going to tell me what happened last night with Ethan?"

We huff as we climb over various rocks to get to the one she wants, and when we reach it, I collapse on my back, allowing the sun and wind to steady my breathing. "It's not like I haven't wanted to tell you, Maddie, I just—" She bites on her bottom lip, staring off into the distance. "I told you I didn't want to ruin our friendship, and I don't want things to get weird between us. You're the most important person to me, and I would never let a boy ruin the bond we have. Even if it *is* Ethan."

"Maya." I reach over to grab her hand. "I'm not going to be mad, okay? You told me you were into him, so I've had time to come to terms with it. If something happened between you two then I'm happy for you."

She arches a brow. "Really?"

"Yes. Plus, you've kept my secret with Cam this whole time, so this is my way of repaying you, okay?"

"Deal," she replies with a smile.

"So what happened? Did he kiss you?"

Her grin grows wider. "Remember what you said about not wanting to hear all the details?"

Oh god.

The pieces click together.

"You *more* than kissed."

"Thus the reason I just said the date went well."

The smile on my best friend's face says it all. She's ecstatic to be with Ethan, and why shouldn't *all* of us be happy? If I can accept Ethan and Maya being together, then shouldn't my brother return the favor and allow me to be with Cam?

I'm tired of hiding.

Tired of being secretive.

Even Cam said he wished my brother knew, so maybe getting *their* secret out in the open will allow us to express ours in the near future.

"Ethan!" I shout across the clearing. His head whips around to meet my gaze. "It's about damn time!"

Confusion passes across his features while it looks like Cameron is explaining that I've known something has been going on between him and Maya for a while now.

"You're cool with it?" he shouts back.

I give him a thumbs-up, and the smile he sends me makes the tension in my shoulders lessen bit by bit.

"Finally." Maya sighs. "Now can we take this picture so we can get out of here? I think the hot tub is calling our names."

"Couldn't agree more."

Rising to my feet again, I wince at the soreness and take a step back to find a good angle, but instead I slip and stumble backward. I try to catch myself with my hand, but my ankle twists, and I release a bone-chilling cry when I glance down to see it stuck between two rocks. It slipped between the cracks, and now when I attempt to tug it out, it doesn't budge.

I can't move it.

"Holy *fuck*!" I scream out in pain. Tears stream down my

cheeks and pain lances up my calf and into my knee as Maya sinks beside me to try to help. I can feel my ankle beginning to swell, making it impossible to free it.

"Mads, hold on!" Cam sprints across the clearing, Ethan following close on his heels. No matter how hard I try, the rock won't move, and Maya is trying to reassure me everything will be okay, but I can't hear her. My ears are ringing as panic begins to seep in.

"Hold on," Maya says. "The boys are coming."

Cam reaches me first, falling to his knees to inspect the damage. I can tell he's trying not to seem worried, but it's written all over his face. I'm stuck between two boulders that might as well be larger than Spaceship Earth at Disney World. I don't know how the hell I'm getting out of this.

"I just want it out," I sob. "Fuck. I can't look at it."

"Should I call 9-1-1?" Maya asks.

Ethan nods. "Yeah. Let them know the trail we're on. Tell them we're at the clearing." He helps her down from the rocks before shifting his attention back to me.

The panic becomes so overwhelming that I begin to hyperventilate. No amount of air I drag down seems to be enough. It feels as if my throat is closing, and I'm terrified that I'll never get out of this fucking mess.

What if I lose my foot?

"Mads." Cam's soothing voice brings me back to reality, and when I meet his emerald eyes, I can finally drag in my first breath after a full minute. Worry flickers in his stare, but he's keeping it together for me. "You're going to be okay, all right? I'll make sure of it."

"What if they can't get it out?"

Cam grasps my chin when it begins to tremble, and for a second, all I can focus on is him. "What did I tell you all those years ago?" he asks. "I've got you, Maddie. *Always*."

Now I'm beginning to hyperventilate for a completely different reason. He remembered my bike accident. He remembered that sentiment I've thought about more times than I can count, and now I'm wondering if he's thought about it too.

Another wave of pain breaks through the slight reprieve, and I cry out in agony, gripping my leg while seeing stars.

"Baby, *breathe*."

Two words.

Two words have my cries of agony subsiding and my body locking up not in pain, but in *fear*. Cameron's mouth slams shut, his lips forming a thin line as he realizes what he just said too.

In front of my brother.

"What the hell did you just call her?" Ethan narrows his eyes and glances between us, and finally, after thirty seconds of silence, it clicks. "Mystery Girl is fucking *Maddie*? My little *sister*?"

"Ethan . . ." Cam starts. He gets to his feet, but Ethan shoves him back with his hands. It shouldn't do much considering Cameron has a few inches on him and a *lot* more muscle, but Cameron doesn't try to defend himself either. He takes the shove and allows it to propel him backward.

"You fucking *lied* to me!" Ethan shouts. "When the hell were you going to tell me you were messing around with her? How *dare* you do this to her. You know she's had a crush on you since we were kids. We've *all* known it. Now you're going to break her heart and store it with all the others you've collected? You're no better than Michael!"

This time, when Ethan shoves him again, Cam holds him

back. "I didn't lie to you, Ethan, I just didn't know how to tell you. It started during break, and—"

My brother lands a punch that comes out of nowhere and sends Cam flying to the ground. Blood drips from his nose onto the slab of rock beside me, and I let out another cry of pain that has nothing to do with my ankle and everything to do with the realization that things between us are coming to an end.

"Fitting, isn't it?" Ethan seethes. "You punched Michael for breaking her heart before I could, so now I'm getting a head start before you inevitably do the same."

Wait.

Cameron was the one who punched Michael?

It shouldn't be my main focus. Not when the two boys in front of me are staring each other down like a UFC fight will break out at any minute, so I tuck the thought away and shift my focus to my brother. Ethan isn't going to be okay with this, and I'm done holding on to the possibility that things can still work between us. The timing has never been right, so why would now be any different? When things settle down, when this news of Cameron and me sinks in for Ethan, I highly doubt his opinion will drastically change.

The look of hatred he's giving us says it all.

"I'm not him," Cameron pants. "If you just let me explain—"

"And *you*." Ethan snaps his eyes to mine, seeming oblivious to the fact I'm in no mood to hear a lecture. "This whole time I've been tiptoeing around making a move on Maya because I was so worried about hurting you when the *whole* time you were fucking my best friend. And you didn't have the decency to talk to me about it first?"

Guilt threatens to swallow me whole.

"There's no service!" Maya pants, quickly taking in the scene.

Her eyes dart from Ethan looming over Cam, to the blood on his face. "What the fuck happened?" Then her eyes meet mine, and the expression on my face must give it away.

She inhales deeply before she says, "Okay. Whatever the hell you found out needs to be dealt with later. We need to help Maddie. Maybe you guys can try to move the boulder."

"Move the boulder?" Ethan looks incredulously at her. "How the hell are we supposed to do that?"

"Fucking *try*!" Maya snaps. "She's your sister, Ethan. Pull yourself together."

Everyone is screaming, and a day that started out so good comes crumbling down around me. I can do nothing but listen to the bickering, unable to walk away.

"Just wait." Cam spits blood onto the sand and walks over to the side of the canyon. There's a piece of wood on the ground, likely from another tourist, and he grips it firmly as he walks back over to me. "Okay," he says, wedging it between the rocks. "I'm going to try to—" He grunts and pushes with all his might, and the slight relief it brings makes me sob from the reprieve.

"It's working." I gasp.

"Good." He grunts. "Ethan, help me push it."

"Don't fucking talk to me," Ethan spits icily at Cameron. The pain written across Cam's face makes my heart shatter into tiny pieces, but my brother helps him regardless, and leans into one side of the boulder.

With Ethan pushing and Cameron using the wood for leverage, they free my ankle after three attempts. It hurts even worse now that it's freed and the blood flow returns. I land on my back, staring up into the sky, and stars continue to form from the pulsating pain.

"Holy fuck." I don't need to look at my brother to know he's staring at my ankle, and when I sit up to inspect the damage myself, the bile immediately rises into my throat. There's a golf ball on one side from the swelling, and a deep shade of purple has already formed from the bruising, traveling halfway up my calf.

My chin wobbles again, but before the tears slip out, Cam whisks me into his arms and holds me close to his chest. "We've gotta get you to a hospital," he says.

"Absolutely fucking not," Ethan hisses, but when he tries to tug me out of Cam's grasp, it causes my ankle to hit his arm, and I scream in agony.

When that scream echoes into the canyon, Cameron *explodes*.

"Fuck off!" he shouts, holding me tighter against him. "She needs to go to the fucking emergency room, and you're that worried about the fact we're together? *That* is what you're concerned about? Fuck off, Ethan. We can discuss everything else later when she's safe and under a doctor's care. Get your priorities in fucking line."

With me cradled against his chest, Cameron climbs carefully over the rocks before storming off in the direction of the trail.

"The trail is miles!" I sob. "Cam, you can't carry me all that way."

Pure determination lines his face when his eyes meet mine. "Watch me."

My eyes are stinging from all the crying and my ankle is throbbing, yet all I can think about is the fact that Cameron stood up for me. For *us*. He didn't cower at my brother's blatant denial of this, and my fragile heart can't help but cling to the frayed hope that maybe, just *maybe*, Cameron will choose us in the face of all this chaos.

The urge to know overpowers my pain when I ask, "Are you going to break up with me?"

His lips twitch, threatening a smile. "Jesus, Mads. That is *not* what you should be worrying about."

"Well, are you?" I press.

He sighs, giving a shake of his head. "No, Maddie. I'm not breaking up with you. I think the pain is making you delusional."

I want to laugh but I'm in so much pain that it sounds more like a chortled sob mixed with a laugh.

Cam bends down to kiss my forehead, his steps steady and sure as he forges down the path. "We're going to get you help," he reassures me, glancing over his shoulder for any sign of Ethan or Maya. "Even if I have to carry you to the car by my damn self, I'm going to make sure you're okay."

Even through the pain, I smile faintly against his bare chest because the more feelings develop between us, the more I realize that I might be more important to him than I imagined myself to be. I've spent years thinking Michael got a black eye from my brother, but it was Cameron who defended my honor that day. It was *Cameron* who has always done his best to protect my heart in his own way. And with that knowledge, maybe we'll choose to face this chaos together.

"I know," I reply as I cling to his chest. "You've got me. *Always.*"

Thirty-two

CAMERON

Blinking my eyes open under the harsh fluorescent lights of the hospital room, I shield my face from the brightness, shifting in the uncomfortable chair for the umpteenth time since we arrived.

I carried Maddie for three miles, and because of that, every one of my muscles is in pure agony. With every movement I make, my body barks out in pain. This overexertion won't help with my training, and if my dad finds out, I'll be sure to get an earful.

Not that I care.

Not when Maddie whimpered and cried the entirety of the way back to the car. In those moments, I didn't even feel the strain I was putting on my body. Adrenaline pushed it to the side, and it stayed that way until we got here and the doctors checked her out. She had to get multiple X-rays and imaging scans done, and when she finally got pain medicine and passed out, only *then* did I find the time to close my eyes and fall asleep.

Mud, sweat, and dirt stick to my skin. Thankfully, one of the nurses gave me a hospital gown since I was shirtless on the hike, and now Maddie and I look like a pair in matching outfits. I'd laugh if I wasn't so plagued by exhaustion, concern, and downright panic as I scan the room for Ethan.

There are no signs of anyone else in the room, but I know better than to assume her family isn't nearby. I called Richard and Mary as soon as we made it back to the car, and Ethan and Maya came to the emergency room with us. Ethan didn't speak to me the entire ride, but with the adrenaline coursing through my veins I barely noticed. My only concern was making sure Maddie was okay.

But now, as I watch her sleeping, all the worry I pushed to the side creeps back in. Ethan found out about us, and he definitely wasn't understanding or happy like I hoped he would be. Instead, he was everything I feared, and now I'm terrified I'll have to make a choice between my best friend and the girl who is slowly but surely bringing me back to life.

I always thought if it came to this that I'd know who I'd choose. I would never choose a girl over my friendship with Ethan, but now . . .

I can't imagine giving her up. I don't even want to think about how lonely I'd be without her friendship and these intimate moments with her. She makes me a better person. She makes me want to believe I'm not the emotionless robot I think I am.

How am I supposed to let her go when I just got her back?

The curtain opens, pulling me from my thoughts, and Mary and Richard are standing there, each holding coffee cups. Mary holds an extra cup out to me, her eyes red rimmed and puffy from crying. "Figured you could use the caffeine," she whispers.

Do they know?

Did Ethan tell them?

I want to ask, but given the events of today, I think better of it and bite my tongue. "Thank you," I reply, gratefully taking the cup. "Did she wake up while I was out?"

"No," Richard says. "She's been out like a light from those pain meds."

Mary places a hand over her heart, stifling a sob. "Thank you, Cameron. It could have been so much worse if you hadn't carried her all that way. Ethan told us the details earlier, and I can't imagine—" She sniffles, and Richard places his free hand on her lower back. "I can't imagine how much effort that took, but just know we are *so* grateful."

Richard nods in agreement. "And happy for you both."

My brows fly to my hairline. "About what?"

"Don't act naive," Mary says with a watery smile. "Ethan may be upset, but that doesn't mean *we* have to be. I've always known there was something between you two."

"You're not mad?"

Richard scoffs. "How can I be mad when you just carried her three *miles* to ensure she was okay? You're already doing pretty damn well in my book."

"You've always been a son to me," Mary adds, tears in her eyes. "I couldn't have chosen anyone better for her myself."

What are the odds that Maddie's parents accepted us against Ethan's opinion? Then again, I didn't attempt to hide this from his parents the same way I did to him. He knew there was a mystery girl, and rather than being up front and honest about it, I schemed my way around it. He has every right to be upset.

"That means a lot. I hope I don't let you guys down."

"You won't," Mary reassures me. "You never could."

My eyes are burning when I look away from them and into

the hallway, where Ethan is sitting on the floor with his legs stretched out in front of him. Maya is beside him, attempting to calm the anger that's still written on his face, but it doesn't seem to be doing any good. His arms are crossed tightly over his chest and his jaw is set in a firm line. Dirt smears his cheek, and the hair on the top of his head is disheveled. It wasn't *only* me walking as fast as possible to the car, so I know they're both exhausted too.

"He'll come around," Mary says, following my gaze.

As if he can sense us speaking about him, Ethan's head lifts then his eyes meet mine, nothing but betrayal and fury staring back at me.

"I'm gonna go talk to him." I rise to my feet, and Mary squeezes me tightly while Richard claps me on the back. "Wish me luck."

"You won't need it. We're going to grab some dinner, but we wanted to stop by and drop off the coffee. Do you want us to bring you back anything to eat?"

"No, that's all right. I'll wait for Maddie to wake up and probably order something with her."

After another crushing hug from Mary, I abandon my coffee cup on the makeshift desk in the room and step into the hallway. Maya takes the hint at the tense expression on my face and heads back into the room with Maddie, giving me a pat of encouragement before pulling the curtain closed behind her.

"Can I sit?"

He scoffs. "Oh, you're asking me for approval *now*?"

"Ethan, come on." I sigh and slide down the wall to sit beside him, resting my head and turning to look at him. "I didn't tell you because I was scared of this exact reaction from you."

"Then why do it at all?" he shoots back.

"Are you really going to pretend you didn't realize I had a crush on her too? It's been obvious to everyone around us, including your parents, and they seem to be just fine with us dating."

"Because they don't *know* you, Cameron. The *real* you. You put on an act in front of them, but me? I witnessed firsthand the guy you became in high school. You've done nothing but fuck everything in sight with no regard for those girls' feelings. And I get it, you're emotionally scarred and have this fear of commitment, but I wouldn't be a good brother if I said I was happy you're messing around with my sister. Her definition of a crush and *your* definition of a crush mean two very different things."

"And you're any better?" Twisting to face him fully, I can feel my anger burning beneath the surface. "We're the same people, Ethan. We both fucked around in high school and broke girls' hearts, and you're screwing around with Maya now. How is this any different? Don't act like you're a saint when we *both*—"

"I haven't." Ethan cuts me off, silencing my words before they leave my mouth. The sound of monitors beeping and nurses chatting at the station nearby fill the silence before he takes a deep breath and says, "I haven't fucked. I'm a virgin. Well, I *was* until last night."

A virgin.

No matter how many times I mentally repeat his words, they don't sink in.

How the hell can he be a *virgin*? I mean, he never went into details with me about the girls he claimed to sleep with, but I always assumed that was because he was uncomfortable speaking about it. I never thought he was lying to me.

Slowly, the sense of betrayal hits me too.

"I never told you because I felt like if I did, you wouldn't want to be my friend anymore. That sounds stupid when I say it, but you were *so* different after your mom died, Cameron. We went from playing video games to you wanting to party and fuck every weekend, and I went along with it because I thought it was part of your healing process. But as time went on, you stayed the same, and telling you the truth became more intimidating."

"*Why?* What did you think was going to happen? You thought I'd make fun of you or something?"

"No, I thought you wouldn't want to be my friend anymore. If you knew I didn't like partying and fucking I was afraid you'd become more distant, and I didn't want to lose you."

"Ethan." I shake my head, trying to come up with words but finding myself short. What am I supposed to say to that? The guilt and shame I've been carrying nearly doubles in size at the thought of disappointing yet another person in my life. How could he not feel comfortable enough to tell me that? Have I really changed to the point he thought I'd push him out of my life because he was a virgin?

"I'm sorry," I admit, clearing my throat. "You've been such a good friend to me, Ethan, and I've been shit in return. I knew something was up with you, but I was selfish."

"No, you weren't selfish. You were dealing with losing your mom, and I understood that."

"Then why didn't you find new friends? I wouldn't have expected you to put up with me. If you had explained, I might have tried to change, or—"

"You're my brother." He levels me with a look that makes a lump form in my throat. "No matter what happens, I'm with you, and if that means pretending to enjoy partying and creating imaginary girls to sleep with, I'd do it all again so you weren't alone, because I know you'd do the same for me."

"Fuck, man." I swipe at a tear that's escaped. "Of course I'd do the same for you, I'm just sorry it's taken me so long to notice and get my head out of my ass. I'm going to be a better friend, though. I promise you."

He sighs, resting his head against the wall. "That's the thing. What I started with Maya? She's it for me. I've been sure about her for a long time, but I was too scared to make a move because I didn't think she'd be comfortable with the virginity thing. I'm happy to say I was wrong, but can you honestly say you're certain about my sister? Can you promise me you won't hurt her? I can't stand by and let you play with her feelings like you have with all the rest. While I understand *why* you look for girls to use as an outlet, I'm not going to allow my sister to get her heart broken. We watched her go through that once already with Michael, and I'm not going to stand by only for it to happen again."

"And I'd be lying to you if I told you with absolute certainty that I won't hurt her. I'm fucked-up in a lot of ways, and you know it, but Maddie knows it, too, and I was honest with her from the very beginning about taking things slow between us. She's been patient with me. If you're looking for a definitive answer, I can't give it, but one thing I can promise you? I'm trying my fucking hardest to be the guy she deserves, and she's nothing like the rest. Not even close."

"And if things don't work out?" he asks. "What does that mean for us?"

"Nothing will change. Maddie knows how important our friendship is. She and I already had a falling out once, and were things a bit awkward? Sure, but you and I were still friends, right?"

"Do I even want to *know* why you guys stopped speaking for years?"

Telling him I gaslit Maddie and kicked her out of my house the day after my mom passed wouldn't bode well for me, and I don't think admitting we had snuck out during their family trip to Myrtle Beach would bode well for me either. While I fully intend on telling him the truth someday, this isn't the right time.

"Probably not," I admit. "But the important thing is that she and I are working through it, and it'll be a hell of a lot easier if we have your blessing."

I hold my breath as he contemplates, blinking at nothing until he finally closes his eyes and releases a heavy sigh. "*Please* don't make me regret this, but fine. I won't stand in your way. Just be cautious, Cameron. She loves hard, and she's a girl you don't want to fuck up with."

"Trust me, I'm aware." Getting back on my feet, I extend a hand to help him up, relief blossoming in my chest. Her entire family is accepting of us now.

No more secrets.

No more hiding.

"Sorry about punching you," he adds.

I shrug. "I deserved it. Sleeping with your little sister is a good reason."

"For fuck's sake," he groans. "Did you have to remind me?" When he pushes the curtain open again, Maddie is sitting up analyzing the walking boot covering her foot, and as soon as she hears her brother's voice, her eyes dart between us, noticing the smiles on both of our faces.

I give her a subtle nod that everything is worked out, and the grin she sends me in return tells me she's loopy from the medicine but fucking adorable all the same. It makes me want to do everything in my power to keep it there.

"How are you feeling?" I ask, easing into the chair beside her. My body screams in protest, and right now the only thing I want to do is step into a hot shower or bask in the hot tub for the rest of the night.

"Better." She frowns, reaching over to rub my nose. "You're bruised and swollen. Why haven't you put any ice on it?"

"You can't seriously be worried about *me*," I deadpan, sending a pointed look to her walking boot. "I'll be fine, Mads. I've taken a hit to the face a lot, given my profession."

She glares at her brother. "You're still an idiot for doing that in the first place."

"I was looking out for you," he replies.

"Well, you're doing a shitty job at it."

Maya rises to her feet, smiling tightly at Ethan. "How about we go grab some food? We can meet your parents down in the cafeteria."

"Fine," he says after a second. The tension between Ethan and me seems to have transferred to him and his sister. "We'll be back in an hour or so."

When the curtain shuts behind them, leaving us alone, I scoot my chair closer and brush a stray curl away from her face. "You scared the hell out of me today."

"Trust me, I scared *myself* enough for the both of us. I don't think I'll ever climb rocks again." Fussing with the edge of the sheet on top of her, she adds, "Ethan is really okay with this?"

"I wouldn't say he's thrilled about it, but he's trying to understand it, and that's better than nothing. We won't have to hide anymore, which is a relief in itself."

"Except if your dad finds out," she says pointedly.

I scoff. "Trust me, he's not coming back until Christmas. This last visit was a spur of the moment type of the thing—something he doesn't do often."

"Hmm," she hums, sinking back into the pillows. That same loopy smile falls onto her face before she says, "No hiding, huh? I wonder what that'll be like."

"Well, for starters . . ." Leaning up to press my lips against hers, I kiss her deeply, and after everything that's happened today, it's exactly what I need. Kissing Maddie grounds me. It brings me to a state of relaxation that no elixir could provide. "I can kiss you without fear of someone walking in on us, so that's nice."

She giggles, bringing her hands up to run through my curls. "Has anyone ever mentioned that you're *insanely* hot?"

I arch a brow. "Do you want the truth?"

"No," she hums happily. "Lie to me."

I kiss her cheek, then her forehead. "Then you're the only one who's ever said I'm insanely hot."

"Okay, the lie didn't make me feel any better." She pouts, frowning at the thought. "Now all I'm thinking of are the numerous girls who've probably called you hot."

"Want to know the truth, then?"

"Fine," she groans. "Let me hear the damage. How many?"

My mother raised me not to be an idiot when it comes to girls. I'm in no way, shape, or form going to tell her how many of them I've heard call me hot. Honestly, I wouldn't be able to count the actual number, as bad as that sounds. I don't want to be cocky, but a *lot* of girls have said I'm hot.

I lock eyes with her, swallowing thickly as the emotions from the day catch up to me. She got hurt today, and those screams . . . I didn't realize how important she was to me until that moment. My body kicked into overdrive, desperate to save her. Hell, I carried her three *miles* back to the car. As much as I want to say I'm not emotionally ready, my actions are telling me otherwise.

Just take the leap.

Fucking tell her.

But looking into her eyes, I'm reminded of my conversation with Ethan and how I can't be certain that I won't hurt her. I don't know if I'm ready to say those three words because of the value they hold, but is *anyone* ever ready to say them?

My emotions may still be on the fence, but I can at least give her one truth that I'm more than confident in.

I hover my lips above hers with that seductive grin she loves so much. "The truth is, plenty of girls have called me hot, Maddie, but you're the only one I've ever wanted to hear it from."

Thirty-three

CAMERON

When I show up on Maddie's doorstep with a dozen roses clutched in my hands, I'm more nervous than I thought I'd be. Dates have always been an obstacle to get to the end goal for me. I never cared about them or took them seriously, but everything with Maddie is different. She's someone I genuinely want to impress, and for her first real date, I don't want to disappoint.

Ethan opens the door, eyeing my button-down shirt and jeans before cracking a grin. "You look like a sap," he says. "I never thought I'd see the day where Cameron *Holden* looks like a love-stricken fool, but here we are."

"Shut up," I grumble. "Did you do what I asked?"

He nods. "She's almost finished getting ready. Although you owe me. She's been giving me the cold shoulder since we got back from the Grand Canyon."

"Maybe you shouldn't have punched me, then," I reply with a teasing grin of my own. "Are you going to let me inside, or . . ."

He leans against the doorway, blocking the entry. "I don't

know, I think I'm going to have a little fun with this. Shouldn't I be interrogating you?"

"Isn't that your *father's* job?"

He stares at his fingernails like he couldn't be more bored. "I'm just as much of her protector as he is, no? What are your intentions with her tonight? Will you be back at a reasonable hour?"

"I am two seconds away from—"

Maddie walks into the foyer behind him, and when she sees me, her eyes grow wide. "*Cameron?* What are you doing here?"

Words fail me as I take her in, and now I'm beginning to wonder if it's my first date or hers. A flirty pink dress flows around her curves, a deep cut with ruffles around the edges outlining her breasts. Her lipstick matches her dress, and her curls are in perfect ringlets, but the best part of her ensemble is the locket my mother gave her. Maddie said she only wore it for special occasions, and I can't help but wonder if she subconsciously knew tonight would be important.

I've never seen someone more beautiful.

But I have to pull myself together and say *something* so I don't embarrass myself entirely. I want to take her on the best damn date she'll ever have.

As I extend the flowers to her, Ethan finally moves out of the way. "These are for you."

"We—" She furrows her brows before she glances at her brother. "I thought Mom wanted to take us out to dinner one last time before I go back to school?"

He shrugs as he heads for the stairs and tosses over his shoulder, "I lied! Have her back by ten!"

"Fuck off!" I shout.

When we're finally alone, Maddie takes in what's happening, her cheeks turning a bright pink. "I didn't realize you had plans for us. I would have worn something different."

"What you're wearing is perfect."

"Really?" She frowns at her feet, the walking boot sticking out like a sore thumb. "I can't wear heels with this thing."

"Good thing you don't need them, then. Do you have everything you need?"

"Yeah, I think so. I just need my—"

"Wait, wait!" Mary bustles around the corner, her phone in her hand with the camera already open. "I need a picture first!"

If Maddie's cheeks were pink before, they're bright red now. "*Mom.* Are you kidding me? This isn't prom, for crying out loud! It's a date."

"All the more reason for a picture! It'll just take a second. Here, get together." She lines up her camera, huffing with annoyance. "Maddie, at least put a smile on your face."

I bend down to her ear to whisper, "It's fine, Mads." And it really is. In fact, it feels nice having a parent be an actual parent and want to capture an important moment. If my mom were still alive, she'd be right next to Mary, snapping pictures of her own. She had a passion for taking photos, and a part of me wonders if Mary is doing this for me rather than for her daughter.

My hand lands on Maddie's waist, and after we take a few cute and silly ones, Mary swipes at her eyes, tucking the phone back into her pocket. "Here." Mary slides a purse off her shoulder. "I figured you'd need it, and I'll put those flowers in a vase for you."

"Thanks, Mary." I lean over to press a kiss to her cheek. "We'll be back later tonight."

Back on the porch, I help Maddie down the steps and lead her over to my car. Before she can touch the handle, I beat her to it and hold the door open. I've done this for her even when we weren't speaking for years. It's the gentlemanly thing to do, but now that we're together it seems to have a different meaning.

She smiles softly, guiding my head down to press her lips against mine. I'm fucking addicted to the way she tastes. It consumes my mind. It's *all* I can think about, and—

I break away from the kiss, earning a scowl in return.

"Why'd you stop?"

Taking a step closer, I press her against the door. Her lips are pink and swollen, and I probably have lipstick smeared on mine, but I don't care. She looks too tempting, and if I stare at her another second longer, I'm going to lose all self-control. "I'm almost certain your mom is watching out the window, and if I keep kissing you, I'll have a full-blown erection."

"Oh," she breathes. "Right."

"Yeah. *Right.*" I open the door wider for her, watching as she slips into the seat.

"So, where are we going?" she asks. "Bowling? Movies?"

Leaning against the door, I roll my eyes and say, "I'm almost offended you think I'd plan something so lame for your first real date, baby. Have *patience.* We'll be there soon enough."

>> <<

"Cameron. Are you kidding me?" Maddie glances out the windshield, seemingly speechless. I put the car in Park in the gravel parking lot, following her open-mouthed stare to the large hot air balloon sitting on the empty field. The sun is just beginning to set, and in ten minutes we should be up in the air. "How the hell did you afford this?"

"It doesn't matter. I wanted tonight to be special, so I'm making it happen."

My dad gave me a credit card for emergency purposes, and although this probably isn't classified as an emergency, I'll find a way to explain it to him should he catch the charge.

"This is—" She shakes her head in disbelief.

"We enjoyed the view of the canyon, so I figured this would be even better. We can see practically all of Arizona in this." She still isn't saying anything, and suddenly, I begin to panic. I know Maddie like the back of my hand, and she never said anything growing up about having a fear of heights, but maybe she does. Maybe I got this all wrong.

"If you don't want to, we don't—"

"Are you kidding? This is the coolest thing anyone has ever done for me. I *love* it, Cam."

"You do?"

I don't know why I'm surprised considering I could take Maddie to the park for a damn ice cream and she'd be overjoyed. She doesn't ask for much, and it's the little things that matter to her, but it's for that reason that she deserves the fucking world.

"Yes!" she squeals with excitement. The passenger door swings open, and it's comical since she can't move as fast as she wants to with the walking boot. She shuffles out of the car, tapping her free foot impatiently.

Hand in hand we head over to our pilot, and I help lift Maddie into the gondola then climb in beside her. We listen to the safety basics before the burners come to life, and since this is a private ride, we have a decent amount of space between us and the pilot when we lift off the ground. Maddie gasps, and I assume it's because of the foreign feeling, but she's pointing to a basket on the bottom of the gondola, holding two flutes and a bottle of champagne.

"You really thought of everything," she muses. Then, when her voice drops lower, she adds, "You know I can't drink yet, right?"

I raise my eyebrows in challenge. "I won't tell if you won't."

Breaking the rules has never been something she's comfortable with, but doing so with me seems to make her giddy with adrenaline. She bites on her lower lip and gives a subtle nod, and as we rise farther off the ground, I pour two glasses and hand one to her.

"I expected it to be loud," she whispers, staring at the ground disappearing below us, "but it's quiet. *Peaceful*, even."

I step up behind her and wrap my arms around her waist, bending down to place my head on top of hers. From up here the world seems so large and full of opportunities. It's *mine* for the taking, and yet I still don't feel like it's completely mine. Things worked out with Maddie, but my life has been planned out since I was a kid. Arizona is my dad's favorite team, so I've been pushed to get drafted by them. What if I don't want to live in Arizona, though? What if I'm like my mom and want to live near fresh grass or even the ocean? I've allowed myself to follow my dad's wishes because if I couldn't make my mom's dreams come true, at least I could make *his* come true.

"Do you like Arizona?" I find myself asking her.

She takes a few seconds to admire the insanely gorgeous view and says, "Up here? Yes. When we're at the Grand Canyon? Yes. The landscape here can be stunning, but I like it in Connecticut more. It's beautiful when it snows, and my school is close to the water too."

"Would you want to live there someday?"

She twists in my arms to face me, the gentle breeze from the burners keeping us warm. "Maybe. I haven't really thought that far ahead yet. Why do you ask?"

"I think it's important to know considering we're in a relationship now, right?"

She tilts her head to the side. "Would my opinion change anything? You've been planning to get drafted by Arizona since high school."

I wouldn't have asked the question if her opinion didn't matter. Maddie being my girlfriend feels like a dream that's too good to be true. I never imagined we'd get *here*—flying in a hot air balloon and speaking about the future—but as our relationship continues to develop, I've come to the realization that I can't see myself playing for Arizona if she's not next to me. I've spent years without her, and the misery that caused is a feeling I never want to experience again.

Knowing where she wants to live one day is going to be a huge factor, and for the first time, it's one that could sway my decision.

"Your opinion would change everything," I tell her firmly.

Fears of this going too fast race through my mind, but Maddie was mine long before I made the first move in the closet. We've known each other since we were kids, and our feelings developed slowly over time. Now that those feelings are finally out in the open after years of keeping them locked away, I want it all with her.

I just need to get the courage to tell her I'm in love with her.

I need to have better self-esteem and *believe* I can be the guy to provide her with everything she'll ever need.

"I wouldn't want to live in Arizona," she says, "but if you were signed to them, I'd manage to find a way to make it work."

"Manage it how?"

"Well, just like we'll have to manage in a few days when we go back to school. I'll drive to you some weekends, or you'll drive to me when you're free. If you're drafted to Arizona, I'll find the time to break away from school and fly out for your games and stay for breaks or any free time I have."

Right. Because Maddie is studying to become a doctor, which requires a hell of a lot more schooling than a degree in physical education.

"And when you're done with school?"

She laughs. "This is a deep conversation for wanting to take things *slow*." Then, after a beat she adds, "When I'm done with school, I suppose where I end up will be determined by my relationship status at the time. Who knows who I'll be with at that point?"

I narrow my eyes while she attempts to hide a smile. "Was that supposed to be a joke? If so, it was a cruel one."

"I'm not trying to be cruel! I guess I'm just surprised you're thinking that far ahead. You aren't the type to get serious with anyone."

"Didn't I say before you weren't like the others? I *want* a future with you, Maddie, I'm just afraid I won't be able to give you what you want out of life. I don't want to let you down and fuck this up."

The wind blows a few strands of hair in her face, so I gently push them behind her ear at the same time she reaches up to cup my cheek. "You're *always* going to be enough for me, even at your lowest, Cameron."

I can't breathe as she holds my gaze, and I have to bite down on my tongue with so much force to stop myself from saying I love her. Withholding it feels more and more futile when my actions speak differently, but until I can find the strength to get out from beneath my father's thumb and become an independent person capable of providing her with the world, I refuse to admit it. I'm terrified of fucking things up. Terrified of commitment. Terrified of what's growing between us and being unable to stop myself from falling head over heels for her.

But despite the fear, I've waited my entire life for this opportunity, and if I continue to push through all this uncertainty, I'll have to reach the better side eventually, *right*?

Clearing my throat of the emotion clogging it, I reach down to grab the champagne and top off our glasses. "What should we toast to?"

She hums appreciatively, bringing the glass inches from her lips. "The future."

"I like that," I say, clinking my glass against hers. "To the future, baby."

>> <<

Now that we've rekindled our friendship and started a relationship as adults, I'm learning new things about Maddie the more time we spend together. She enjoys reality television now, and the books she reads have become far more scandalous than the ones she read in middle school.

And now, as she erupts into a fit of giggles walking back to the car, I've discovered she's a lightweight.

"Careful." I bite back a laugh when she stumbles in the gravel, but it quickly subsides when she presses me up against the side of the car, her hands landing on my chest. "You okay?"

"More than okay," she says, working at the buttons of my shirt. It's pitch black outside now, and with the pilot already gone for the night, we're alone in the middle of a field with not a soul around us for miles.

My cock thickens at the possibilities.

"Mads," I warn when her nails drag down my abs. "If you keep doing that I'll—"

"Give me what I want?" she teases. "I don't see anyone else out here, do you? There's a perfectly suitable car behind you, and I fully intend to make good use of it."

Fucking hell.

I'm opening the door of the backseat before I can think twice about it. The possibility of getting caught and having the cops called on us should make me take a pause to consider the consequences, but I'll accept *any* consequences that follow if it means I'll be able to fool around in the backseat with her.

"You're so fucking hot," she groans, as if it's painful, shoving me down. After only two small glasses of champagne, there's no way she's drunk. Tipsy maybe, but not drunk. I can't tell if her confidence is from the small bit of alcohol or becoming more comfortable with this and doing it with me.

I sincerely hope it's the latter.

Even lying across the backseat, my legs still can't be stretched out the entire way. I keep both legs bent with one foot on the floor, allowing her to straddle my thighs. Her hands find the buckle of my belt, desperately trying to undo it.

"I want you," she pants. "So badly."

"You have me," I reassure her. "All of me."

Her eyes briefly flick to mine at the admission, but she's too wrapped up in lust to process it, and so am I. I lift up my hips to drag my pants and briefs down, springing myself free, and just as I'm about to push *her* onto her back, she surprises me and flings her underwear to the front seat before grabbing my cock with greedy fingers.

"I want to try this," she whispers shakily, lining herself up with my cock.

"Wait," I blurt, cursing myself for stopping this. "Condom. Fuck. Please grab it before I change my mind. Jeans pocket."

She giggles, the sound making me even harder. "You brought one?"

"I'm learning to take one everywhere with me when it comes to you."

She finds it and passes it over, and when I'm finally protected, she lines herself up again. "If I'm bad at it, then—"

"There's no possible way you could be bad at this. Trust me." Not when it's her. Not when I've been fantasizing about her riding me since freshman year. This is new for her, and I have to keep reminding my dick of that when its only urge is to slam into her and fuck her senseless.

So I tamp down those urges and allow her to touch me wherever she pleases. I let her explore those lines between my abs she loves so much, tentatively pressing my crown into her wet heat. It's fucking torture slowly sliding against her walls. I'm stretching and filling her, cursing while she learns what she likes.

Slow circles, back and forth, side to side . . . her hips find what suits them best, and finally, when she's fully seated on my cock, she tips her head back with her jaw falling open.

"*Cam*," she whimpers.

"Fuck me." I brace myself when she picks up speed, feeling my balls draw up tight at the sight. With her hands supporting her weight on my chest, her breasts are right in front of me, and I can't help myself when I force her dress down to let them fall exactly where I want them to.

My tongue darts out to lick her nipple, and she cries out in bliss before riding me harder. Her ass is smacking against my thighs, the car windows beginning to fog out around us, and I swear, I've only got about ten seconds in me before I fill up this condom to the fucking rim.

"It feels so good," she moans. "I don't know how to—"

"It's okay," I soothe her. "Fuck me, baby. Let yourself feel all of it. Take me."

Then I cautiously lift my hips to give her more, and the sound she makes nearly tips me over the edge.

"So good," I praise her, swiping my fingers against her clit. "You ride it so fucking good. Look at you."

"*Cam*, I—"

Her pussy clenches around me before the scream flies out of her, and I'm damn sure relieved no one is around us for miles, because if they were, I have no doubts they would hear her.

I pound into her in frenzied, erratic thrusts. Sweat forms on my brow as I admire her postorgasmic smile while she rides out her high. Her nipples are erect, goose bumps pebble her skin, and her nails are digging into my chest when I find release, moaning her name like a curse and a blessing wrapped into one.

I've been uncertain about a lot of things in my life, but Maddie Davis has never been one of them. Ethan asked me the other night at the hospital if I was sure about her the same way he was about Maya, and at the time, I didn't know how to answer it because I was scared of making a promise to him that I couldn't keep.

But right now? As she collapses on my chest and my face is muffled by her curls?

She's it for me, and there isn't another girl in this entire world who could ever take her place.

Thirty-four

CAMERON

Thirty minutes is all it takes for my night to go from fantastic to shitty.

As soon as I pull into the driveway after a night I'll never forget with Maddie, I feel the buzzing in my pocket. The negative energy seems to ooze from my phone before I even check the contact, and sure enough, my father's face appears on the screen.

With an elaborate sigh, I swipe to answer, my keys jingling in the background. "Hello?"

"What the hell has gotten into you, Cameron?" The tone of his voice makes me pause halfway to the front door. I've heard him angry with me plenty of times, but I've always been able to appease him somehow. This time, though, I have a strong suspicion that won't be the case. "A credit card charge for *five hundred* dollars? I don't know what to do with you anymore!"

"I'll pay it off myself," I reply. "You don't have to worry about it."

"And how are you planning to do that with football? I thought we agreed that this card would only be used for *emergencies*."

"We did."

"And a fucking *hot air balloon* ride was an emergency? For fuck's sake, son. I'm going to ask this one time and one time only. Are you still seeing Maddie? Is she the reason for the charge?"

I bite down on my tongue when the urge to let it all out in the open overwhelms me. Everyone knows, so what's the point in hiding it? I don't care if my dad disapproves. I'm a grown adult capable of making my own decisions. He doesn't get to dictate whether or not I date someone.

I'm tired of trying to make everyone happy but me.

"I took her out," I reply, fumbling with the keys to unlock the door. All the lights are off when I step inside, a blaring reminder of how alone I am physically *and* emotionally. "We're dating, and we're happy. She's more than just another girl to me, and—"

He cuts me off, his words as sharp as a knife. "We talked about this. You don't need distractions. You're so close to getting everything you've ever worked for, and now you're going to risk messing that up for her? Wait a few years when you're established and drafted. You can't handle a girl and football at the same time. Not when you both live so far away from one another."

"And you know that how?" He hardly knows me. Aside from memorizing my exercise routine so I can be fit enough and have the endurance for football, he knows nothing about what I'm capable of handling anymore. Truthfully, he'd be shocked to know just how much I can carry on my shoulders.

"You're not ready for a relationship," he continues, ignoring my question. "We've worked too hard for this moment, and I'm not going to sit by and let a girl get in the way of it."

"How has Maddie gotten in the way of *anything*?" I explode. "I'm still working out. I'm still eating healthy. I'm still doing everything my trainer has instructed. Nothing has changed."

"But hasn't it? Your workout routine used to be in the morning, not at night, and all these charges for McDonald's, pizza, and other junk food certainly wouldn't be there if you weren't with her. Whether you see it or not, she's messing up the balance, and you can't afford it."

"How would you know anything—you aren't even *here*?"

"I saw enough when I stopped by last week, and it's not going to continue."

Letting out a laugh of disbelief, I let my duffel bag drop to the floor. "Who I'm in a relationship with is none of your business, Dad. You can't tell me who I can or can't date."

"I can if I'm paying for your tuition."

My knuckles turn white around the phone. I'm staring into nothing but darkness as I let the threat sink in. My own father, the one who introduced me to my love of football in the first place, the man who used to be everything I looked up to and more is now *threatening* to pull my tuition if I continue this relationship.

"You can't—"

"I can, and I will. Since the day you made the team your freshman year of high school, your dream has been to make your mother proud and get drafted to the NFL. Your mind is clouded by the potential of what could be with Maddie, and even though you can't see it now, this is in your best interest."

My chest is heaving, heart racing, and I'm two seconds away from chucking this phone at the goddamn wall. There is no way in hell this is happening. Maddie and I have overcome *so* much in just a short amount of time, and it's all going to come down to *this*? To my dad controlling my life?

I want to tell him maybe my dreams have shifted. It's not that football isn't still one of them, but Maddie and building a life with her is a dream too. There has to be a way to have both. It can't be all or nothing.

But I do want to make him proud, and I want to make my mother proud too. My heart is being ripped in half, and when it splits, I unfortunately know which path I'll choose. If my dad were to pull my tuition, I'd have no chance at making it on my own. I'd have to work three jobs to keep up, and if I had to keep up training and football too? It would be impossible.

"I know you're upset now, and that's fine, but someday when you have kids of your own, you'll understand. You'd do anything to see them succeed, and I haven't busted my ass for fifteen years to be able to put you through school for it to come crumbling down because of Maddie. You've both waited this long. A few more years won't hurt."

"And you realize making me choose between the two means I'll never forgive you?"

It's silent for a few seconds before he says, "As I said, this is for the best, whether you understand it now or not. I mean it, Cameron. Break it off with her or your tuition is pulled. And don't think I won't be able to tell. I track your cards, and I'm not afraid to check your messages and calls too. Whatever's going on between you both? It's over."

My molars are clamped down so tightly I fear I might chip one. Who was I to ever think I could be the guy Maddie deserves? The right guy would tell his father to fuck off. The right guy wouldn't even contemplate giving her up. But the right guy also wouldn't have emotional trauma to unpack. The right guy wouldn't have a desperation to please his father because deep down, he knows he's grieving too.

I was never the guy for her, and I'll never be worthy of her.

Maddie is an angel, and I'll always be a sinner trying to steal her light.

She deserves someone better.

"Understood." The word tastes like acid on my tongue but I force it out regardless, letting the loneliness and regret eat away at me as the silence grows over the phone. I haven't even told her yet, and I know without a shadow of a doubt I'll be haunted by her sobs just as I was when she left my living room after my mother's death.

All I do is disappoint others, so I don't know why I'm surprised. I warned Maddie for this exact reason that I'm not capable of being in a relationship, and although I'm strong physically, I'm weak as hell when it comes to my emotions. I don't understand them. After losing my mom, feelings became foreign, and dealing with them was a whole other story. I don't know how to process the betrayal from my father, and the heartbreak of the impending doom with Maddie hasn't sunk in yet.

As always, my first instinct is to run.

Leave before they get a chance to hurt me first.

Disappoint them so I won't have the pressure to live up to someone I can't be.

"I'll see if I can find a break in my schedule to fly out before you leave for school on Monday," he starts. "We can go over the routine and adjust it again, and maybe—"

"Don't bother," I reply, my voice void and lifeless. It's robotic, the same tone I carried after losing my mother. "I don't want you here."

"*Cameron.*" If I didn't know better, I'd almost think he sounded hurt. "I know you're upset, but—"

Ending the call, I sit numbly on the couch. Ironically, it's the same couch Maddie walked away from bawling her eyes out, and the irony doesn't escape me.

The one person I need guidance from isn't here. I'm a lost soul with nowhere to go, no one to direct me which path to choose, and I'm *alone*.

An hour ago I was on top of the world, but now, I let the darkness swallow me whole with the knowledge that tomorrow I'm losing the dream I didn't even realize mattered most until tonight.

Thirty-five

MADDIE

I should be packing considering I leave for school tomorrow, but instead all I can think about is the anticipation of how Cameron and I will celebrate our last day together.

My suitcase is open and empty on top of my comforter, stacks of clean clothes scattered around the floor, but I can't focus on packing when my mind keeps replaying last night.

I still can't believe Cameron rented a hot air balloon and we sipped champagne while flying over what felt like the entirety of Arizona. Those types of dates are only written about in books or shown in a major film. I never thought one would happen to *me*.

When we started fooling around two weeks ago I was hesitant to give my all to him when I wasn't sure if he would be able to fully commit, but last night erased all those doubts. He's in this. *Fully*. He wouldn't have brought up a future together if he wasn't planning on this working out between us, so there's no more holding back. I'll wait for him until he's ready to say he loves me, because he's worth it.

"Maddie! Cameron's here!" my mom shouts from downstairs.

It's embarrassing how quickly I make it to the front door. I'm a ball of energy, and Cameron is the only person who can wind me down. I want to fling myself into his arms, kiss him senseless, and—

I skid to a halt as soon as my gaze meets his.

Bags line his bloodshot eyes, and his hands are stuffed in the pockets of his shorts. From his demeanor, I can tell he hasn't slept, and for the life of me, I can't figure out why.

Our date last night was incredible.

"I'll be in the kitchen," my mom says, worry lining her features before she disappears down the hallway.

Cameron shifts his weight, clearing his throat before he asks, "Can we talk?"

The three words no one ever wants to hear leave me utterly in denial.

I'm not naive enough to assume this will be a good conversation. *Can we talk* is code for *I'm breaking up with you*, but I refuse to accept that. We both had an amazing time last night, didn't we? Or was it all in my head?

Numbly, I follow him out to the driveway where his car is parked. He leans against the hood, so I follow suit and do the same beside him. Silence stretches for what seems like an eternity, but I can't think of any words to break it. I don't want to listen to whatever he has to say. I don't want to stand here and feel my heart shatter into a million pieces *again*.

"My dad called last night," he says, cutting right to the chase. "He threatened to pull my tuition if I don't end things between us."

I glance up at him; his profile showcases a clenched jaw. His eyes remain locked on the garage door, almost as if he can't bear to look at me.

"And I—" He runs a hand through his curls, tugging on the ends in frustration. "I can't have my tuition pulled, Mads. It's everything I've ever worked for, and football is the closest thing I have to my mom. I—"

He doesn't have to finish.

I get the gist.

Thousands of emotions run through my mind, but the most prominent is *embarrassment*. I knew going into this that it could end this way, but I foolishly held on to the hope that this time things would work out for us. The tears pricking the backs of my eyes are no one else's fault but my own.

Cameron studies my face, cursing when he notices the tears threatening to spill.

There are plenty of questions I could ask right now. Why not go to another college that's cheaper? His stats already have him on everyone's radar. Why not take a chance on *us* and figure out a way to make this work?

But I've already fought for him once. I begged him to remain in my life all those years ago, and I refuse to do it again. I have enough pride to walk away, and I have enough self-respect to keep my tears at bay when I meet his stare again.

"Okay," I whisper.

"Okay?" His brows furrow, perplexed. "That's all you have to say?"

"What would you like me to say? We agreed to take things slow. I knew what to expect, so I have no reason to be hurt. I would never try to take you away from your dreams, Cameron, and if your dad is saying to break things off, I understand."

Because at the end of the day, I love him, and I want him to be happy. If he didn't have football, he'd lose his passion, and as much as I want to be mad at him, I can't be. I'm studying to become a doctor for the same reason he's striving to play football professionally—an attempt to cling to a bond that's already been severed.

"You have every reason to be hurt," he starts. "Mads, I took your vir—"

"*Please*," I beg. "I don't need a reminder of what happened, okay? I'm aware of what transpired between us, and no, I don't regret it. You told me this could be a possibility."

"It doesn't mean I can't be sorry. Despite what you're probably thinking, I never wanted to hurt you, and the last thing I want to fucking do is walk away from you."

The breeze whips between us, sending a shiver down my spine.

"You deserve someone who chooses you over everything else," he says, "and although I want to, I don't know how to be that person yet. My dad is depending on me because it's *his* dream, too, and I can't let him down."

A bitter laugh comes out. "Cameron, maybe you're right. Maybe I do deserve better, but again, I knew what I was signing up for when we started this. I knew about your baggage, I knew about the red flags, I knew about it all, and I still chose you. You needed time, and I was willing to give it to you because to me, we're worth it."

"We *are* worth it, Mads. You think I don't know that? But I'm stuck here. Football is something I can't give up, and I'm not going to ask you to wait until I'm drafted. It's not fair to you. I'm not worth your time."

With a heavy sigh I look up into the sky and blink a few times, trying to find the compassion I need in order to word this correctly. "I wish you knew how special you are," I find myself saying. "If you could look in the mirror and see half of what I see, there wouldn't be any insecurities."

"*Mads.*" My name is a plea on his lips, but I can't stop now that I've started.

"You're the type of guy everyone is lucky to have in their life. You're loyal, devoted, and selfless, even if you think you aren't. It's the reason you're breaking up with me now. You want to keep the dream alive for your dad because you're afraid that if you don't he'll break after keeping himself together for so long after your mother passed. I just . . . I wish sometimes you *would* be selfish, because if you're constantly trying to please everyone else, you're going to run yourself ragged, and then you'll end up getting burned-out."

He wipes his cheeks with his sleeve to gather the tears. "Trust me, I'm already burned-out. It happened a long time ago."

"Then choose *you.*" As I reach up to wipe his tears myself, he leans into my touch, and damn if it doesn't crumble the tough exterior I'm trying to keep up. "If that includes me, great, and if doesn't, I'll learn to accept that. This is *your* life, Cameron. The only person stopping you from easing all this pressure you carry is yourself."

"Will you hate me?" he blurts. "If I choose to carry out my mom's dream, will things go back to the way they've been? Silence and ignoring each other like the other doesn't exist?" I smile softly when he bends down to rest his forehead against mine. "I can't live like that again, Maddie, but if it's what you need, then—"

"Give me time," I say. "I don't want things to be like that

again, either, but—" But how am I supposed to forget the past two weeks? No matter how fleeting, the moments were real. Talking about the future, stolen moments of intimacy, losing my virginity, laughing our heads off together at the lake. I don't know how I could ever FaceTime him or see him in person again without feeling the urge to touch him like this. Hold him like this.

And the realization that this is probably the last time we'll ever get to do this washes over me like a tsunami.

As if the same thoughts are dawning on him, his lips crash against mine like a desperate, urgent necessity. Our tears meld together, a never-ending saltwater ocean of our own as my hands drag through his hair to pull him closer. His hands find my hips, pulling me closer against him to make the kiss deeper, but my tears are flowing freely now, and a sob working its way up my throat forces him to pull back.

I was supposed to be strong.

I knew this could happen, but I let it destroy me regardless.

"I'm sorry," he repeats. "Fuck, I'm so sorry."

"It's okay," I gasp, but it's not. We both know it isn't. "I'm going to go back inside."

This relationship was doomed from the start, but we gave it a shot. We tried, and we failed. No harm, no foul, right? I should be grateful I've experienced something so special, and it kills me to say goodbye, and although it's not goodbye forever, it's walking away from everything I've ever wanted.

"Don't leave like this, Mads. We can . . . fuck, I don't know. We can talk this through. Figure out a way to make this easier on both of us."

Nothing will ever make it easier.

The damage has been done, and although I promised myself

I'd keep my guard up, I failed, and now I'm left to pick up the pieces of my heart.

"You said you'd give me what I need. Being alone right now is what I need."

His chest heaves with a shaky exhale, but with a jerk of his chin, he releases me from his hold, his fingers flexing as if he regrets the decision to do so immediately. "Can I call you tonight?"

He can try, but I can't guarantee that I'll answer.

It'll be too soon.

Too fresh.

Seeming to get the hint, he nods. I leave him on the hood of his car before I make a mistake and kiss him again, prolonging the inevitable.

Getting my heart broken has always been the outcome of this scenario, but I stupidly ignored it. My brother was right. *Maya* was right. I should have kept that fucking guard up, but I didn't.

When the front door clicks shut behind me, only then do I let the repercussions of my decisions fully reach the surface. My heart implodes into a thousand tiny shards just as my mom rounds the corner and sinks with me to the floor, scrambling desperately to pick them up.

Thirty-six

CAMERON

It didn't take me long to find someone with alcohol.

I texted my entire contact list, but truthfully, I would have taken some from a stranger on the street if they offered it to me. It didn't matter who the source was, just as long as I obtained it.

Fucking *Mark* was the first one to text back. He was playing poker with his friends and extended an invitation, which included free liquor. At first I didn't dare entertain the possibility of hanging around him, but after some more thought, I figured going to Mark's was what I deserved.

Playing poker with him and his buddies was a reminder of the type of guy Maddie could have had if I wasn't a selfish prick. I don't care what she claimed I was. For the second time I fucked around with her heart, so I played poker and sat next to the guy she should have given her chance to instead of me. Twist the knife a little deeper.

I deserved every ounce of pain it delivered.

And then, to top it all off, when I got so drunk I could hardly stand, Mark offered to drive me home because he was sober. He's the good guy. The type of guy who would choose Maddie over anything else. The type of guy who isn't hounded by the pressure of making it big and pleasing everyone else but himself.

She should have chosen him.

And now, after stealing a bottle of whiskey from my father's liquor cabinet, I'm sitting on the same couch where she left me the first time, drinking myself into oblivion.

Christ.

I took her goddamn virginity.

She was filled with light and hope and *everything* good the world has to offer, and in return I dragged her down into my world of misery, tainting her angel wings with hopelessness and despair.

With another long pull from the bottle, I enjoy the burn it brings as it travels down my throat. The world is tilting on its axis, threatening to pull me under, but I force myself upright to face the disappointment and regret head-on.

When my mom passed, I thought becoming a robot and feeling nothing was the worst I've ever felt.

But now that Maddie and I are officially done, I'm feeling everything, and that, I've come to learn, is far worse.

The jingling of keys echoes on the other side of the front door. I'm so drunk I fear I'm hallucinating when my dad seems to teleport in front of me. *How did he get in here so quickly?*

He frowns, turning on the lamp beside me. "It's three in the morning, Cameron. What are you doing?"

"What are *you* doing?" I slur, waving my hand around. "Shouldn't you be, I don't know, anywhere but here?"

Snatching the bottle of whiskey out of my hands, he sighs

excessively. "I told you I was going to come back so we could discuss the routine and get you back on track. You shouldn't be drinking. *This* is why I told you not to get involved with her."

The laugh I release is one of disbelief. "You think I'm drinking because of *her*? None of this would be happening if you didn't give me a fucking ultimatum!" Anger courses through me, and with the addition of liquid courage, I've reached my breaking point. How dare he waltz in here and act as if he cares about my life. As if he cares about my well-being. The only reason he's here is to ensure I have the best chance at being drafted.

"You know, football used to be something we loved to do together," I continue. Now that the dam has burst, I can't seem to close it. "It was fun, and after mom passed, I learned to love it even more because it connected me to her. But *you* became obsessed. My training sessions, tracking my calories, tracking my location to make sure I wasn't partying. I let you control my life, and now—" I blink away tears. "I don't know who I am anymore. I don't know what my dreams are. I'm in a constant cycle of pleasing you because if I don't, if I don't have football to connect us, I'm afraid you'll leave for good."

The truth comes out. My one fear—the one I can't get rid of no matter what I do—makes its way into the void, and my father stands in front of me with the bottle of whiskey in his hand, stunned into silence.

"I understand you worked so hard to try to give me a better life, but I would rather have gone to community college if it meant you'd be home more. I could have cared less about the name brand clothes. I just . . . I just wanted *you*." My voice is gravelly from trying to hold the tears back, but when I glance up, my dad has a liquid sheen coating his eyes as well.

"I didn't—" A hand rakes over his hair before he takes a swig of the whiskey, wincing on the swallow. "All I've ever wanted was the best for you, but clearly it hasn't come across that way. Do you honestly think getting into a relationship is a good idea when you're so close to being signed by Arizona?"

"Who says I want to be signed by them?"

Silence falls between us, taking up every section of space in the room. "What do you mean you don't want to be signed by Arizona? It's been your dream ever since you were a teenager."

"No." I laugh, cold and lifeless. "It's been *your* dream. Every decision I've made has been based on what would make you happiest. I was terrified of disappointing you, so I went along with your diet plans, workout routines, and anything else you suggested because it was the only thing that we had in common after Mom died. But you know what? I don't know where I'll be drafted, but the one constant nagging thought I have is that I hope for damn sure it's close to Maddie because I can't live without her. I'd be devastated without football, but losing her? I won't survive it. I'm barely surviving now."

Telling him this is pointless when I know he'll never change his mind. I'm wasting my breath. "Anyway, none of this matters," I say while reaching for the bottle again. Shockingly, my dad allows me to take another swig.

He takes a seat beside me, hands clasped between his legs. "It *does* matter."

My hand holding the bottle freezes in front of my lips.

"You're my kid," he continues. "And I didn't know you felt that way. The fact you kept those feelings inside this long should tell me all I need to know about how good of a parent I've been." My father has never cried in front of me, not even when my mother passed. He's always tried to be strong for us, but now a tear slips onto his cheek. "I thought that providing you with everything you could ask for would give you what you needed. I wanted to make your mother proud, but instead I think I've failed her, and I've failed you in the process too. She would have loved to see you carry out your dreams by playing football professionally, and I became so wrapped up in it that I somehow lost what *you* wanted. I never asked, and I should have."

Am I hallucinating again?

My father and I are having a conversation that is actually going well for once.

His reflection isn't one I disagree with, so I'm not going to make up some bullshit excuse and stroke his ego that he's been a good father when he hasn't been. Instead, I give him the time to work this out himself.

"I miss her more than you can possibly imagine, and I've let my grief consume me, which resulted in me neglecting you when you needed me the most. Your mother was my soul mate. She was the type of person who could make the sun come out in the darkest of storms, and it became painstakingly obvious when she passed that the sun had no intentions of ever breaking through the clouds again. It broke me, Cameron."

My vision is blurry, so I desperately blink down at my shoes to try to clear it.

"I'm sorry I haven't been there for you in the ways that matter, and I'm sorry I became so shattered by her loss that I stopped focusing on the most important thing, which is keeping our family together. I could come up with a thousand ways to try to solve this between us, but what do *you* want? What do you need from me to fix this?"

The anger that's been brewing in me for years at his absence throbs with a glimmer of hope he's giving, and that fifteen-year-old boy who lost his mom can't seem to let go of it. Mending things isn't something that's going to happen overnight, and while I'll never understand why he chose to leave me, I can understand his pain. I can understand changing into a different person. Becoming emotionless. Becoming an empty shell of the person I used to be.

So I think about his question for a few moments before I say, "Time. I understand you work a lot, but I wouldn't mind a visit here and there at school. And maybe we could talk about something other than football during those visits."

He nods thoughtfully, and even though he's not speaking, I can see his mind working as he deciphers my words. "Done. Anything else?"

"Maybe therapy? I think, you know, after all that's happened, we could both use it. Together *and* individually." Because the more this conversation unfolds, the more I realize that Maddie was right. The only person stopping me from relieving this pressure is *me*. All it took was a single confession to my dad to get my point across and begin the healing between us, and if I can openly speak about all the other shit going on in my head with someone else, maybe I can mend myself too.

"And no ultimatum," I add. "It might be too late since I ended things with her this morning, but I can't achieve my dream of football if Maddie isn't by my side. They're both my dreams, and if you strip me of one, it'll take away the other."

He leans back into the couch, taking the whiskey back to take another gulp. "Are you sure she's the one?"

Last week I wouldn't have been able to answer that confidently, but with this major step taken and gaining a semblance of control back in my life, I'm proving to myself that I *can* be the guy who chooses her over everything else. I refuse to accept anything less.

"She is," I reply. "I'm in love with her."

I'm expecting a rebuttal or some sort of lecture, but what I didn't expect? A *smile* on my father's face. "I'll be damned," he mutters more to himself than me. "It seems your mother was right." Before I can ask what he means, he clears his throat and adds, "I'll take your word for it. Even though I don't think it's the smartest decision to become involved with someone, if she's truly the one you want to be with, I'll learn to be okay with it."

"Really?"

He shrugs. "I've always loved Maddie for you, I just didn't think it was the right time. If she and football are what will make you happy, then I'll compromise, and we'll figure out a way to make it work. However, if your grades start to *slip*—"

"They won't."

He holds up the empty bottle, examining the damage I did on it. "All right then. You need to get some sleep. We can talk about things in the morning when you're sober."

"You aren't leaving?"

"No." He shakes his head, regret shining in his eyes. "I'm going to make an effort to be part of your life more, Cameron. I mean that. I'll be here when you wake up, although something tells me you'll be busy pining for the girl I made you let go of. If you need me to apologize to her, I'd be more than willing—"

"Thanks, but this is something I need to fix myself." Because just like Maddie said, I've been standing in my own way, but not anymore.

Now that I've taken the control back, there's nothing stopping me from achieving my ultimate dream of happiness.

Her.

>> <<

When morning comes, I realize drinking an entire bottle of whiskey wasn't smart. My head is pounding and my stomach rolls with nausea, but this hangover is going to have to wait.

I'm a man on a mission.

Operation Get Maddie Back is in full effect.

But when I turn onto my side, I see a letter on my nightstand. It's not just *any* letter. The familiar cursive handwriting of my name makes my heart cease beating in my chest. For a millisecond, I assume I'm dreaming, but the letter feels real when I twirl it between my fingertips.

This is my mom's handwriting.

I'd recognize it anywhere.

My thumb traces over my name, and because I can't help myself, I bring the envelope to my nose to see if it still smells like her. I'm disappointed there isn't any trace of lilac, a perfume she always loved, and before I can drive myself mad any longer, I open the letter with shaky fingers.

My dearest Cammie,

You're likely wondering why you're reading this letter, but along with this one comes plenty of others that will correlate with big moments in your life. I didn't want to miss a thing, so I'm entrusting your father to deliver these to you during these milestones, as I fear I don't have much time left.

There are moments you'll experience when your father might not be much help, and realizing you're in love is one of them. Sure, he might have some advice, but I taught him everything he knows. How else would he have married me?

Writing this while you're so young breaks my heart because more than anything I want to be there for the day you marry the love of your life, but I've come to terms with the fact I can't be. Please remember that even if I'm not there physically, I'm with you spiritually in every step you take. Not even time and space could prevent me from watching over you.

You're the sweetest, most kindhearted boy this world has ever seen, and with this letter, I've written some things down about my marriage that I hope you experience in your own someday. Whoever has stolen your heart, I know they're lucky, and I wish I could have met them.

For starters, I hope you've found someone who is willing to stick by your side no matter what obstacles come your way. In life, things don't always go the way you expect them to, and it's important to have a partner who will not only lift you up in those tough moments, but love you through them too.

I hope you've found someone who finds you just as attractive at your worst as they do at your best. Beauty fades as we grow older, so I pray the person you've chosen admires the beauty that is within you.

Lastly, I hope you've found someone worth fighting for. Love is the strongest force on earth. It's capable of moving mountains if you try hard enough, and your partner should be the driving force of it all. Love can pounce quick, with no mercy, or it can sneak up on us over time, but if it's true love, any milestone you pass, any decision you debate, and every breath you take will be made with them in mind without you even realizing it. That person becomes the center of your universe, and although terrifying, it can be the greatest experience you'll have in this lifetime.

Since I won't have an opportunity to do so later, can I take a wild guess as to who has become the center of your universe?

Is it Maddie?

If not, please continue to the next paragraph (I am so sorry). But if it is her, I couldn't have chosen better for you myself. She looks at you like you're the moon to her stars, and call it motherly instincts, but I've always known there was something special between you two.

I love you, Cammie. I am overjoyed you've found someone worth fighting for, regardless of if it's who I'm assuming or not.

You will always be my proudest accomplishment, and if I can't be there to take care of you, it warms my heart knowing you've found someone to take my place.

Love always,

Mom

Thirty-seven

MADDIE

I put off packing until the last minute, and now I'm racing around my room like a madwoman trying to get all these clothes shoved inside my suitcase.

After my mom tried to console me yesterday, I spent the night crying into my pillow and stuffing my face with ice cream. I didn't want to tell Maya or Ethan about what happened. They went on a date last night, and I didn't want to ruin it. Telling them Cameron and I are over and speaking the words aloud will make it real, and I'm not ready for that yet.

Plus, admitting I was wrong is like pulling teeth for me. They both warned me, and I ignored all the signs because some idiotic part of me thought it could work between us.

The joke's on me.

Cameron called four times last night but I didn't have the strength to answer. Hearing his voice would only make this more difficult than it needs to be. I still want him as part of my life, but it'll take some time before we can get to the point where things return to being platonic.

I'm attempting to sit on my suitcase when knocks on the doorway pull me from my failing effort. Ethan strides into the room, leaning against the wall with his arms crossed over his chest, lips pursed into a frown. We haven't spoken since he decked Cameron at the canyon, and I don't plan on starting now.

"Is there a reason you're in my room?" I ask, aggressively removing a sweater and tossing it to the floor.

"I wanted to apologize to you."

My eyes shoot up to his, the aggressive unpacking coming to a halt. "Come again?" An apology from my brother is like finding a needle in a haystack.

An impossibly rare occurrence.

"I'm apologizing," he reiterates. "I shouldn't have punched Cameron when I'm doing the same thing with Maya. He's my best friend, and regardless of his track record, I should have listened and heard you both out. Although it'll take some getting used to, I'll be fine with it eventually."

I force a smile, swallowing thickly when he comes to the bed to help me zip my suitcase. Little does he know there's nothing to be okay with anymore. Fighting on those rocks was all for nothing, and soon enough, things will go back to how they used to be.

"Thanks," I manage to reply. When I'm ready to talk to him about it, I will. For now, I need to heal through this heartbreak on my own. "That means a lot, Ethan. I know apologizing isn't your strong suit, but if I'm being honest, I owe an apology to you too. You went about things with Maya the right way, and I'm sorry I wasn't more considerate of your feelings before starting things with Cameron. You deserved better than that from me."

"I appreciate that," he says. "So, are we good now?"

"We're good," I confirm.

After another two attempts, we finally manage to get my

suitcase shut, and he hauls it off for the bed for me, taking a glance around the room. "Are you all packed?"

I nod, looking for anything I might have missed. "Yep. That was the last of it."

"Well, you better get going then. He's outside waiting."

"Dad? I thought Mom was driving me to the airport."

Ethan stares at me as if I'm losing it. "No, Cameron is. We pulled in at the same time, but I asked if I could talk to you first before you leave."

Cameron.

Cameron is *here.*

Outside.

"I'm confused," my brother continues. "Didn't you know he was taking you?"

I thought he was leaving for school today too. I thought he'd be long gone by now, not outside in my driveway waiting for me. Ethan apparently doesn't know we broke up, so I have to act like everything is fine until I figure out what Cameron's here for.

And despite me chastising my heart to stop getting ahead of itself, it's beating like a drum at the possibility of why Cameron would show up here unexpectedly.

Stop it, I warn. *It doesn't mean he changed his mind.*

"No, I did. I just forgot."

"You forgot," Ethan enunciates slowly, clearly not believing me.

"Yeah. I probably shouldn't keep him waiting, though. I'll be back." My palms are sweaty, and my heart is racing when I leave Ethan behind in my bedroom and try to walk calmly down the stairs. I'm a trembling mess as I step onto the porch, seeing Cameron leaning against the hood of his car. He's twirling something between his fingertips, seeming deep in thought, but as soon as he hears the front door click shut behind me, his eyes lift to mine, and then he *smiles*.

It's such a switch from the version I saw yesterday that I almost don't believe it's him, but that smile can only belong to one person, and those green eyes are ones that live in every fantasy I have. He's wearing a white T-shirt that's snug to his muscled body and a backward white cap holds his curls at bay. That damn chain glistens beneath the sunlight, and damn him for making me feel like this. Damn him for breaking my heart and showing up here as if nothing happened. Damn my *heart* for ignoring the heartbreak and instead trying to persuade me to run right into his arms.

Traitorous bastard.

"Hi," he says softly.

"What are you doing here?" I'm rooted on the porch, unable to move another muscle until he tells me why the hell he showed up.

He flinches at the hurt behind my words, but the breath gets stuck in my throat when he opens his palm, showcasing a crystal. Not just any crystal, but the crystal I gave him after his mom passed. I assumed he threw it away after he told me to get lost that day, but he kept it.

"It's always been you," he whispers so softly I almost don't hear him. "You check all the boxes, Maddie."

"I . . .what does that mean?"

When he takes a step closer, I try to control my breathing, but it's useless. I'm a panting mess as the distance closes between us, fully consumed by every word that leaves his lips.

"You've always seen the very best in me even when I gave you no reason to. You cared enough to give me this crystal when I pushed you away. You thought I was hot even with my braces and my obsession with Pokémon cards because you liked me for me, and I'm so fucking sorry it took me this long to realize it."

Tears well in my eyes as he continues to turn the crystal in his hand, a symbol of how much he's cared about me over the years. It's something so small, but it holds the weight of the world in this moment.

"You have every reason to turn me down, but I told my dad there can't be an ultimatum. He came home last night, and for the first time, I was honest with him. You were right about me standing in my own way, and I don't want to be that person anymore, so I did something about it. I'm going to put in the effort to become the man you need because you're worth it. *We* are worth it, and although I have no idea what the future holds, I promise to fight like hell to ensure we make it because—" He's right in front of me now, eyes locked on mine when he says, "I'm in love with you, Maddie Davis. I always have been, and I always will be."

The breath whooshes from my lungs. If it wasn't for his hands coming out to steady me, I might fall over from the admission.

"I don't deserve it, but if you give me another chance, you won't regret it. I'll never break your heart again."

I laugh, and it's such a bad moment to do it, but I can't help myself.

Cameron seems concerned. "I can't tell if you laughing is a good or a bad thing."

"I'm sorry," I say with another giggle. Tears are threatening to spill but I hold them back when I add, "It's just funny that you think I would ever be able to say no to you."

Finally, that arrogant grin I used to hate appears on his face, and I decide I never want it to disappear again. I want it to stay put forever.

"Is that a yes, then? You'll give me another shot?"

I hook my arms around his neck and he lifts me off the ground so my legs can wrap around his waist. It's a little awkward with my walking boot, but the extra weight doesn't seem to faze him. In his arms, I feel whole, and right now, I realize it was useless for him to ask me where I wanted to live after college. The truth is, anywhere he goes, I'll gladly follow because home isn't a place. It's with *him*.

"I love you, Cameron Holden. Always have, always will."

His cheeky grin grows wider before he kisses me, and like the heavens above want to get in on the celebration, a beam of sunlight hits us both, encasing us in a blanket of warmth. The locket around my neck shimmers, and Cameron pulls away to squint into the sky. I'm not sure what happened in the past twenty-four hours to give him this revelation, but the acceptance that he seems to have fills me with joy.

In the long run, it doesn't matter what made him get to this point.

I'm just glad he did.

>> <<

Two hours later we're on the interstate, my suitcases packed in the back of Cameron's car. The windows are rolled down, whipping my curls in all directions, and Cameron has one hand on the steering wheel, the other on my thigh. After explaining more about the conversation with his dad, Cameron told me he's not flying out until later tonight so they can spend some much needed time together, so I'm grateful he wanted to take the time to drive me to the airport.

A long-distance relationship is going to be an entirely different battle, but with the love we have for one another, I'm confident we can make it work. We've gone through far worse than distance, and if anything, we've proved we can overcome it.

I turn to admire the profile of my insanely hot boyfriend. His jaw is working overtime chewing gum, and his sunglasses make him look sexier than usual. His thumb strokes my thigh in calming, happy patterns, and the sky remains a bright blue with no clouds in sight.

Our future may still have uncertainties, but today?

Today is a *good* day, and I'm going to enjoy every second of it.

That's why, when Cameron leans over to switch on the radio, I allow the country music to play at full blast.

WATCH FOR BOOK 2 IN THE
HIDDEN ATTRACTIONS SERIES

Game Changer

COMING SOON FROM W BY WATTPAD BOOKS!